When the breathtaking kiss finally ended, Roarke looked into Cleo's eyes and saw desire there. And something more.

"Why did you do that," she demanded, "after I expressly told you not to?"

Roarke tilted her chin upward. "Every bride should be kissed on her wedding day, Mrs. Roarke, and every groom should have the pleasure."

But there was more to it than that, and he knew it. Damn it all, he had desperately wanted to kiss her. He'd warned himself not to give in to the temptation, to his need to discover just how deep Cleo's frigid, controlled exterior went.

Well, he had just found out. His new wife's icy facade was only skin-deep. Buried just below the surface was a volcano of passion waiting to explode. And heaven help him, he was glad that he was the man who was going to set off that explosion....

Dear Reader,

With the coming of fall, the days—and nights—are getting cooler, but you can heat them up again with this month's selections from Silhouette Intimate Moments. Award winner Justine Davis is back with the latest installment in her popular TRINITY STREET WEST miniseries, *A Man To Trust*. Hero Cruz Gregerson proves himself to be just that—though it takes heroine Kelsey Hall a little time to see it. Add a pregnant runaway, a mighty cute kid and an opportunely appearing snake (yes, I said "snake"!), and you have a book to cherish forever.

With *Baby by Design*, award-winning Paula Detmer Riggs concludes her MATERNITY ROW trilogy. Pregnant-with-twins Raine Paxton certainly isn't expecting a visit from her ex-husband, Morgan—and neither one of them is expecting the sensuous fireworks that come next! Miniseries madness continues with *Roarke's Wife*, the latest in Beverly Barton's THE PROTECTORS, and Maggie Shayne's *Badlands Bad Boy*, the newest in THE TEXAS BRAND. Both of these miniseries will be going on for a while—and if you haven't discovered them already, you'll certainly want to come along for the ride. Then turn to Marie Ferrarella's *Serena McKee's Back in Town* for a reunion romance with heart-stopping impact. Finally there's Cheryl St.John's second book for the line, *The Truth About Toby*, a moving story about how dreams can literally come true.

Here at Intimate Moments, we pride ourselves on bringing you books that represent the best in romance fiction, so I hope you'll enjoy every one of this month's selections, then join us again next month, when the excitement—and the passion—continue.

Yours,

Leslie J. Wainger
Senior Editor and Editorial Coordinator

Please address questions and book requests to:
Silhouette Reader Service
U.S.: 3010 Walden Ave., P.O. Box 1325, Buffalo, NY 14269
Canadian: P.O. Box 609, Fort Erie, Ont. L2A 5X3

ROARKE'S WIFE

BEVERLY BARTON

Published by Silhouette Books

America's Publisher of Contemporary Romance

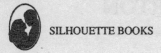

SILHOUETTE BOOKS

ISBN 0-373-07807-2

ROARKE'S WIFE

Copyright © 1997 by Beverly Beaver

All rights reserved. Except for use in any review, the reproduction or utilization of this work in whole or in part in any form by any electronic, mechanical or other means, now known or hereafter invented, including xerography, photocopying and recording, or in any information storage or retrieval system, is forbidden without the written permission of the editorial office, Silhouette Books, 300 East 42nd Street, New York, NY 10017 U.S.A.

All characters in this book have no existence outside the imagination of the author and have no relation whatsoever to anyone bearing the same name or names. They are not even distantly inspired by any individual known or unknown to the author, and all incidents are pure invention.

This edition published by arrangement with Harlequin Books S.A.

® and TM are trademarks of Harlequin Books S.A., used under license. Trademarks indicated with ® are registered in the United States Patent and Trademark Office, the Canadian Trade Marks Office and in other countries.

Printed in U.S.A.

BEVERLY BARTON

has been in love with romance since her grandfather gave her an illustrated book of *Beauty and the Beast*. An avid reader since childhood, she began writing at the age of nine and wrote short stories, poetry, plays and novels throughout high school and college. After marriage to her own "hero" and the births of her daughter and son, she chose to be a full-time home-maker, a.k.a. wife, mother, friend and volunteer.

When she returned to writing, she joined Romance Writers of America and helped found the Heart of Dixie chapter in Alabama. Since the release of her first Silhouette book in 1990, she has won the GRW Maggie Award, the National Readers' Choice Award and has been a RITA finalist. Beverly considers writing romance books a real labor of love. Her stories come straight from the heart, and she hopes that all the strong and varied emotions she invests in her books will be felt by everyone who reads them.

To
Linda Winstead Jones,
who has become my dear friend, my trusted
confidante and my faithful sounding board.
Thank goodness for fax machines!

Chapter 1

"She's outside." Dane Carmichael stood in the doorway of Simon Roarke's office. "The lady brought her aunt with her."

Roarke nodded to his boss, who had recently taken over the reins as head of Dundee Private Security. Raking his fingers through his thick, brown hair, Roarke shoved back his chair and stood. "I'll be damned if I don't feel like some Thoroughbred stallion about to be paraded around and sized up to see if I'd make a good studhorse."

Dane chuckled. "I think the lady's pretty much made up her mind that you're the man she wants for the job. This little inspection is probably just a formality."

"I haven't accepted her proposition. I'm not sure that I can. She's asking an awful lot for her million dollars."

"I wouldn't do it." Dane clamped his big hand down on Roarke's shoulder. "But then, we're very different men, with totally different agendas. I'm not eager to retire from this business, and I'm not paying the bills for an ex-wife's medical treatment."

Roarke tensed at the mention of his former wife. Dane was one of the few people he'd ever told about Hope. He had always felt that his relationship with his ex-wife was nobody's business.

"I might as well get this over with." He took a deep breath and tried to grin at Dane. Was he a fool even to consider hiring himself out as a husband to a **woman** he'd never met?

"I'll tell the two Miss McNamaras to come in."

"Hey," Roarke called out.

Hesitating at the closed door, Dane glanced back at Roarke. "Yes?"

"What does she look like?"

"Does it really matter?" Dane asked.

"Yeah, it really matters. Good Lord, man, if I take her up on her offer, I'm going to be having sex with her for the next few months."

Dane cleared his throat in an obvious effort not to laugh. "She's okay, I suppose, if you like the type."

"And just what type would that be?"

"A petite redhead in a business suit, with an attitude so frosty that I could have chipped icicles off my fingers after our handshake."

"Damn," Roarke groaned. It might have made things a little easier if she was a luscious blond bombshell, the kind who could raise a man's temperature just by walking into the room.

"What did you expect—a hot-blooded temptress?" Dane asked. "Don't forget that she'd rather pay a man to marry her than seduce one with her charms."

"This particular woman is paying for more than just a husband," Roarke reminded him. "Ms. McNamara expects her money to buy her a husband, a bodyguard and a sperm donor."

Cleo McNamara shifted uncomfortably in the straight-backed chair. She couldn't remember a time in her life when she'd been so nervous. But then, a lot was riding on her interview with Simon Roarke. If he accepted her offer, she could save McNamara Industries and the jobs of several hundred employees. If he refused...? No, she wouldn't allow herself to think in negative terms. Cleo, more than most women, knew the power of money. After all, she had been born with the proverbial silver spoon in her mouth. Few men could turn down a million dollars for less than a year's service.

"Cleo, dear, will you sit still?" Beatrice McNamara patted her niece's quivering hand. "You'll make yourself sick if you don't calm down."

"I cannot believe I'm actually doing this," Cleo said. "I'm about to hire myself a husband. If the matter wasn't so dead serious, it would be hilarious. I'm sure Daphne will laugh herself silly if she ever finds out."

"Let Daphne laugh," Beatrice said. "Let the whole family laugh. It doesn't matter. The only important thing is that by fulfilling the stipulations in Daddy's will, you'll be able to retain control of McNamara Industries. Besides, there's no reason for anyone to know this marriage isn't a love match."

"If Uncle George hadn't been such an old-fashioned male chauvinist, he wouldn't have put me in this situation."

"Now, dear, give credit where credit is due." Beatrice straightened the soft neck bow on her silk blouse, her tiny fingers touching the material with delicate finesse. "Daddy might have been a bit old-fashioned, but if he'd been a true male chauvinist, he never would have allowed you to become CEO of McNamara Industries in the first place."

"I know, Aunt Beatrice, but—"

"He simply didn't want to see you wind up an old maid like me." Beatrice sighed dramatically. "Besides, when he made out his will, I'm sure he thought you'd marry Hugh."

Cleo supposed it was reasonable for Uncle George to have thought she would marry Hugh Winfield in order to fulfill the stipulations of the will. But she had dated the man only to please Uncle George, who'd been determined—for years—to see her marry. She'd known Hugh most of her life and had always liked him, but she certainly wasn't in love with him. In all honesty, if he had dumped her—a week before Uncle George's death—for anyone other than her cousin Daphne, she would have been relieved.

Beatrice fidgeted with the braid trim on her lavender jacket. "I'm most eager to see what Mr. Roarke looks like, aren't you? His credentials are quite impressive, but one can't really judge a man until one meets him face-to-face."

"I don't see that Mr. Roarke's physical appearance matters

much one way or the other,'' Cleo said, lying to herself as well as to her aunt. "He meets all the qualifications I need in a temporary mate. He's intelligent and healthy. And he's a seasoned bodyguard.''

"Well, say what you like, but I know that if I were planning on having—'' Beatrice lowered her voice to a whisper "—*sex*…with a man, I'd want him to be at least passably good-looking.''

Before Cleo could think of a reply, the inner office door opened and Dane Carmichael invited them into Mr. Roarke's office.

Standing, Cleo stiffened her spine, and when Aunt Beatrice grabbed her hand, she squeezed tightly, trying to reassure them both. She stepped back, allowing her aunt to enter first, then followed her into the plainly decorated, modern office.

The man stood with his back to them. A very large, wide back. He wore a long-sleeved blue shirt, the sleeves rolled up to the elbows, exposing dark, hairy forearms. He was a big man, broad and thickly muscled beneath his clothes. He turned slowly. His blue eyes captured Cleo in their mesmerizing glare. The bottom dropped out of her stomach. She swallowed hard.

Beatrice McNamara gasped, then said ever so softly, "Oh, my, my.''

My, my, indeed, Cleo thought. Simon Roarke was, without a doubt, the most masculine man she had ever encountered. He stood six-three, a good foot taller than she. With his top shirt buttons open, his thick, dark chest hair was partially exposed. Despite telling herself not to stare, Cleo could not stop herself from inspecting the man.

There was a rugged, almost fierce beauty in his appearance. His face was not a pretty one by anyone's standards, but a strikingly handsome, extremely manly one. A five o'clock shadow darkened his jawline.

"Roarke, this is Ms. Cleo McNamara,'' Dane said. "And her aunt, Miss Beatrice McNamara.''

Gathering up her courage, Cleo stepped forward. She tilted her chin defiantly, daring anyone to think that she wasn't strong, capable and fearless.

"Mr. Roarke.'' She offered him her hand.

Simon glanced down at her small hand, tiny almost and quite delicate. Pale. Creamy. Soft. Unadorned. Well manicured, the nails painted with clear polish.

He accepted her greeting, his own big hand swallowing her small one when he grasped it. He felt a barely discernible tremor when their palms touched, but it was so slight he thought he might have imagined it. He realized he wanted this woman, who was trying so valiantly to appear tough, to show him some sign of weakness. But his gut instincts told him that Cleopatra McNamara seldom allowed anyone to see her vulnerable.

"Ms. McNamara. Won't you sit down?" He found himself strangely reluctant to release her hand, so he guided her to the chair and assisted her in sitting.

Dane had been right about her. Cleo was a frosty little redhead in a neatly tailored black business suit. But where Dane had failed to notice Ms. McNamara's nicely rounded behind and the high thrust of a pair of not-too-inadequate breasts, Roarke *did* notice. Maybe if a man knew he was destined to bed a woman, he paid closer attention to her physical attributes.

Cleo was no ravishing beauty—that was true. But good Lord, there definitely was something about her that stirred Roarke's baser instincts. Maybe it was because she was so small, so thin, that he could easily break her in half with his bare hands. Or maybe it was the fact that she was trying so damn hard to show him how strong and tough she was. A lot of women in her situation would have used the "I'm so helpless and need a big strong man like you" approach. Whatever the cause, Roarke found himself interested in and oddly attracted to this woman who could soon be his for the taking.

Cleo stared up at him with fearless, moss green eyes, her expression questioning him, his honesty, his sincerity. And for the briefest instant he felt as if she were warning him not to hurt her.

"We haven't any time to waste," Beatrice said in her authoritarian, schoolteacher voice. "It's taken us nearly three weeks to find you, Mr. Roarke, and Cleo *must* be married within thirty-one days of Daddy's death." Beatrice stood behind her niece's chair, her fingertips biting into the leather surface.

Roarke glanced at Beatrice McNamara, a softer, older version of her niece. He knew she was sixty-three, but would have guessed her a good ten years younger. Although her auburn hair was streaked with gray, she kept it cut stylishly short, and her petite body was still youthfully slender.

"I understand the urgency." Roarke spoke directly to Beatrice, then turned his attention to Cleo. "You must be desperate to retain control of your uncle's little fertilizer plant if you're willing to marry a man you don't know and have him father your child."

What sort of woman must she be, Roarke wondered, to pay such a high price for the stewardship of a small chemical plant in a one-horse Alabama town? If she didn't marry within a month of her uncle's death and become pregnant within a year, she wouldn't lose her inheritance, just control of the company. In fact, by selling the business, as the other family members wanted to do, she'd be a far richer woman than if she kept the company and lived off the quarterly dividends.

"If I don't fulfill the stipulations of Uncle George's will by marrying and getting pregnant, then McNamara Industries will be sold. And the company that wants to buy it plans to downsize drastically. That will mean hundreds of River Bend residents will lose their jobs. Our 'little' fertilizer plant is the major employer in the county, Mr. Roarke."

"I see." Roarke scanned Cleo's face for any sign of deception and found none. So Cleo McNamara was a do-gooder. A wealthy businesswoman who actually gave a damn about her employees.

Beatrice cleared her throat. "You understand that your background in the Green Berets and here at the Dundee agency is what tipped the scales in your favor as our choice for a husband. Cleo needs a full-time bodyguard."

"I'm well aware of Ms. McNamara's reasons for selecting me over the other candidates." Roarke glared at Dane Carmichael, who stood by the wall, his arms crossed over his chest and a smirky grin on his face.

"We're quite certain that someone in the family is trying to kill Cleo," Beatrice explained. "Two days after Daddy's funeral, someone tried to shoot her. And with one of Daddy's rifles, too! The sheriff checked every weapon in Daddy's collection immediately after the shooting and discovered one of the rifles had been fired recently. The bullet they found in the wall behind where Cleo had been standing was a match.''

''But according to the report you sent me, there were no fingerprints, other than your father's, found on the rifle.''

''That's right.'' Beatrice nodded.

''And the authorities don't have a clue as to who fired that shot?'' Roarke posed his question to Cleo.

''Not a clue,'' she said. ''But it had to have been either a family member or someone they'd hired. Only Aunt Beatrice and I want to keep McNamara Industries a family-run business. The rest of the family want to sell it.''

''Is saving your uncle's company worth risking your life?'' Roarke fervently wished he didn't find Ms. McNamara to be so damned noble. There was certainly something irresistibly appealing about a strong, intelligent, noble woman.

He realized that he'd never met anyone quite like her, and it was at that very moment he decided to take Cleo McNamara up on her offer of marriage. Even though he'd be doing it for the money, perhaps by making it possible for her to fulfill the stipulations of her uncle's will, he, too, would be doing something just a little noble.

''Yes. Saving McNamara Industries is worth any price I have to pay.'' Balling her hands into tight little fists in her lap, she stared up at Roarke. ''Do we have a deal? As Aunt Beatrice pointed out, I don't have any time to waste.''

''Has your lawyer drawn up all the documents?''

''Yes. I have them with me. In my briefcase.''

''Then leave them and I'll read over them tonight. Come back tomorrow morning and, if you haven't changed your mind, we'll sign the papers.''

''I won't change my mind,'' Cleo assured him. ''Once we've finalized our deal, I'll want you to return to Alabama with me and we'll be married immediately.''

Cleo stood and offered her hand to Roarke. Reluctantly, he accepted, once again holding on to her longer than necessary.

''I want one thing understood up front,'' Roarke told her, his thumb caressing her knuckles. ''I'll marry you, father your child and protect you while we try to discover who wants to kill you. But I won't be around once the child is born. That's the only way I'll agree to this deal.''

Cleo couldn't understand how a man could father a child and then desert it, never wanting anything to do with it. But for her sake and the child's, she was glad Simon Roarke wasn't the sentimental type. She had wondered how she'd handle the situation if he asked for visitation rights. Obviously, that wouldn't be a problem.

"You never want to see the child?" she asked. "Never want to be a part of his or her life?"

"That's right." Roarke clenched his jaw; the pulse in his neck bulged and throbbed. "The child will not be mine. It will be yours—completely yours."

"Very well. We have a deal." She pulled her hand free, squared her shoulders and turned away from him.

Roarke watched while Dane escorted the McNamara ladies out of the office. The moment the door closed behind them, he turned toward the window, took a deep breath and thought, *Good Lord, am I making the biggest mistake of my life?*

For a good thirty minutes, he stood looking out the window. His thoughts raced backward in time. To another marriage. To a twenty-one-year-old soldier madly in love with the prettiest girl in the world.

The pain rose inside him, a deep, twisting knot of agony that started in his belly and spread through him like an insidious poison. With unsteady hands, Roarke removed his wallet from his pocket and slipped out a frayed photograph. Blue eyes identical to his own stared back at him from the face of a golden-haired angel. His little Laurie. The picture had been taken only a few weeks after her third birthday. Her last birthday. Roarke had been halfway around the world in an insect-infested jungle when his daughter had died. If his military career hadn't been more important to him than his child, Laurie would still be alive. And Hope might not be vegetating in a mental hospital.

Cleo lay in the double bed in Atlanta's Doubletree Hotel, listening to Aunt Beatrice's wispy breathing as she slept peacefully. Cleo could not imagine life without her aunt, who actually was her father's first cousin. Beatrice, whom she'd referred to as *aunt* all her life, had been the nearest thing to a mother Cleo had ever known. When she was three, her father had been killed in Vietnam and her mother, young, beautiful and a bit wild, had deserted Cleo.

She had grown up on the McNamara estate in River Bend, a sleepy little Alabama town in northwest Alabama, near the Tennessee River. Aunt Beatrice had adored her and taken over her upbringing. And because she not only looked like the McNamaras but Uncle George believed she had the McNamara brains and grit, she soon became his favorite. "You're your father's daughter," he'd told her often. Uncle George had thought the world of young Jimmy McNamara Jr., his only brother's son.

Cleo couldn't ever remember wanting for anything money could buy. If she wanted it, needed it or asked for it, it was hers. But she would never forget the nights she had prayed her mother would return for her and love her the way mothers should love their daughters. But the beautiful, wild Arabelle had never returned. And when Cleo was nineteen, they received word that her mother had died accidentally of an overdose of drugs and alcohol.

She supposed one of the reasons she'd fallen in love with Paine Emerson and had agreed to marry him at twenty was that she'd longed for the kind of family life she'd been denied. She'd seen herself as a happy homemaker and the mother of half a dozen little Emersons. She'd been such a young fool. More in love with love than with Paine. And totally infatuated with the dream of being the kind of mother she'd never had.

She had thrown herself into their relationship with total abandon, giving Paine her virginity as well as her heart. She didn't know which she regretted losing the most. But in the long run, it didn't matter. She had retrieved her broken heart and mended it quite well. And her lost virginity was of little importance, since, for all intents and purposes, she was still what some would call a semivirgin, a woman with very little sexual experience.

She had hated Daphne for quite some time after her cousin had seduced Paine into eloping. But when Paine had left

Daphne for another woman only four years into their turbulent marriage, Cleo had actually felt sorry for her cousin. She had welcomed Daphne home, if not with open arms, at least with civility.

She couldn't remember a time in her life when Daphne hadn't wanted what she had. If Cleo got a pony, Daphne wanted a horse. If Cleo got a new dress, Daphne had to have two new dresses. When Cleo became engaged to Paine Emerson, Daphne promptly seduced him into eloping with her. So why had Cleo been surprised that, less than six months after she started dating Hugh Winfield, she found him in bed with Daphne?

Cleo supposed Uncle George had known that the only reason she dated Hugh was to please him. He'd made it perfectly clear how much he wanted to see her married. One of his greatest regrets had been that his only child, Beatrice, had remained single and childless. Understanding his reasoning and his assumption that she'd marry Hugh, Cleo could almost forgive her great-uncle for placing her in such an awkward predicament.

Tomorrow she and Simon Roarke would sign the documents that sealed their fate and doomed them both to a temporary marriage. She had weighed the pros and cons of this situation again and again. She didn't want to get married. And she certainly didn't want to bring a baby into this world with only one parent. Her actions would be unfair to her child. But she and Aunt Beatrice would surround the child with love, and she was wealthy enough to afford to raise a child alone. When she had considered taking Aunt Beatrice's advice to hire a husband who could father her baby, she'd thought the man would want to be a part of the child's life after the divorce.

What sort of person could walk away from his own flesh and blood? *A person like Arabelle McNamara,* she told herself. Was Simon Roarke as callous and unfeeling as her own mother had been?

Cleo wasn't sure what she had been expecting when she'd met Mr. Roarke. She knew a great deal about him, but only superficial information. His age, birthday, weight, height, schooling, occupational background, financial situation, medical history. But she knew absolutely nothing about the man himself. About Simon. She supposed, considering their marriage was a business arrangement and would be of short duration, that she really didn't need to know the things a woman usually wanted to know about her husband.

But their child was bound to ask about him someday. What would she tell her son or daughter? *The only reason I had you was so that I could save McNamara Industries. Your father and I were strangers who married each other for strictly business reasons, and he wanted no part in your life.*

Dear God in heaven, am I making a terrible mistake? Should I sell the company? That would make the rest of the family happy and no doubt end the threats on my life. Then there would be no need to marry a man I don't even know and conceive a child who would be born out of necessity and not out of love.

Reaching to the foot of the bed, Cleo grabbed her yellow cotton robe and slipped into it. She got up and walked quietly across the room, hoping not to disturb her aunt. Opening the drapes enough to allow the moonlight to filter through the sheer curtains beneath, Cleo then pulled a chair over to the window and sat down, placing her feet on the bottom cushion as she hugged her knees to her chest.

No, she hadn't known what to expect when she'd met Mr. Roarke today, but she certainly hadn't anticipated her reaction to him. She had long since passed the age of being a silly romantic and she'd never considered herself a very sexual creature. So why had every feminine instinct within her come to full alert the moment he'd touched her? Falling for the man she married wasn't part of her plan. But how on earth could any woman be immune to a man like Simon Roarke?

"I don't know," she answered herself aloud, her voice a whisper. "But, Cleo, my girl, if you want to come out of this marriage with your heart intact, you'd better find a way."

"Do you, Simon Alloway Roarke, take this woman to be your lawfully wedded wife?"

Simon listened to the Alabama judge's words, reciting the marriage vows and making the appropriate responses when called upon to speak. Not long after he'd taken Cleo Mc-

Namara's hand in his, a soothing numbness had claimed him. Thankfully the event, being a civil ceremony, wouldn't last very long. He didn't think he could have endured anything elaborate. Lucky for him, Cleo was a sensible woman, not one for turning their wedding into a major production.

Of course, once they arrived at her home, they would have to begin acting the parts of madly-in-love newlyweds.

"My family may suspect the truth—that I bought and paid for you," Cleo said. "But I will not give them the satisfaction of knowing for sure. Whenever we're around others, I expect you to pretend to be in love with me. Aunt Beatrice has told the family that you used to date a college friend of mine, that you and I were acquainted years ago. And when we met again, by chance, while Aunt Beatrice and I were on our Atlanta shopping trip, you and I found ourselves attracted to each other. You simply swept me off my feet in a whirlwind courtship."

Roarke wasn't too sure how sharp his acting skills were, but he'd give it his best shot. After all, Cleo was paying him for his services, and it wouldn't exactly be a hardship to fake affection for a woman as appealing as Cleo.

"And do you, Cleopatra Arabelle McNamara, take this man to be your lawfully wedded husband?" the judge asked.

"I do," she said clearly in her deep, raspy voice that Roarke thought was very sexy.

Cleo and Roarke exchanged the simple gold bands she had purchased at the local jewelry store in River Bend earlier that day. He made sure he didn't hold her hand longer than was necessary.

Remembering a first wedding on the day of a second wedding might be only natural, but Roarke refused to allow himself to remember anything about his first wedding. It would be unfair to Cleo to compare her with Hope. And it would be unfair to him to have to recall the circumstances that had led to the demise of his former marriage.

Simon didn't look at his new bride. He hadn't made eye contact with her at all. What was the point? They both knew why they were there and what they had to do. This was a business arrangement, one that would benefit them both.

All the legal documents had been signed beforehand. The

equivalent of one year's salary plus a nice bonus had been deposited in a bank account in Simon's name and Cleo had agreed to a million-dollar divorce settlement once he had successfully fulfilled his part of their bargain.

And that was the reason he was going through with this farce—for the money. If he was ever going to free himself from a life of danger and violence and still continue to meet his obligations to Hope, he needed money. A lot of money.

Cleo McNamara had offered him a small fortune to marry her—and to keep her safe. In the weeks, possibly months, ahead he would be not only her husband, but her bodyguard. Being her bodyguard, no matter how difficult, would be the easy part. Being her husband would be a complicated situation. But he could handle it. He could handle just about anything if it meant making sure Hope would be taken care of for the rest of her life. The most difficult part of the bargain would be dealing with Cleo's pregnancy. No matter how painful it would be for him, he could force himself to father Cleo's child—as long as he never saw the child, never became a part of its life, never allowed himself to love it.

He and Cleo were virtual strangers, having met only three days ago. But now they were man and wife. Legally bound in an unholy alliance. He had married her for money. She had married him for control of her family's business. No matter what the mitigating circumstances, no matter who else would benefit from their marriage, they had gone into this most sacred union without an ounce of love or commitment between them.

He kept reminding himself that Cleo wasn't his type, but he couldn't deny that she was attractive. Slender. Elegant. Cool. Controlled. Bossy and independent. It hadn't taken him long to size her up and decide that he liked her. But there wasn't much chance of her stealing his heart. Hell, he wasn't sure he even had a heart anymore.

His lips twitched slightly, but he didn't smile. He was no longer very susceptible to women in general. Once, he had preferred his women soft, warm, sweet and needy. Hope had been like that. But he had learned his lesson—learned it the hard way. Now he steered clear of emotional entanglements.

He didn't love anyone, and he never would love anyone. Not ever again.

But he had to admit that a part of him was intrigued by the challenge of melting the ice princess, of finding out if there was any fire inside Cleo.

"You may kiss your bride," the judge said.

Roarke looked at Cleo then, and for just a split second her expression was soft, almost tender. He noticed a damp glaze covering her moss green eyes. Tears? Surely this steel magnolia wasn't crying.

"Well, Boss Lady, do you want a kiss?" Roarke asked, looking down, staring directly at her and determined to start this marriage off on the right foot. He reminded himself that this was strictly a business arrangement and she was his employer.

Cleo's expression hardened instantly. Taking a deep breath, she closed her eyes, then opened them to face him with a chilly glare.

"That won't be necessary." She pulled her hand out of his loose hold. "There are only three things this job requires of you, Roarke, and kissing me isn't a mandatory part of any of them."

"Well, I can see where marrying you and protecting you don't necessarily require kissing, but I'm afraid playing the part of your lovesick husband *will* require a few kisses. And getting you pregnant is definitely going to require more than a handshake."

The judge coughed several times and then cleared his throat. Cleo glared at Roarke. He met her glare head-on, neither flinching nor smiling.

Roarke had to continue thinking of getting her pregnant as just part of his job. He would never allow himself to think of the child as his. The baby would be Cleo's—Cleo's alone—from the moment of conception. Things had to be that way. Otherwise, he'd never be able to go through with their deal.

He took a good, hard look at the woman he had just married. Even on her wedding day, she wore a simple navy blue suit with a cream silk blouse. No frills. Not even a bouquet or corsage. She had dressed as if this were a business merger, not a wedding.

The fact that she had taken no pains to make herself feminine and alluring, hadn't bothered with flowers, music or even a little dab of perfume, made Roarke want all the more for her to act like a woman, a bride—his bride. Dammit, how could any female not wear something lace or satin on her wedding day? How could she not at least pin a rose on her lapel? And why the hell wouldn't she want to be kissed?

Maybe she did, he thought. Maybe she was just too proud to ask.

Before Cleo had a chance to object, Roarke slid his arm around her tiny waist and drew her up against him. Gasping, she gazed up at him, her cheeks coloring slightly.

"What—" She started to question his actions.

Quickly lifting her off her feet, he leaned over to meet her open mouth, capturing it in a kiss that left her breathless and shocked. When she jerked her head back, trying to end the kiss, Roarke deepened his attack, thrusting his tongue inside. She struggled momentarily, then melted into him, her lips softening, her moist warmth accepting him.

When he felt himself growing hard, Roarke slowed his pace. Tracing her lips with the tip of his tongue, he looked into her eyes and saw desire. And something more.

Good Lord, what had he done? The last thing he wanted was for this woman to care about him, and he figured that Cleo was the kind of woman who'd tie lust and love together in one neat little package.

"Why did you do that, after I'd expressly told you it wasn't necessary?" she demanded.

Roarke set her on her feet, then clutched her chin, tilting it upward so that she was looking directly at him.

"Every bride should be kissed on her wedding day, Mrs. Roarke, and every groom should have the pleasure."

"Oh" was all she said before pulling away from him.

Dammit all, he had desperately wanted to kiss her. He'd warned himself not to give in to the temptation, to his need to discover just how deep Cleo's frigid, controlled exterior went.

Well, he had just found out. His wife's icy facade was only

skin-deep. Buried just below the surface was a volcano of
passion waiting to explode. And heaven help him, he was glad
that he was the man who was going to set off that explosion.

Chapter 2

The iron gates swung open, admitting Cleo's sleek, green Jaguar. Roarke could barely see the Steadman-McNamara house from the road. Cleo had told him that Jefferson Steadman, Aunt Beatrice's maternal grandfather, had built the country manor house around the turn of the century.

"How many acres have y'all got here?" Roarke asked, taking note of the vast, well-manicured green lawn, the huge, old trees that lined the driveway and the wooded areas in the distance.

"Three hundred and fifty acres," Cleo replied. "At one time this place was a working farm. We still have the fruit orchards, and Pearl cans and freezes a great deal of the harvest each year."

Three hundred and fifty acres. Not enormous, but large in comparison with the sixty-acre farm he'd grown up on in Tennessee. He had hated the way his overbearing, religiously fanatical aunt and uncle had treated him—like an indentured servant. But he had loved the land, the animals, the clean air and sunshine. That's what he missed, what he wanted again someday. Just a small place where he could raise a crop or two and keep a few chickens and horses and some cattle. He might even buy himself a dog. When he was a kid, he'd wanted a dog.

"Brace yourself," Cleo said. "We're almost there."

A two-story portico added a certain grandeur to the facade of the old manor house. Glistening white in the afternoon sunshine, the home boasted three stories, neat black shutters and four brick chimneys.

Roarke let out a long, low whistle. "This is mighty fancy digs for an old country boy like me."

Glancing at the man sitting beside her, Cleo noted the way he rested in the leather seat. His big, long body lounged in a half sitting, half lying position.

A quivering sensation hit Cleo's stomach. She quickly returned her attention to the driveway ahead of her. Just because Simon Roarke was devastatingly masculine didn't mean she had to overreact to the mere sight of him. If she allowed her hormones to dictate her actions every time she was around him, she'd be a nervous wreck by the end of the week.

"Do you really still consider yourself a country boy?" Cleo asked, remembering that Roarke's personal history stated that he'd been born in Chattanooga, but had grown up on a farm outside Lawrenceburg, Tennessee. "After a career in the Special Forces and having lived in Atlanta for several years, I don't see how you can think of yourself as a country boy."

"You know the old saying." Roarke scooted his massive frame up in the seat and spread one long arm out above Cleo's shoulders.

When she widened her eyes in a quizzical expression, he grinned. "'You can take the boy out of the country,'" he said.

"'But you can't take the country out of the boy.'" Smiling, she completed the sentence for him.

Cleo had a nice smile, Roarke realized. Warm, genuine and sort of sexy. Her wide mouth parted at a slightly crooked angle, curving the left side up more than the right. Her full, pink lips were moist and very inviting. Roarke's body tightened. Groaning silently, he warned himself to concentrate on something other than Cleo's luscious mouth.

"One of the reasons I took this job as your hired husband is so I can buy myself a little farm somewhere and retire."

"Thirty-nine is a bit young to retire, isn't it?" Cleo asked.

"Not from my line of business," he told her.

"Yes, I suppose you're right. I can't begin to imagine the things you've seen, what all you must have endured, the types of people you've met."

Yeah, he'd probably seen just about everything, experienced nightmares other people never even knew about. He wondered what Cleo would think if he told her that neither the horrors of being a professional soldier nor the dangers he faced in the private security business could compare with the never-ending hell a man lived in when he felt responsible for the death of his only child.

"Let's just say my life has been nothing like yours, Boss Lady."

"I wish you'd stop calling me that!"

"I'll be careful not to use the term around your family." He gave her shoulder a reassuring squeeze.

Suddenly realizing this homecoming was going to be a worse fiasco than she'd thought, Cleo groaned as they drove up to the house. The whole clan waited on the veranda, like a group of overeager fans prepared to pounce on their favorite rock star.

Smiling warmly and waving enthusiastically, Aunt Beatrice stood at the top of the steps. Several feet behind Beatrice, Oralie and Perry waited in front of the double doors. As always, Aunt Oralie, in her flowing silk dress and her thirty-inch pearls, looked the part of an aging Southern belle. She gazed at the approaching couple with cool, calculating hazel eyes, but put on a proper smile of welcome. Uncle Perry possessed a good poker player's face. One never quite knew what was going on behind his faded brown eyes.

Cleo pulled her Jaguar to a slow, smooth halt. Aunt Beatrice rushed down the front steps. Laughing giddily, she clapped her hands. "Congratulations, children, and welcome home."

Gripping the steering wheel, Cleo took a deep breath and willed herself to stay calm. If she was going to make this charade work, she could not allow anyone to suspect that she wasn't a deliriously happy bride.

"I thought you said you told your family that you didn't want any fuss made." Roarke surveyed the group of people hovering about on the porch.

The older couple had to be Oralie and Perry Sutton. Roarke thought that the woman's smile was too strained to be genuine, and he wondered what secrets lay hidden behind Sutton's unemotional demeanor.

The couple half-hidden behind one of the white columns were probably Trey Sutton and his wife, Marla. Young Sutton resembled his father a great deal, but he was a good three inches shorter. His wife looked very young and perhaps a bit too wholesome for this group of wealthy snobs.

"Knowing Aunt Beatrice the way I do, I imagine she's planned some sort of celebration." Releasing her tenacious hold on the steering wheel, Cleo turned to her husband of less than an hour. "I'll forewarn you. They're going to be suspicious and will probably ask far too many personal questions. My cousin Daphne will, no doubt, flirt outrageously with you today. And sooner or later, she'll invite you into her bed."

"I assume you would prefer that I didn't accept her invitation."

Cleo glared at Roarke, her dark green eyes glowing hotly. "You assume correctly. That is one advantage of your being my *hired* husband. You're my employee, and if you want to get paid, you follow my orders."

"I take it that your cousin Daphne isn't one of your favorite people," Roarke said. "Does that mean we should put her at the top of our list of suspects?"

"Other than Aunt Beatrice, all my relatives should be on our suspect list." Cleo opened the car door and stepped out, then plastered on a phony smile and turned to face her family.

Aunt Beatrice met Roarke the moment he emerged from the Jaguar. She slipped her arm round his waist and gave him an affectionate hug. "So wonderful to see you again, Simon, my dear boy."

Roarke's gaze swept the veranda and stopped on the tall, bosomy brunette who had slunk out from behind a white column. She had to be Daphne. Exotic. Sultry. Seductive. He'd known women like her before. And they were all pure poison.

Daphne's mouth curved into a mocking smile when her gaze met Roarke's. She licked her red lips. Roarke grinned.

When Cleo rounded the Jaguar's hood, Beatrice reached out, motioning her niece toward her. "Come, Cleo, everyone's waiting. They're all simply astonished by your whirlwind romance and marriage.'' Slipping her other arm around Cleo's waist, Beatrice whispered, ''Oralie and Daphne have asked me a million questions, and Trey is fit to be tied. You're going to have to put on a good show to convince this—'' Beatrice nodded toward the veranda ''—skeptical audience.''

Bending to reach Beatrice's cheek, Roarke kissed his bride's aunt, who blushed and giggled. ''You leave everything to me,'' he told her.

Without warning, Roarke swept his wife up in his arms. Gasping, Cleo flung her arm around his neck and glared into his smiling face.

''What are you doing?'' she murmured.

He nuzzled her neck. Cleo squirmed. His nose glided underneath her hair and circled her ear. Cleo swallowed hard.

''I'm convincing your family that you and I are madly-in-love newlyweds,'' he said.

''Don't you think we could find a less dramatic way of doing that?''

''Don't frown, Boss Lady. All those people waiting on the veranda are going to wonder why you look unhappy on your wedding day.''

''Oh, all right. Proceed.'' She forced her phony smile back in place as Roarke turned around and walked toward the house. Aunt Beatrice, all smiles and fluttering hands, followed the couple.

When he put his foot on the first step, Roarke whispered to Cleo, ''I'm warning you so that you'll be prepared. I'm going to move my hand down from your waist to your hip, then I'm going to caress you. And when we get to the top of these steps, I'm going to kiss you.''

''Roarke, I—'' The moment she felt his big hand gripping her hip, Cleo stiffened.

Her whole body tingled from his caressing touch. Relaxing, she gave herself over to these moments of sweet pretending. Almost unaware of her actions, she turned just enough to press her left breast against Roarke's hard chest and glided her fingers up his neck and into his thick, dark hair.

If only this were real, she thought. If only we were in love and wildly happy and unable to keep our hands off each other. If only this marriage *were* real and not a farce.

True to his word, the moment he reached the top of the stairs, Roarke took Cleo's mouth in a tongue-thrusting kiss that left her flushed, breathless and trembling.

For a split second, Roarke felt stunned himself and not quite in control. He had expected Cleo's acquiescence, but not her wholehearted cooperation. She had returned his kiss eagerly, her mouth opening in a warm, moist invitation, her tongue mating savagely with his.

He looked directly into her eyes—compelling green cat eyes—and saw a reflection of his own desire.

"You two might want to save that for later," a soft, saccharine, feminine voice said. "Right now, we have a little party waiting inside for the bride and groom."

Still slightly disoriented and sexually aroused, Cleo stared at her cousin. She focused on Daphne's moist, red lips, which were curved into a mocking smile. Daphne glared at Cleo, then turned to Roarke, and her expression changed. She sent him an invitation with her notorious come-hither look.

Cleo stiffened in Roarke's arms. She tightened her hold around his neck and glanced at her husband, who was surveying Daphne from head to toe. When he grinned at Daphne, Cleo wanted to scratch his eyes out. Dammit, wasn't there a man on earth immune to her sultry cousin?

Threading his big fingers through Cleo's short hair, Roarke pulled her face toward his. She quivered when his mouth touched her ear.

"If you laugh and then look longingly into my eyes, she'll wonder if I told you something about her," Roarke said.

As though on cue, Cleo smiled, then laughed and gazed at Roarke as if he were the only man in the world. In her peripheral vision, Cleo noticed the smile on Daphne's face vanish, quickly replaced by a sullen frown.

Still carrying Cleo, Roarke headed straight for the double entrance doors. A tall, skinny, gray-haired man, wearing faded, patched work clothes, hurried ahead of them and opened the leaded-glass doors, then stood back and nodded a greeting.

"Oh, hello, Ezra," Cleo said. "Ezra, this is my husband, Simon Roarke. And this—" she smiled warmly at the old man

"—is Ezra Clooney. He's worked here on the estate since before I was born."

"Nice to meet you, Mr. Roarke," Ezra said. "We're sure glad to see Miss Cleo got herself a husband."

"I'm glad that I'm the man she chose for a husband." Roarke carried his bride over the threshold and into the enormous foyer, where a sparkling crystal chandelier lit a hallway decorated with Persian rugs and antique furniture.

Once inside, he put Cleo on her feet, but kept his arm around her waist, securing her to his side. Beatrice McNamara scurried into the house behind them, followed by the other family members.

"Come on into the dining room," Beatrice said. "I have a little surprise for y'all."

"Heaven help us," Cleo moaned.

"Let's go see what Aunt Beatrice has done for us, darling." Following Beatrice's lead, Roarke led Cleo down the hallway and into the dining room.

A string quartet, set up in a corner in front of the Hepplewhite breakfront, played a Tchaikovsky composition. A classically romantic piece of angelic sweetness.

Cleo closed her eyes and said a silent prayer for the strength to see her through this ordeal. Wasn't it bad enough that she'd had little choice but to marry a stranger? Did she have to go through the motions of celebrating a marriage that was destined to end in divorce?

An enormous wedding cake awaited them in the center of the Sheraton dining table that was obviously large enough to accommodate a good two dozen persons or more. The four-foot cake was traditional in style, with a bride and groom perched on the top layer. Several bottles of champagne were waiting to be opened and a small feast had been placed on the sideboard. A variety of floral arrangements filled the room with a sweet, springtime aroma.

"This is lovely, Aunt Beatrice. Thank you," Cleo said, all the while wishing she and Roarke could escape upstairs to her suite and not have to endure this phony celebration. But it was her own fault, really, for letting her pride get in the way. Maybe she shouldn't have insisted on playing out this little drama with Roarke as her devoted lover.

Roarke glanced around at the assembled guests and discovered one person whose identity he couldn't discern. A blond man with a thin mustache. Somewhere in his midthirties. A three-piece-suit type. A slick, cultured pretty boy.

"Perry, you must do the honors as man of the house, now that Uncle George is no longer with us." Oralie Sutton slipped her arm through her husband's.

Perry Sutton opened the first bottle of champagne and filled flutes for everyone, then lifted his glass for a toast.

"To Cleo and her husband," Perry said. "We wish them every happiness."

There were several murmurs of "To Cleo" from among the small crowd.

Aunt Beatrice practically shouted, "Happiness to Cleo and Simon."

One by one, Cleo's family gathered around the table, waiting for the bride and groom to cut their wedding cake.

Slipping his arms around Cleo, Roarke placed the silver knife in her hands, then covered her hands with his, and together, they sliced the first piece of cake.

"You must feed it to each other." Beatrice's eyes glistened with unshed tears. "And I'll freeze the top layer for y'all to share on your first anniversary."

Of all the silly things for her aunt to have said, Cleo thought, when Beatrice knew good and well that there was no chance she and Roarke would celebrate their first anniversary. As soon as the identity of the would-be killer was discovered and Cleo was pregnant, Roarke's job would be completed.

Continuing their charade of being happy newlyweds, Cleo put a piece of cake up to Roarke's mouth and he bit into the delectable concoction. Without thinking, she lifted her hand to the side of his mouth and wiped away a smudge of frosting. Realizing what she'd done, Cleo stared into Roarke's sky blue eyes—eyes that were smiling at her. He grasped her hand, brought it to his mouth and slid her finger between his lips, licking off the frosting. Cleo shivered. Her mouth gaped. She sucked in a deep breath.

For the next hour and a half, Roarke and Cleo gave award-winning performances. All the while Cleo prayed for deliverance, Roarke observed the group of suspects. And that's how he thought of Cleo's family. As suspects. After all, one of them had already tried to kill her.

He wasn't sure what lay at the root of Cleo and Daphne's problem, but even to an untrained eye, the animosity Daphne felt for her cousin was obvious. Roarke's gut instincts told him that a man was involved somehow. He couldn't help wondering if that man wasn't the pretty boy, whom he'd found out was a lawyer named Hugh Winfield, the son of the head of the law firm that handled all of the McNamaras' personal and business concerns.

Daphne had kept herself draped around Winfield like a vine around a trellis. But the odd thing was that Cleo seemed totally unconcerned. Maybe Winfield wasn't the man.

Cleo leaned over and whispered to Roarke. "I can't take much more of this. My feet are hurting. I've got a killer headache, and if I have to keep smiling this way much longer, my face is going to crack."

"Would you like for me to swoop you up in my arms and carry you upstairs?"

"No! I think we've put on enough of a show for one day," Cleo said. "Why don't you see how many more of Trey's and Aunt Oralie's questions you can answer, while I run out to the kitchen and ask Pearl to bring our supper upstairs to my suite? I think everyone will understand that we want to be alone on our wedding night."

"Do you suppose Pearl could round up some beer for me? I'm not much of a wine drinker."

"If necessary, I'll have her send Ezra into town to buy some. Any particular brand?"

"Anything domestic will do." Roarke grinned.

When Cleo started to walk away, he grabbed her wrist and pulled her up against his chest, then kissed her. "Don't be long, darling," he said loud enough for everyone to hear.

The moment Cleo exited the room, Trey Sutton, dragging his thin, blond wife with him, approached Roarke on one side, while Oralie Sutton closed in on him from the opposite side. Across the room, Daphne ran the tips of her long, red nails up and down Hugh Winfield's chest while she stared provocatively at Roarke.

"So, you knew Cleo when she was in college?" Trey asked. "Surely you weren't a student, too."

"No, I wasn't a student," Roarke replied.

"How did the two of you meet?" Oralie smiled ever so sweetly as she played with her cultured pearls.

"Mr. Roarke was dating a friend of Cleo's, Mother," Trey said derisively, his hazel-brown eyes twinkling with humor. "Don't you remember Aunt Beatrice telling us the whole story? Cleo and Mr. Roarke were attracted to each other years ago, but didn't pursue a relationship because he was dating a friend of hers."

"Oh, yes, of course." Oralie patted her son's arm affectionately. "But then, Beatrice is such a romantic little creature and prone to…well, shall we say…fantasies."

Oralie's mocking chuckle got on Roarke's nerves far more than Trey's unmannerly inspection. What the hell was the guy doing—measuring him for a suit or a coffin? From the short time he'd been around Cleo's family, Roarke already knew one thing. He didn't like any of them. With the exception of Beatrice.

"I'd love to hear your version of this wild, whirlwind courtship." Daphne sauntered across the room, her long, curly black hair swaying with each movement of her broad shoulders. "I've never thought of Cleo as the type who could inspire such hot passion in a man. Especially a man like you."

Oralie's cheeks flushed. She cleared her throat. "Daphne! What a vulgar thing to say."

"Was I being vulgar, Mr. Roarke?" Daphne brushed by Marla Sutton, who clung to her husband's arm, her eyes wide with wonder and her mouth slightly parted.

Slipping her arm through Roarke's, Daphne manacled his wrist. She scratched his skin just above his wristwatch. He grasped her hand, holding it tightly, then tilted his head downward enough so that he could whisper in her ear.

"I find everything about you vulgar, Ms. Sutton." He spoke so low only Daphne could hear him. "Especially the way you're coming on to me." He jerked her hand away from his wrist and smiled when he saw the look of disbelief on her face.

Roarke stepped back, away from the smothering bodies and

the prying eyes. He saw Aunt Beatrice looking forlornly at him from across the room where she stood beside Perry Sutton. With her eyes, she pleaded with him to continue the charade, to consider Cleo's pride before speaking.

"I think we should get a few things straight. Up front," Roarke said.

Aunt Beatrice's mouth opened on a silent gasp. Her green eyes widened in fear. She took several hesitant steps in Roarke's direction.

"I'm a private man and I don't think the details of my relationship with Cleo are any of your business. But since y'all are her *family*—" he practically snarled the word "—and know all about Uncle George's will, then I should tell you that Cleo and I rushed into this marriage so that she could fulfill the stipulations of that will."

Beatrice gasped. Tears glazed her eyes. Oralie nodded, a self-satisfied smile on her face. Trey laughed aloud.

"I knew it!" Daphne stared at Roarke.

"Oh, you misunderstand, Cousin Daphne," Roarke said. "If it hadn't been for Uncle George's will, Cleo and I would have had a chance for a longer courtship, but the end results would have been the same."

"What do you mean?" Trey asked.

"Cleo and I would have married. We just wouldn't have been in such a hurry. You see, I've been waiting all my life for a woman like Cleo." Roarke glanced at Daphne. "I'm damn lucky she agreed to marry me."

Silence hung heavily in the room, like a rain-filled cloud on the verge of explosion. Roarke scanned the room, quickly taking note of each person. Seeing Beatrice's bosom heave with a sigh of relief. Catching the little secret glance between Trey and Daphne. Observing the tightening of Hugh Winfield's soft jaw. Noting Marla's nervousness. Detecting Oralie's vaguely disguised anger. And recognizing Perry's unemotional demeanor for what it was—a habitual mask he used to hide behind.

"While I have y'all's undivided attention, I might as well go ahead and make something else perfectly clear," Roarke said.

A communal hush filled the air, as if everyone had taken a

deep breath and were waiting for his revelation before exhaling.

"I know that someone in this family took a shot at Cleo right after her uncle's funeral. Let me warn you. If you're smart, you won't ever try to harm my wife again. Because if you do, when I catch you—and I will catch you—you're mine."

"How dare you accuse one of us of wanting to harm Cleo!" Oralie said.

"Just who do you think you are, coming in here, making threats like that?" Trey lifted his chin defiantly, but made no move to shorten the distance between himself and Roarke.

"I'm Cleo's husband." He crossed his arms over his broad chest, stretching the material of his dark blue suit taut over his wide shoulders. "And in case anyone doubts that I'm capable of backing up my promise of retaliation, I think you should know that I spent over a dozen years in the Special Forces. I know a hundred and one different ways to kill a person."

Oralie and Beatrice gasped in unison. Marla cried out. Trey, his face ashen, instinctively stepped backward. Daphne licked her lips. Perry remained silent.

"Now, if y'all will excuse me, I'll go out in the kitchen and find Cleo. We would appreciate not being disturbed tonight."

When Roarke exited the room, he paused briefly in the hallway, trying to discern where the kitchen might be. Hugh Winfield's voice rang out loud and clear.

"I'll speak to Father about what can be done legally to rectify the situation. Surely once I tell him about this man he'll be more forthcoming with information about Cleo's personal legal matters. And I'll run a check on Simon Roarke immediately."

Roarke grinned. *Yeah, you do that. Unless you've got some powerful friends, you'll never get any information on me. My army files won't be available, and Dane Carmichael will make sure you learn only what I want you to know.*

He heard Aunt Beatrice making angry, mother-hen sounds about respecting Cleo's marriage, but he didn't hang around to listen to anything else.

The kitchen had to be on the first floor somewhere. It was just a matter of opening a few doors. Suddenly, he wanted to whisk Cleo away from all the madness downstairs, away from her suspicious, uncaring family. Part of his job as Cleo's hired husband was to act as her bodyguard, to protect her from harm. And he intended to do just that. But after meeting her relatives, Roarke wanted to do more than simply protect her physically. He wanted to protect her emotionally. His gut instincts warned him that Cleo's kindred felt very little love for her.

If Roarke had his way, that bunch of vultures would never get their claws into Cleo again. They would never rip her apart and leave her bleeding. In the weeks to come, he would do everything in his power to take care of Cleo and keep her safe.

But what he intended to do right now was find his wife, take her upstairs and enjoy his wedding night.

Chapter 3

"Why didn't you come out and meet my husband?" Cleo watched Pearl while the housekeeper hand-washed the pots and pans she had used in preparing the upcoming evening meal.

Other than Aunt Beatrice, Cleo supposed she loved Pearl better than anyone else in the world. Pearl had been Cleo's true friend for as long as she could remember.

"I don't approve of this hasty marriage of yours." Pearl kept her back to Cleo. "No matter what you or anyone else tries to tell me, I know why you married that man."

So, that was how it was, Cleo thought. Pearl had never been one to mince words, to keep her true feelings to herself. Uncle George had relished his and Pearl's heated disagreements over everything from politics to religion. Pearl came from a long line of Southern Baptist conservatives and would fight to the death for her convictions.

Taking one tentative step at a time, Cleo made her way across the polished wooden floor, past the tile-topped center island and toward the row of daffodil yellow cabinets.

"And just why do you think I married Roarke?" Cleo halted a couple of feet behind Pearl.

"You married him because of your uncle George's will." Pearl placed the last pan in the drainboard, wiped off her age-spotted hands on the large, white apron and turned to face Cleo. "You went and bought yourself a husband. That's what you did. You paid for a man to get you pregnant. And as soon as he does, you'll get yourself one of them quickie divorces."

"Is that what Aunt Beatrice told you?"

"Your aunt Bea said this Mr. Roarke swept you off your feet and the two of you were madly in love." Pearl frowned, turning the corners of her wide, thin lips downward and creating a row of wrinkles across her brow. Looking directly at Cleo, her sharp gray eyes narrowing, she shook her head and grunted. "Yep, that's what she told the rest of 'em, too, and they didn't believe her any more than I did."

"Don't you think I'm special enough that some man would fall madly in love with me and sweep me off my feet in a whirlwind romance?"

"Child, I doubt that the man's been born who's good enough for you." Swallowing her sentimental emotions, Pearl tilted her silvery white head to one side and surveyed Cleo from head to toe. "You deserve better than a bought husband. You deserve a man who'll worship the ground you walk on."

"Oh, Pearl!"

When Cleo threw her arms around the old woman's thick waist, Pearl wrapped Cleo in her embrace, stroking Cleo's hair as if she were a child.

"Your uncle George was a stubborn old fool to have written such nonsense in his will." Pearl wrapped her arm around Cleo's waist and led her over to the pine drop-leaf table. "He thought sure you'd marry Hugh Winfield. Had that boy all picked out for you, he did. I tried to tell him that old Hubert's son wasn't man enough for my Cleo Belle. I told him, one morning when he was sitting at this very table…I said to him, a Thoroughbred filly like our Cleo needs her a rogue stallion, not some 'lead him around by the nose' gelding."

Pearl's comment made Cleo smile, not just because she had fairly accurately described Hugh Winfield and Simon Roarke, but because her comparing people to animals reminded Cleo of the game she and Pearl had been playing since she was a small child.

"I'm sure if Uncle George hadn't taken ill suddenly and been in the hospital when I found Hugh in Daphne's bed, he would have reconsidered the stipulations in his will." Cleo pulled out one of the maple splat-back chairs for Pearl, and after the housekeeper sat, Cleo pulled out another chair and joined her.

"Now, there's a pair for you." Pearl's round, fat face crinkled with tiny lines when she smiled. "Daphne and Hugh. I'd say those two deserve each other. A black widow spider and a cockroach."

Cleo burst into laughter, the action releasing all the bottled-up tension inside her. "And Trey is a weasel and poor little Marla is a timid mouse and—"

"Your aunt Oralie's been a snake all her life, and all the years they've been married, Perry Sutton's been a whipped dog. And dear Beatrice has always been a little lamb. Even now, and her sixty-three years old." Pearl reached across the table and took Cleo's hands in hers. "Mr. George was so afraid you'd end up an old maid like Bea. It near broke his heart that she never married and had children."

"Aunt Beatrice has no idea you told me about what happened all those years ago." Cleo squeezed Pearl's hands, then released them and took a deep breath.

"She was brokenhearted when she lost her man." Pearl shook her head sadly. "And the way it happened. Poor little lamb ain't never gotten over it. But thank the good Lord, you're made of tougher stuff. When that Emerson fellow up and eloped with Daphne, you didn't roll over and play dead for the next thirty years like Bea did."

Cleo needed Pearl's support as much as she needed her aunt Beatrice's. She realized she should have talked things over with Pearl before getting married, made the old woman understand the necessity of her drastic actions. But when Aunt Beatrice had suggested the idea of hiring a bodyguard who could also double as husband and potential father, Cleo hadn't been one hundred percent certain she would be able to go through with the plan. Only after a weeklong search and nearly two weeks of screening half a dozen contenders did Cleo decide she'd found the perfect man. Simon Alloway Roarke.

"Pearl?"

"What is it, Cleo Belle?"

"You can help make things a lot easier for me if you can accept my marriage to Roarke."

"What sort of man can this Roarke of yours be if he's willing to be bought and paid for? That's what I want to know."

"I'm sure he has his reasons for accepting my offer," Cleo said. "Can't you see that he's essential to me right now? You don't want McNamara Industries to be sold and half the employees to lose their jobs, do you?"

"No, of course I don't."

"And you want me to be protected against the person who tried to shoot me, don't you?"

"I suppose this Roarke fellow is a bodyguard as well as a hired husband."

"That's exactly what he is, Pearl. He's a former Green Beret and has worked for the past several years as a top agent for Dundee Private Security."

"You must be paying the man a small fortune for all his expertise." Pearl slapped her meaty hand down on the table. "I don't approve of divorce. You know that. But...well...all things considered, I'm willing to hold off making a final judgment until after I get to know this Simon Roarke of yours."

Cleo let out a sigh of relief. "You'll go along with our little charade, then? You'll accept Roarke as my husband and co-operate with us?"

"I won't let on like I know a thing," Pearl agreed. "But you've got to know that the whole bunch suspects something's fishy about your marriage to a man none of them ever heard of before yesterday."

"It doesn't matter what they suspect, as long as they don't know for sure."

"You'd have been better off to have told them the truth—what you did and why. And that if they didn't like it, that was just too bad. Wasn't no need for you to go letting your pride get in the way of the truth." Pearl reached out and tenderly caressed Cleo's cheek. "It's Miss Daphne you don't want knowing that you had to hire yourself a husband, ain't it?"

"I could lie and say that I don't care what Daphne thinks, but—"

"But you're human and you do care."

Smiling sadly at Pearl, Cleo shoved back her chair and stood. "The agency Roarke works for not only provides security, in my case a highly trained bodyguard, but it also does investigative work. While my new husband is protecting me, he's also going to work on discovering the identity of the person who tried to kill me."

"I know there's little real love lost between that bunch of vipers and you, but it's hard for me to believe that one of them is capable of murder," Pearl said.

The kitchen door swung open. Cleo and Pearl turned abruptly to see who might have overheard their conversation. Pearl's eyes narrowed to a squint as she observed their intruder.

Smiling warmly, Cleo crossed the kitchen. She rushed over to her husband and took his arm. "Come meet Pearl. She's been running this house since before I was born."

Roarke allowed Cleo to lead him over to where the plump, elderly woman was rising out of her chair.

"Pearl, this is Simon Roarke. My husband." Cleo waited for the housekeeper to say something, but when Pearl kept staring at Roarke, obviously evaluating every inch of him, Cleo cleared her throat. "Roarke, this is my dearest and oldest friend, Pearl Clooney, Ezra's wife and our housekeeper for the past forty years."

"Nice to meet you, Mrs. Clooney." Roarke held out his hand in greeting.

She tilted her head, then grunted and smacked her lips. "Call me 'Pearl.'" She didn't accept his outstretched hand.

"Yes, ma'am."

"You're going to take good care of my Cleo Belle?" Pearl's words were part statement and part question.

Realizing the old woman wasn't going to shake his hand, Roarke withdrew it, then slipped his arm around his wife's waist and drew her up against him. "Yes, ma'am, I plan to take good care of Cleo."

Letting her gaze travel from Roarke's intense blue eyes to the tips of his size-twelve shoes, Pearl pursed her lips and then grunted again. "Yep, I do believe you just might be man enough, all right."

Shaking her head, Cleo rolled her eyes heavenward. Roarke grinned.

"You two escaped your own wedding reception, huh?" Pearl asked. "Can't say I blame you. A little of that bunch goes a long way."

"We're planning to go upstairs and stay there," Cleo said. "Do you suppose you can serve our dinner in my room?"

"Getting an early start on your wedding night?" Pearl looked directly at Roarke.

"Yes, ma'am. You understand how it is with newlyweds," he said.

"I'll bring supper up around six," Pearl said. "That should give you time to unpack. Ezra done took your bags upstairs."

"Roarke likes beer," Cleo said. "Do we have any?"

"Ezra's got some." The corners of Pearl's mouth lifted in an almost smile. "You let me know what else your man likes to eat and drink, and I'll be sure to pick it up at the grocery store."

Cleo pulled away from Roarke, gave Pearl a big, loving hug, then turned back to her husband. Arm in arm, they walked across the room and opened the door.

Pearl called out to them, "A wife should use her husband's Christian name. If she doesn't, people wonder why." With that said, the housekeeper turned her back to them and busied herself by checking the apple pie in the oven.

Neither Cleo nor Roarke replied. They looked at each other and smiled.

"She's right," Cleo said. "I've got to stop calling you 'Roarke.' It's just that somehow I don't think of you as Simon."

It had been a long time since anyone had called him "Simon." He preferred to be called "Roarke," even by the women he dated. Using his last name was more impersonal. And that's the way he liked his relationships. Impersonal.

Roarke led her out into the narrow hallway between the kitchen and the sunroom. "Maybe it would be easier for you to call me 'honey' or 'darling' or something like that instead of forcing yourself to call me 'Simon.'"

"No, I'll call you 'Simon.' I suppose this is just the first in a long line of concessions I'll have to make while we're married.''

"We're both going to have to make some concessions for the duration of our marriage," Roarke said. "After I unpack and we settle in upstairs, I think it would be a good idea for us to discuss setting up some ground rules. Each of us needs to know exactly where we stand, so that we can present a united front to your family and to your employees."

Roarke followed Cleo up the back staircase. "Pretending to be happily married isn't going to be easy, is it? Maybe Pearl was right. Maybe I should have been totally up front with everyone. Just told them that I hired you."

"I overheard you admitting to Pearl that it matters to you what your cousin Daphne thinks," he said. "And I have a hunch that it matters to you what your employees think. You'd prefer for people to speculate about our marriage than to pity you for having no choice but to buy yourself a man."

Directly in front of the door leading to her suite, Cleo whirled around to face Roarke. "I did not have to buy myself a husband. I know at least half a dozen men who would have jumped at the chance to marry me. I chose to hire you because none of the men I know had your particular skills. I need someone who can protect me and unearth my would-be killer."

"I didn't mean to imply that you couldn't attract a man, my dear Ms....pardon me...my dear Mrs. Roarke."

"No matter whom I married, it would have been a business arrangement."

"Even if you'd married Hugh Winfield?"

"How do you know about Hugh?"

"I guessed right, then, didn't I?" Roarke's broad chest rumbled with laughter. "You and Daphne both wanted Fancy Pants Winfield, and your cousin won the prize."

"Hugh Winfield is no prize." Cleo opened the door to her suite. "Please come in and make yourself at home. We'll share these rooms for however long our marriage lasts."

She took a step forward, only to be swept up in Roarke's arms once again. When she glared at him, he only smiled.

"It's customary for the groom to carry the bride over the threshold."

"You did that downstairs," she reminded him.

"That was for your family's benefit," he said.

"Oh? And for whose benefit is this little show, Mr. Roarke?"

"It's for your benefit, Boss Lady. I thought it might help you get in the right mood for our wedding night."

Feeling the heat rise in her face, Cleo looked away from Roarke as he carried her through the open door. She should have said something to him earlier about not wanting to rush into having sex. Obviously, he intended to take that part of their marriage seriously. Of course she realized that she'd have to have sex with him sometime if she wanted to get pregnant. She'd considered asking him to go through an artificial insemination process, but had changed her mind. Everything about her marriage to this man was a charade and as impersonal as a relationship could be. She didn't want the process of creating a child to be a clinical, impersonal act. She wasn't quite sure why it mattered so much; it just did.

Roarke carried her across the room and deposited her in the middle of a mahogany spindle bed. Placing his knees on the quilt coverlet, he braced himself with both hands spread out beside her hips. Leaning forward, he kissed her. She pulled back and sucked in a deep breath.

As she scooted toward the headboard, he followed her, trapping her against the ornately carved wooden surface. "It's been a while since you've done this, hasn't it?" he asked.

"What?" Her eyes widened, the dark irises glistening like polished jade.

"Sex," he said, resting his body beside hers, his head against the headboard. "You haven't had sex in a long time. You're too skittish for an experienced woman. You act as if you're afraid of me." Laying his head on her shoulder, he cocked it to one side and looked up at her.

Every muscle in her body tensed at his accusation. Every nerve rioted, sending shock waves of embarrassment through her entire system. "Just because I'm not quite prepared to—to—"

"Jump my bones." Roarke chose the words for her.

"Okay. Just because I'm not quite prepared to jump your bones right this minute does not mean that it's been years since

I've been intimate with a man. It simply means that I can't rush into having sex with a man who's a stranger to me.''

Lifting his head off her shoulder, he shrugged. "You don't have to know a person to have sex with him. Believe me, you can have great sex with a perfect stranger.''

"I'm sure you would know. But unlike you and, from what I understand, most men, sex for me isn't just some bodily function, it's—''

"A deep and profound emotional experience?''

"I do not appreciate your making fun of me. And I don't appreciate your implying that I'm practically a virgin!''

Uh-oh, Roarke thought. He certainly had pushed all her buttons, hadn't he? He had hoped that Cleo McNamara wouldn't turn out to be the type of woman who couldn't separate her physical needs from her emotional needs. But just as he had suspected, she was a romantic under that icy exterior.

He had no intention of becoming emotionally involved with this woman. He hadn't allowed himself to care about anyone, really care, since Laurie died. Loving others meant pain and suffering when you lost them. His divorce from Hope had made him cynical. His daughter's death had made him emotionally barren.

He didn't want Cleo to care about him, didn't want her confusing good sex with love. It would make things easier for him if she'd had a legion of lovers, men who had meant nothing to her. But no, just his luck, she had admitted to being inexperienced. Just how inexperienced was she? *Practically a virgin?* What did that mean?

His stomach did an evil flip-flop. Practically a virgin usually meant only one former lover. Winfield? No, Roarke thought. Not Winfield. Someone else. Someone a long time ago. Someone she had loved.

Roarke scooted to the edge of the bed and stood. "I'm sorry if I sounded like I was making fun of you. I wasn't. Not at all. I just thought that since I'm going to be your lover, it would be better for both of us if I knew it had been a while since you'd been with someone.''

"All right. Yes, it has been a while…years,'' she admitted reluctantly, her gaze fixed on the carved back of the needle-point-upholstered French chair that sat behind her desk at the foot of the bed. "Ten years. He was my fiancé." She swallowed, bit down on her bottom lip and crossed her arms, hugging herself about the waist. "A few weeks before we were to be married, he eloped with Daphne."

That would explain, in large part, the animosity between Cleo and Daphne. And it explained Cleo's cool, controlled attitude. Apparently, Daphne was no longer married to this man, whoever he was. What Roarke wondered was whether Cleo still loved him. Surely not. Not after ten years. But the hurt would still exist. And the awful humiliation.

He, perhaps better than anyone, knew that sometimes old wounds never healed. Not completely.

Roarke walked over to the French doors that led out to a balcony overlooking the backyard. Lined drapes in an expensive floral fabric hung on each side of the doors. He glanced down at the brick patio and the small flower garden. Off in the distance, he saw the orchard Cleo had told him about earlier in the day.

"Any man who'd dump you for Daphne is a fool." Roarke's voice was deep, calm and totally void of emotion. "You're better off without him."

"Yes, I know." She got out of bed, removed her navy heels and slipped into a pair of green satin house shoes.

When Roarke opened the French doors and stepped out onto the balcony, she followed him. "You've been with a lot of women, haven't you?" she asked.

He grasped the white wooden banisters that circled the balcony and leaned over, looking straight down at the screened back porch. "Several."

"How many are several?" She stood directly behind him, a couple of feet away.

"I don't know. Half a dozen before I got married, then more after my divorce. Not very many in the past five or six years. If you're worried, don't be. I always practiced safe sex."

"Did you ever love anyone other than your wife?"

"Not really. A couple of heavy involvements before I got married. Kid stuff, really. Hormones, mostly." He couldn't remember the last time he'd spoken so openly, so honestly with anyone, least of all a woman. But Cleo had been honest with him, had shared probably the most painful and humiliating experience of her life. He owed her the truth. He'd answer her questions. As long as she didn't start probing into his marriage, asking about things he couldn't bear to remember.

"Simon?"

A sudden hot, searing pain hit him square in the gut. It was as if she had branded his name into his flesh. The women he'd known in the past fifteen years had called him "Roarke" or "honey" or "lover," if they'd called him anything at all.

Hope had called him "Simon." She still did, on the rare occasions that she recognized him when he visited her at the sanitarium.

"Yeah?" He'd have to get used to Cleo calling him "Simon." It was all part of the act. This was just a job, he reminded himself. When it was over, he would walk away and forget he'd ever known Cleo McNamara. Forget that he'd left her with his child growing inside her body.

"I can help you unpack, if you'd like," she said. "I'll empty a couple of drawers in the chest for you. And I have an enormous walk-in closet with plenty of room for your clothes."

"I travel pretty light." He turned slowly and faced her, thinking how very pretty his new wife looked in the fading early-evening sunlight. Her red hair shone like bronze silk. He had the sudden urge to reach out and pull her into his arms. "I've got two suits. The blue one I'm wearing and a black one. Some dress pants, a sport coat, a couple pair of jeans and a few shirts. Other than socks and underwear, that's about it."

"We'll have to get some new suits made for you," she said. "Uncle George has a tailor in town that all the men in the family use."

"Tailor-made suits?" Roarke widened his eyes in mock surprise, lifting his dark, thick eyebrows in the process. "You really want me to look the part of your husband, huh?"

"Let's just call any new clothes you acquire during our marriage a bonus," Cleo said. "Besides, we'll have to find something for you to do at McNamara Industries to explain why you're going in to work with me every day and nosing around at the plant. You'll need to look like a successful businessman."

"I'll certainly live up to the image of a kept man, won't I? We're living in your family's mansion. You're buying me new clothes and giving me a job. What else? Are you giving me a car, too?"

"Would you prefer using my Jaguar or my Mercedes?" she asked. "I prefer the Jag, but if you'd rather drive the Mercedes, then I have no objections."

"We'll use the Jag," he said. "Since I doubt I'll be going anywhere without you, we'll just use your favorite vehicle."

"Maybe everyone will think we're so in love that we can't bear to be apart, not even for a few minutes."

Moving closer, he clutched her shoulders in his big hands. "Look, Cleo, I know this situation isn't easy for you. And I know you have the noblest of reasons for choosing this course of action. I intend to do whatever I can to make things as easy for you as possible, and if that means convincing the whole world that we're madly in love, so be it."

She laid her hands on his chest, intending to push him away. But once she touched him, she felt the warmth of his body, the steady beat of his heart. "Thank you…Simon."

"We need to discuss each member of your family." He released her shoulders, then grasped her hands, which lay on his chest. "The more information you can give me, the better. I'll have to find out everything about your aunt and uncle and cousins, including Trey's wife."

"Surely Marla isn't a suspect. She's harmless. She doesn't make a move without Trey's approval."

"Then she'd do whatever he asked her to do, even try to kill you."

"Everyone is a suspect?"

"Everyone, including Hugh Winfield." He clasped her hands tighter, pressing them against his chest.

"Hugh?" Cleo gazed directly into Roarke's eyes, and for one brief moment longed to stand on tiptoe and find his mouth with her lips.

"He's involved with Daphne, and if he marries her, her inheritance will be his, too."

Cleo was looking at him as if she wanted to be kissed. But he wouldn't kiss her. He was beginning to know this woman—

his wife. Her eyes might be begging for him, but she would deny their hunger if he attempted to give her what she wanted.

"Aunt Beatrice is above suspicion, and Pearl and Ezra, too, I hope."

"Probably. I don't think Beatrice would have suggested bringing in a bodyguard who could fulfill the stipulations in her father's will if she wanted you dead. And I don't see that either Pearl or her husband has a motive."

Cleo had to get away from Roarke—Simon—before she embarrassed herself. She couldn't figure out what was wrong with her, why she was acting like some female animal in heat. Maybe their discussion of their respective sex lives had triggered the rush of hormones that had her practically climbing the wall. This would never do! How was she going to convince her husband that she wanted to wait a couple of weeks before consummating their marriage if she went up in flames every time he touched her?

"I think I'll shower and change clothes before Pearl brings up dinner." Cleo shoved on Roarke's chest, and for a couple of seconds she thought he wasn't going to release her.

He dropped his hands to his sides and waited for her to remove her hands from his chest. "Sounds like a good idea. As soon as you finish up, I'll take a shower."

Lift your hands, she told herself. Lift your hands, turn around and walk away.

He kept looking at her, his gaze moving over her face, then down to her chest. He was staring at her breasts, at the pebble-hard nipples pressing against her sheer bra and silk blouse. A gripping sensation throbbed intimately within Cleo, sending tingling desire radiating from her feminine core to her taut breasts and then throughout her body. Balling her hands into fists, she shoved against his chest. He stepped backward, putting a few inches between their bodies.

Without saying a word, she turned and ran into her bedroom, leaving Roarke alone on the balcony. The moment she slammed shut the bathroom door, he let out a long sigh, then cursed under his breath. He was aroused to the point of pain. Somehow he had to make it through dinner and a discussion of the suspects. How many hours would that take? How long would it be before they went to bed? He could wait a little longer, if he had to. A few hours. Waiting would make the loving all the sweeter. For both of them.

Chapter 4

Roarke finished off his second beer, placed the bottle on the table and leaned back in the French bergère chair. Crossing his arms over his chest, he looked at Cleo, who sat in a matching chair across the round Sheraton table in her sitting room. She played with a piece of Pearl's delicious apple pie, destroying the flaky crust with the tip of her fork. She had picked at her entire meal, leaving most of it on her plate. Roarke wondered if she always ate so light or if she was nervous tonight.

His cast-iron stomach was all right; he never had a problem eating. As a matter of fact, all Roarke's appetites were in top form, and there was one particular appetite that he was more than ready to appease.

Cleo hadn't said much to him after they'd showered and changed clothes. Unfortunately, they'd showered separately. In the future, he'd have to rectify that situation. Before he'd had a chance to unpack, Ezra had delivered their dinner on an enormous silver tray, and Cleo had busied herself arranging the meal on the table in her sitting room.

Cleo's suite consisted of three rooms: a large, luxurious bath; a huge bedroom decorated with antiques; and a small sitting room, with a table and two chairs, a fat, overstuffed love seat and a Queen Anne wingback in the corner. All three rooms had been done in pale, delicate shades of green, peach and cream. Although there wasn't any lace or bows or satin or frilly touches in the suite, the rooms were decidedly feminine. The orderly neatness, the expensive decor, the cool, fragile colors corresponded with similar traits in Cleo herself. She was cool, neat, fragile and rich.

She gazed nervously at him, and Roarke instinctively knew that while they'd shared supper, she'd been thinking about tonight. About their first night together. Once or twice, he had noticed her glancing into the bedroom, at her bed. The bed she would share with him during their marriage.

"If you're finished, I'll ring for Pearl to clear away these things."

"I'm through. Pearl's a fabulous cook." Roarke laid his linen napkin on the table. "You didn't eat much. Weren't you hungry?"

"Not really. Nerves, I guess," Cleo admitted. "It's not every day that I get married."

"Or every night that you share your bed with a husband."

"Yes, I'm afraid I'm not accustomed to having someone share my suite, and certainly not my bed." She stood abruptly. Her napkin fell from her lap and landed at her feet on the soft, thick carpet. She crossed the room hurriedly, pulled open a drawer in the mahogany inlaid-and-banded chest, then turned to him. "I'll rearrange a few things so that you can have this drawer. And there's plenty of room in the closet—" she nodded toward the door that led to the room-size walk-in closet "—for you to hang your clothes."

"Thanks." Roarke couldn't help but notice how different Cleo looked after she'd changed out of her navy blue suit and into a pair of jeans and oversize top. Young. Fresh. Innocent. She'd washed away any residue of makeup, leaving her face scrubbed clean. And she had removed her gold jewelry, the earrings, watch and bracelet—everything except the wide gold wedding band.

He looked down at his left hand, at the band circling his third finger. Eighteen years ago, Hope had slipped a similar ring on his finger and he had promised to love her forever. He'd been so sure their love would last a lifetime—it hadn't survived the first year. Now he was married again, but not for love. This time he knew in advance that this marriage was headed straight for the divorce courts.

Cleo notified Pearl that they had finished dinner, then she emptied the second drawer in the chest for Roarke. She opened the closet door and, after flipping on the light switch, walked inside and pushed some of her suits down the rack on the left. Although she watched Roarke while he unpacked his suitcase, she pretended to be otherwise occupied.

Roarke was even more masculine, more devastatingly male in a pair of tight, faded jeans and an Atlanta Braves T-shirt than he'd been in his suit. His shoulders were massive, his arms bulging with muscles, his stomach flat and his butt tight. She didn't believe she'd ever spent as much time assessing a man's body as she had the past hour inspecting her husband.

After his shower, he hadn't bothered putting on any shoes. When he'd commented on how soft the carpet was, Cleo had stared down at his big feet. Even his feet looked masculine. Large. Wide. His toes sprinkled with brown hair.

After he'd emptied his underwear and a pair of blue-and-white-striped pajama bottoms from a duffel bag and placed them in the chest, he pulled out a shaving kit.

"Would you mind putting this in the bathroom for me?" he asked.

"Of course." When she walked out of the closet, he tossed the kit to her.

Entering the bathroom, she paused to look at her very private domain, one that would be private no longer. For the next few months, she would have to share her living quarters with Roarke. Even her bathroom was no longer sacrosanct. She placed his shaving kit on the vanity, alongside her cosmetic basket. Her hand trembled. Marrying a stranger to fulfill the stipulations in her uncle's will had seemed the only solution to her problems, and she'd been certain she would be able to adjust to sharing her suite with a man. But she wasn't as sure now. Now that Simon Roarke's underwear was in her English mahogany chest. Now that his razor and toothbrush and after-shave rested on her vanity. Now that she had to face a night alone with him in her bed, lying beside her, his big body only inches away. What would happen if they accidentally brushed against each other during the night?

Stop worrying, she told herself. You're the boss. He's the employee. Once you explain that you want to wait a couple of weeks and become better acquainted before you have sex, then he'll have no choice but to comply with your wishes.

Exiting the bathroom, she halted in the doorway when she saw Roarke remove a gun and trim leather holster from his suitcase. She sucked in her breath. A gun! Of course he'd have a gun. He was a professional bodyguard.

With the holster in his hand, he looked across the room at Cleo. "Under normal circumstances, I would have worn this today, but... I'd like to put it in the nightstand, on my side of the bed. And I'll need to start wearing it whenever we're out of these rooms."

"Do you really think that's necessary?" If others saw his pistol, what would they think? How would they ever explain why her husband was carrying a gun?

"Yes, Boss Lady. It's a necessary part of my protecting you." He pulled the gun from the holster and lifted it up so she could get a better look at it. "Do you know anything about guns?"

"Not a great deal," she said. "Uncle George had a small collection of rifles that he kept in a gun cabinet in his study downstairs."

"Come here." He motioned for her to come to him.

She complied with his request, crossed the room and stopped at his side. He grabbed her hand and laid the gun in her palm. She quivered.

"A gun is no better or worse than the person who uses it," he told her. "This gun will be used only for your protection. It's not your enemy."

She handed the gun back to him. "I'm not afraid of guns, Roarke. It's just that I'm not used to living with someone who carries one."

Roarke returned his Beretta to the holster, then gave it back to Cleo. "Put this in the nightstand, will you? I don't know which side of the bed you want me to sleep on."

Holding the gun cautiously, Cleo carried it to the nightstand on the left side of the bed, opened the drawer and carefully placed the holster on top of several paperback books.

"How will you explain wearing a gun if someone in the family or at the office notices?" Closing the drawer, she glanced across to where Roarke stood in the closet, hanging his clothes beside hers.

"I brought along that model of Beretta, a Cougar 800, because it's compact and easy to conceal, but uses a high-powered 9 mm clip. No one should notice it, but if someone does, I'll just say I'm wearing it to protect my wife."

She nodded agreement. What sort of man was he, this husband of hers? A former Green Beret. A private security agent. A professional bodyguard. He had nothing in common with the men of her acquaintance. Ordinary men, who lived ordinary lives. No danger. No violence. No weapons.

"You know a lot about guns, don't you?" she asked.

"In my line of business, it pays to know a lot about guns."

A loud, distinct knock at the bedroom door ended their discussion. Before Cleo could reply, the door opened and Pearl sauntered in, a large, empty basket in her hand. She looked Cleo up and down, then gave Roarke the same visual treatment.

"Your aunt Oralie was complaining that y'all didn't join the family for dinner," Pearl said. "Bea told her that she suspected you two wouldn't be joining the family for meals for several days."

When Pearl turned her gaze on Roarke, her eyes narrowing as she inspected him, he grinned at her and winked. Grunting, she spread her lips in a closed-mouth smile.

"Y'all's ears ought to be burning." Pearl chuckled quietly. "They've been discussing the two of you. Taking y'all apart, piece by piece. They're trying to figure out whether this marriage is for real or not."

"And what have they decided?" Roarke asked.

"Well, before y'all showed up this afternoon, they were one hundred percent sure that Cleo had hired herself a husband. But now they're not so sure. Not after the way they said you two were carrying on downstairs at the reception."

"We were not carrying on," Cleo said.

"From what they were saying, I'm sorry I missed seeing

Mr. Roarke carry you up onto the veranda. That must have been some sight.''

"What can I say, Pearl? How could a man keep from being romantic with his new bride?" Roarke grabbed Cleo around the waist and drew her to his side. "Especially when his bride is as lovely as our Cleo Belle?"

Cleo gasped at his use of Pearl's pet name for her. She had wanted and asked for Pearl's understanding and support, but, dammit, it wasn't necessary for Pearl to actually like Roarke.

"What I really hate that I missed was hearing you warn off that bunch of vultures," Pearl told Roarke. "I'd have given just about anything to see their faces when you told them that nobody had better try to hurt Cleo again, and that you knew a hundred different ways to kill a person."

Gasping loudly, Cleo clutched Roarke's arm. "Oh, my God, you didn't say that to my family, did you?"

"I said it and I meant it," Roarke admitted. "I thought that a little warning up front was in order. If we're lucky, just knowing that you have a protective husband watching out for you might give our potential murderer second thoughts."

"Couldn't you have discussed this with me before you went and shot your mouth off?" Cleo's short, neat nails bit into his forearm.

"I'll just go get those dishes cleaned up." Pearl nodded toward the sitting room. "Cleo, why don't you come help me, if you can tear yourself away from your handsome husband for a few minutes?"

Cleo knew Pearl wanted something other than her assistance in clearing away the remains of her and Roarke's meal. More than likely the housekeeper was going to preach her another sermon on marriage, something along the lines of a wife being subservient to her husband. Cleo laughed silently. As if Pearl Clooney had ever been subservient to Ezra one day in her life!

Once they entered the sitting room, Pearl and Cleo cleared away the table, placing the china, silver, crystal and linens in the large wicker basket. Cleo set the basket on the floor.

Pearl pulled a soft rag from her apron and ran it across the inlaid tabletop. Cocking her head so she could look at Cleo, she continued wiping the table. "By the looks of him, I'd say you got yourself some man there, Cleo Belle."

"Do you think so, Pearl?" So, that's what this was all about, Cleo thought. Pearl was on the verge of giving Roarke her seal of approval.

"A smart girl like you should be able to figure out a way to keep that man." Pearl swiped her rag across the wooden trim along the backs of the bergère chairs. "When you get pregnant with his baby, he's bound to want to stick around."

Cleo glanced into the bedroom. The look Roarke gave her chilled her to the bone. His blue eyes darkened to a deep indigo when he glared at her, reminding her that he had said he wanted nothing to do with any child she conceived. Roarke stomped across the floor and disappeared into the closet.

Lifting the basket off the floor, Cleo walked Pearl to the door, then opened the door and handed the housekeeper the wicker basket.

Pearl leaned close to Cleo's ear and whispered, "I believe Simon Roarke just might be that rogue stallion I told your uncle George you needed."

For several minutes after Pearl disappeared down the hallway, Cleo stood in the open doorway. Earthy, erotic images danced wildly in her mind. A stallion and a mare. Lightning illuminating a dark sky. She and Roarke, standing in the rain, naked, their bodies straining to touch.

She had to stop thinking like this, stop wondering what it would be like when she and Roarke made love. No, it wouldn't be making love. It would be sex. They would be lovers, but only in the most basic, animalistic sense.

"Would you care for a brandy?" she called out to him as she closed the door.

He walked out of the closet and stood on the other side of the room. "Sure, if you're having one."

"In the sitting room," she told him. "Why don't we go sit down, have our drinks and discuss the details of how we plan to handle our situation?"

Roarke nodded agreement, but waited several minutes before joining her in the sitting room. He needed a little more time to erase Pearl's words from his mind: *When you get pregnant with his baby, he's bound to want to stick around.*

He could never allow himself to think of the child Cleo would conceive as his baby. Getting her pregnant was just a part of his assignment, a part of the package deal that meant lifetime security for him and for Hope. He would never see Cleo's child, never be a part of his or her life. It had to be that way. He'd been a father once, and he'd done a lousy job of it. He had failed his little girl and his failure had cost Laurie her life.

A man could die a hundred ways and a thousand times, but Roarke doubted that any agony could equal the pain a man felt when he lost a child and knew he could have prevented the tragedy.

Roarke joined Cleo in her sitting room. She sat curled up, in her sock feet, on the fat, pale green love seat, a brandy snifter in her small hand. Her leather loafers lay half-hidden beneath the sofa's fringed edge. His brandy waited for him on the table. He lifted his glass, saluted her with it and slumped down into the corner wingback. He placed his feet on the needlepoint footstool and took a sip of the brandy, savoring the smooth taste of the aged liquor.

"Good stuff," he said, and took another sip.

"Uncle George's private stock. He bought only the best."

"Did he think he'd bought Hugh Winfield for you?" Roarke asked. "Is that why he put those ridiculous stipulations in his will?"

Cleo supposed she should feel insulted, but she didn't. How could she? In a way, what Roarke had suggested was true. "I was dating Hugh when Uncle George made out his new will, and yes, I'm sure he thought that I'd marry Hugh and that Hugh would jump at the chance to marry an heiress."

"What went wrong?"

"You already know the answer to that question."

"Daphne?"

"When Uncle George was in the hospital, dying, I discovered Hugh in Daphne's bed. She had seduced him and set things up so that I'd find them together." Lifting the snifter to her lips, Cleo slowly downed the remainder of her brandy. "Hugh was embarrassed, but not all that remorseful. He even accused me of being to blame."

"How the hell could he blame you?"

"He said that he would never have turned to Daphne if I hadn't refused to have sex with him."

"Aaa...hhh. A reasonable excuse for a man caught with his pants down," Roarke said.

Cleo laughed, despite the vividness of the humiliating memory of that night less than a month ago. "I think at the time Hugh believed one potential heiress was as good as another, so why shouldn't he choose the one willing to sleep with him? Of course, he had no way of knowing that Uncle George would make me his major beneficiary and leave me complete control of McNamara Industries."

"Did Hugh change his tune once your uncle's will was read?"

"He tried once, but I didn't give him a chance," Cleo said. "I would have given up McNamara Industries before I would have married that...that...that weasel!"

"So, Hugh stands to profit only if he marries Daphne and the family can force you to sell McNamara Industries?" Roarke finished off his brandy and set the snifter on the small cloth-draped, glass-topped table beside his chair.

"Hugh's not a bad man." Cleo smiled when she noticed Roarke's widened eyes and raised brows. "He's a weak man. Nothing like his father. Hubert Winfield was Uncle George's attorney for years and he trusted him implicitly. Hugh is a junior partner in his father's firm, but he's not the brilliant lawyer Hubert is. Hugh works exclusively with McNamara Industries. That's about all he can handle, and his father keeps pretty good tabs on him to make sure he doesn't screw up. And Hugh is not privy to any of my personal legal affairs."

"And this is the man your uncle chose for you?"

"Uncle George knew Hugh's bloodlines. Our families have been associated for several generations," Cleo explained. "Besides, I *was* dating Hugh. Uncle George wanted me to find a man, and Hugh was...well, he was there."

Roarke stretched his arms, threaded his fingers together and placed his entwined hands behind his head. "What do you suppose Uncle George would think of me as your husband?"

"I shudder to think. More likely than not, his first reaction would have been the same as Pearl's, but then, just as Pearl has done, once he had a chance to size you up, he'd advise me to hang on to such a prime specimen."

Roarke laughed, the sound a mixture of embarrassment and

amusement. Relaxing, he burrowed into the big, comfortable chair and took a long, hard look at Cleo. He liked what he saw. Liked it far too much. Instead of sitting there discussing potential suspects, he'd much rather carry his wife to bed, undress her slowly and make love to her all night long.

Later, he told himself. Be patient. First things first. Business before pleasure.

Idiot, he reprimanded himself. Pleasuring Cleo would be business. Part of his job was to impregnate her.

He had to get his mind off making love to Cleo. "Does your cousin Daphne hate you enough to kill you?" he asked, determined to get back to the business at hand—gaining more personal information about the suspects.

"I honestly don't know." Cleo shifted uncomfortably, then bent one knee, lifting it high enough to drape her folded hands around it. "Daphne and I have had a love-hate relationship all our lives. Since we were children, whatever I had, Daphne wanted. For years, I couldn't understand why she was jealous of me.

"I envied her so much. She had two loving parents. A mother who doted on her. A brother who adored her. And she's always been beautiful and the center of attention."

"So why do you think she's so jealous of you?" Roarke asked.

"Because of Aunt Oralie's insecurities. My father was Uncle George's favorite and Aunt Oralie resented that. Then when I came to live with Uncle George and Aunt Beatrice, I became Uncle George's favorite."

"Would you say that Oralie Sutton hates you?"

"No, of course she doesn't. I'm her brother's only child. In her own way, she loves me. It's just that…well, she's an unhappy woman, very fragile and high-strung. Uncle Perry is so protective of her, and he resents me a great deal. I'd say if anyone in this family truly hates me, it's Uncle Perry. He hates me because my existence has caused so much pain for Aunt Oralie and kept his children from being the only McNamara heirs."

"Do you think Perry Sutton tried to shoot you?"

"I don't know," Cleo said. "But I think it's possible."

"Why not Trey? Or even Marla?"

Shaking her head, Cleo giggled. Her short, cinnamon hair gleamed with healthy vibrance in the soft glow of the lamplight. "Marla wouldn't hurt a fly. She's too sweet and timid. And I doubt that Trey knows one end of a rifle from the other."

"Whoever tried to shoot you might have been hired by one of your relatives," Roarke told her. "Of course, since the shooter missed his target, I'd say he wasn't a trained professional. But Trey or Perry or even Daphne could have hired some local hoodlum who wasn't a very good shot."

Crossing her arms over her chest, Cleo rubbed up and down her arms. "I hate to think that one of my relatives is willing to kill me in order to sell the company. Can you imagine how that makes me feel? Knowing that someone I've lived with most of my life, someone I've loved and trusted, wants to see me dead."

"I won't kid you, Cleo. These next few months aren't going to be an easy time for you. But I promise that I'll do everything in my power to keep you safe."

"Roarke, I…"

"What?"

"Thank you for agreeing to this arrangement." She slid to the edge of the sofa and stood. "I know that acting as my bodyguard is what you're trained to do, but the other…the personal terms of our business deal… Well, I'm grateful that, for whatever reasons, you decided to take me up on my offer, you were willing to marry me and…and—"

"I did it for the money," Roarke said unemotionally. "I'm nearly forty. I've got my share of battle scars, some obtained when I was in the Special Forces and some since I've been with Dundee. I'm tired. I want to retire. Invested wisely, the million you're paying me should take care of me for the rest of my life."

"Yes. I understand." She walked past him, pausing briefly before exiting the sitting room. "There's more brandy in the cabinet—" she pointed to the chinoiserie cabinet beneath the window "—if you'd like more. And there's a television in the armoire in my…our bedroom, and a fairly good selection of books on the bottom shelves. Please, make yourself as comfortable as possible."

"In other words, make myself at home, huh?"

"Yes, certainly." She glanced at him briefly and wished she hadn't. The way he looked at her made her feel all fluttery inside, as if a dozen tiny butterflies had been set free in her stomach. "I'm tired. I think I'll turn in."

Before she had taken three steps out of the sitting room, Roarke called out to her, "It's been a long day for both of us. I might as well call it a night, too."

Tell him, dammit, Cleo! Tell him that you are not going to have sex with him tonight.

Maybe he doesn't expect to have sex with you. Since you're his employer, maybe he plans to wait for your explicit orders.

"Roarke?"

"You take the bathroom first." He raked his hand over his jaw. "I need to shave before I go to bed."

Nodding agreement, she hurried to retrieve her gown and robe from the closet, then rushed into the bathroom, closing the door quietly behind her.

While preparing for bed, she thought about the fact that this was her wedding night. She almost cried. No, she told herself, don't give in to self-pity. Things could be a lot worse. What if Hugh Winfield was the bridegroom who would join her in her bed tonight? Heaven forbid!

At least with Roarke, she would be the one in charge. There were certain advantages to buying yourself a temporary husband.

The moment she walked out of the bathroom, Roarke, who sat on the edge of the bed, stood and smiled at her. He looked her over from head to toe and almost laughed aloud. She certainly hadn't dressed like a bride on her wedding night. No sheer, see-through nightie. No lace teddy. Nothing the least bit sexy or provocative. But dammit all, if there wasn't something appealing about little Miss Cleo Belle in her unadorned, pale lavender cotton gown and matching robe that skimmed the floor as she moved toward him.

"The bathroom's all yours," she said, then glanced away shyly.

He liked that about her. That hint of timidness. He'd already figured out that some of what people considered coolness in Cleo was actually shyness.

"I usually sleep in the raw," he told her, and couldn't repress a muted chuckle when he saw her mouth gape in a silent gasp. "But until you get used to me, I'll make a concession and sleep in these." He held up a pair of blue-and-white-striped pajama bottoms.

"Thank you for your consideration," she said.

She waited until he disappeared into the bathroom before she removed her robe, draped it over the desk chair at the foot of her bed and turned down the covers.

Roarke usually slept naked. She tried valiantly not to think about how he would look—tall, muscular and completely unclothed. Perspiration broke out on her upper lip. Moisture coated her palms. Her nipples puckered painfully. And her femininity tightened and released, then tightened again.

She crawled into bed, turned off the lamp on her nightstand and pulled the covers up to her neck. She lay there quietly, trying not to move. She should have told him that they were not going to have sex tonight. She should have told him!

Less than ten minutes later, Roarke emerged from the bathroom, clean-shaven and whistling some unfamiliar tune. Cleo tensed. Suddenly, she felt very hot.

She hazarded a glance in his direction. Dear Lord, he was magnificent. Dark brown hair curled over his chest, narrowed down to a vee across his flat belly and disappeared beneath his low-slung pajama bottoms. His massive shoulders looked six feet wide and his big, muscular arms bulged with power.

Two ugly, semicircular scars, located below his right pectoral muscles, marred the absolute perfection of his chest. How had he gotten those scars? she wondered. In the army? Or on an assignment for the Dundee agency?

"Do you prefer the light on or off?" He sat down on the left side of the bed.

"Off, please," she said.

He turned off the lamp, then slipped under the covers and slid across the bed. Cleo lay there beside him as rigid as a corpse. Good God, what was wrong with her? Roarke wondered. Was she afraid? If she'd had only one other lover, she might be feeling more than a little uncertain about their making love.

"It's all right, honey." He reached out and ran his fingertips softly over her cheek.

She sucked in her breath and held it. He raised his head and leaned over her. She gazed up at him, able to see the outline of his face in the faint moonlight coming through the French doors. What would she do if he kissed her? she wondered. *Oh, please, don't let him kiss me.*

Roarke ran his fingers down the side of her neck, slowly caressing her soft skin as he lowered his hand over her shoulder. "Relax. We'll take things easy. I'm not going to do anything you don't want me to do."

Releasing her breath, she turned and buried her face against his shoulder. He lifted her body just enough to take her in his arms and hold her close. She trembled. He soothed her with long, sensitive strokes across her back.

"What's the matter, Cleo? You're trembling."

"I—I—" Tell him, you ninny! Tell him!

He felt the wild beat of her heart, the quivering of her fragile body, the tightening of her nipples as they pressed into his chest. He could not resist the urge to kiss her, but realizing how nervous she was, he tempered his passion with tenderness and took her mouth gently. She responded instantly, her lips softening and opening. He could tell that she wanted him.

Go slow, he told himself. Take it easy. She's not an experienced woman who takes lovemaking lightly. He continued the kiss, deepening it by degrees, gauging her reaction moment to moment. When she made no protest as the level of his passion increased, he cupped her breast in his hand, squeezing it tenderly.

Cleo broke the kiss and cried out. Shoving against his chest, she struggled to free herself from his embrace. He allowed her to withdraw from him. When she sat straight up, he took a deep breath and sat up beside her.

"What is it? What did I do wrong?" he asked.

Bowing her head, she stared down at her clasped hands resting in her lap. "I'm sorry. This was my fault. You didn't do anything wrong. I should have told you before we came to bed, but I thought that…maybe…you wouldn't… I mean, since I hired you to be my husband, to take your orders from me—"

Roarke grabbed her shoulders and shook her just enough to get her attention. "Stop babbling, Cleo, and just say whatever it is you're trying to say."

"I want us to wait to have sex." She looked directly at him. "I should have said something before we came to bed. I thought a great deal about the situation and decided that, since we're practically strangers, it would be easier for me to have sex with you after I got to know you a little better. I think we should wait a couple of weeks."

Dammit to hell! Why hadn't she told him sooner? Before he'd worked himself up into a sexual frenzy. He was hard and throbbing. She hadn't protested when he'd taken her in his arms and kissed her. She had responded eagerly. She wanted him! Dammit, he knew she wanted him.

Releasing her instantly, Roarke shot out of bed and stomped across the floor. He opened the French doors and went outside. He gripped the banister with white-knuckled anger. Frustration rioted inside his body.

Suddenly and without warning, he felt Cleo's hand on his shoulder. The rush of adrenaline roaring in his ears had blocked out every other sound, including her footsteps on the balcony. He tensed at her gentle touch.

"You're angry with me, aren't you?" she asked.

"No, Boss Lady, I'm not angry with you." He kept his back to her and measured each word he spoke very carefully. "You call the shots in this relationship. If you say no sex for two weeks, then we wait two weeks."

"Please understand why I need some time. My body may want you, but—" She hadn't meant to say that, to be so candid. What would he think of her? Did he already consider her a tease?

She did want him! He knew she did! He turned slowly, anger and frustration still riding him hard. The moment he looked into her tear-glazed green eyes, the anger vanished, but the frustration deepened. She was incredibly lovely standing there in the moonlight, her ivory skin gold kissed, her auburn hair shimmering like mahogany silk and her eyes darkened to a deep, dark jade.

"Go on back to bed, Cleo," he told her. "I'm fine. We'll wait until you tell me that you're ready for us to have sex."

"I want you to sleep with me," she said.

"What?"

"I want us to sleep in the same bed for the next two weeks, even though we won't be—"

"Yeah, sure. It wouldn't do if Pearl realized I was sleeping on the chaise longue or on a pallet on the floor. Or if a member of the family caught us sleeping separately."

"Yes, that's one of the reasons I think we should sleep together."

"One of the reasons? What other reason could there be?"

When she looked down, averting her gaze from his face, Roarke grabbed her chin, lifting it, forcing her to look at him.

"If we sleep together every night, we'll get used to each other." She tried to look away from him, but he held her chin tightly. When she could find no other way to escape his visual assessment, she closed her eyes. "I'll become accustomed to your body lying next to me."

Did she have any idea what kind of effect she was having on him? Did she know how badly he was hurting? It had been a long time since he'd wanted a woman the way he wanted her. And it was his own damn fault for assuming he would have sex with his wife on their wedding night.

"I understand," he said, and he did. But understanding her reasons didn't lessen his desire to take her—here, now, where she stood.

"Come back to bed," she said. "Please."

"Yeah, sure. In a little while." He released her chin. "You go on. I need some more fresh air."

"All right." She left him alone on the balcony.

He had meant to stay only a few more minutes, but by the time he had his body under control and his mind calmed, over an hour had passed. When he crawled into bed beside Cleo, he thought she was asleep, but within a few minutes, he realized she was still awake. He had a feeling neither one of them would get much sleep that night.

Chapter 5

One week down and one week to go, Roarke thought. Dammit, he hadn't been this preoccupied with sex since he was a teenager. But he had never slept beside a desirable woman night after night and been *ordered* not to touch her. Well, actually, she hadn't ordered him not to touch her—he *had* touched her, and that was part of the problem. But she had made it perfectly clear that they were not going to have sex for the first two weeks of their marriage.

He'd never been a Don Juan with the ladies, but he certainly hadn't led a celibate life, either. He wasn't accustomed to having someone dictate the terms of his sex life. But then, his sexual partner had never also been his employer. This arrangement with Cleo was frustrating, to say the least, with the potential to become explosive.

For a week now, they had lain in bed together every night, kept apart by nothing except Cleo's edict and his own willpower. But every morning they awoke to find their bodies touching, often lying spoon-fashion, her back to his chest, his arms draped around her, or vice versa, with her breasts pressed against his back, her hand lying on his stomach. This morning when he awoke, her leg had been draped over his, her fingers twined in his chest hair and her head on his shoulder.

He had found it damn near impossible to let her slip away from him, but he'd had no choice. She always seemed slightly embarrassed to discover that her body had sought the warmth of his during the night.

They continued their charade of being a happily married couple, but Cleo had seen to it that they'd had their breakfasts and dinners alone in her suite. She used their newlywed state as an excuse for them not to share mealtimes with her family. But being alone so much only added to Roarke's frustration, and he suspected Cleo wasn't immune to the sexual tension pulsating between them.

Roarke sat on the leather sofa in Cleo's office, trying his damnedest to concentrate on the files she'd asked him to look over. Maybe, if he wasn't aware of what she looked like first thing in the morning, with her hair mussed and her slender body clad in nothing but a thin cotton gown, he could look at the prim-and-proper Ms. McNamara—correction, Mrs. Roarke—sitting behind her impressive desk and see nothing more than a neatly attired businesswoman. She certainly didn't dress provocatively. She had a dozen simple little suits that she wore with matching heels and handbags and accented with pearl, diamond and gold jewelry, all small and delicate, like the lady who wore it.

Every time he looked at her, he saw a desirable woman. A woman he had a legal right to claim. But not a moral right.

Trey Sutton stormed into Cleo's office, disregarding the dire warning from Cleo's secretary that Mrs. Roarke was not to be disturbed. Audrey Woodward raced in behind Trey, waving her arms and threatening to do him bodily harm.

Trey marched straight over to Cleo's desk, pounded his fist on the wooden surface and glared coldly at his cousin. "You had no right to invent a position here at McNamara Industries just so you could give your husband a job."

"I'm so sorry, Mrs. Roarke," Audrey said. "I tried to stop Mr. Sutton, but he wouldn't listen to me. Do you want me to call Charlie?"

Roarke tossed the file folder on the sofa, uncrossed his legs and watched his wife very closely.

Cleo calmly laid aside the computer printout she'd been reading and looked up at Audrey. "No, there's no need to call the guard. After all—" she glanced meaningfully at Roarke "—our new head of security is sitting right here in my office."

"Yes, of course. I'd forgotten."

Audrey smiled at Roarke, and he thought once again, as he had when they'd first been introduced, how very young and sweet she seemed.

"Head of security, my rear end." Trey turned his heated glare on Roarke. "McNamara's never needed more than a guard at the front gate and a night watchman. Why, suddenly, do we need a head of security? You can hardly call a guard and a night watchman a security force."

Cleo smiled faintly, not parting her lips, and Roarke knew she was preparing to strike. In the ten days he'd known his wife, he'd learned the meaning of her different smiles.

"Why do we *suddenly* need a head of security?" Cleo asked mockingly. "Because, *suddenly,* after Uncle George's death, someone took a shot at me. And I have been informed that in the past two weeks, we've *suddenly* had a rash of phone calls from regular customers concerning inaccurate billing. Someone has gone into the computer system and altered the accounts. And in a plant that has been accident-free for over three years, we've *suddenly* had two mysterious accidents since Uncle George's funeral. If I didn't know better, I'd say someone was suddenly trying to sabotage McNamara Industries—someone who would like to see me forced into selling the company."

"Why do you assume that someone is monkeying around with our computer system? More than likely an employee simply made a mistake in billing and is too frightened of losing his job to own up to it." Standing straight, his back ramrod stiff, Trey bent his neatly manicured fingers into his palms, stopping just short of making tight fists. "And accidents do happen, you know? An electrical hoist can short-circuit. Mechanical equipment can and does fail."

"I'm well aware that equipment can malfunction. But not without a reason. As well-maintained as our maintenance crew keeps this plant, two of our workers shouldn't be in the hospital right now, recuperating from 'accidents' that never should have happened.''

''All right, even if someone deliberately screwed with the accounts and there's no logical explanations for those two accidents, that's no reason to put your husband in charge of the investigations. I'd like to know just what his qualifications for the job are.'' Trey's tanning-bed brown face flushed scarlet. He kept his gaze focused on Cleo, not once glancing in Roarke's direction.

''As CEO of McNamara Industries, I do not have to justify my actions to you, a senior vice president, but as my cousin and a stockholder, I'll tell you this—'' Cleo pushed her swivel chair away from her desk and stood ''—I am satisfied that Simon is qualified to head up security, and that's all that matters. As soon as possible, he will be hiring several new people to form a small security force. We've been behind times for years now. I'm simply bringing us up to date.''

''Don't you think you're going overboard in forming a security force, in hiring new employees, when it's all we can do to afford the people already on the payroll?'' Trey asked. ''We should be downsizing, not hiring!''

''The decision has been made,'' Cleo said. ''There's no point in discussing this further. Whoever is behind the accidents, the computer tampering and the attempt on my life is not going to succeed in forcing me to sell this company!''

Roarke rose from the sofa. Standing to his full six-feet-three-inch height, he towered over a much shorter Trey Sutton. ''And you don't have to worry about Cleo's safety.'' Roarke's deep, commanding voice vibrated through the room. ''The only way anyone is going to be able to get to her is over my dead body.''

''Well, I...er...I'm relieved to know that as Cleo's husband, you're taking her safety so seriously.'' Trey cleared his throat. ''But I still think Cleo is going too far in forming a security force.''

Roarke placed his hand on Trey's back. The younger man tensed. Roarke patted his back. ''Well, why don't you let Cleo worry about running this company? After all, her uncle did leave her in charge, didn't he?''

''Right.'' Nodding agreement, Trey took a step away from

Roarke's big hand, then glanced at Cleo. "You'll keep me notified of any developments?"

"Of course," Cleo said.

The moment Trey left her office, Cleo sat down on her desk, letting her short legs dangle off the edge. "He's afraid of something, isn't he?"

Roarke walked directly in front of Cleo, leaned toward her and braced his hands on top of her desk. His arms straddled her hips. With his face only inches from hers, he said, "Do you think Trey is our man?"

For a split second Cleo couldn't breathe, couldn't think. Roarke was too close, his body almost touching hers, his breath mingling with hers, his lips a hairbreadth from hers.

Night after night they lay together—man and woman—and Cleo's body cried out for his, longing for his possession. But she had made such a big deal out of waiting two weeks, to become better acquainted before they consummated their marriage, that her pride wouldn't allow her to back down now. Besides, Roarke had not made the slightest effort to pressure her or seduce her. If he really wanted her, wouldn't he have tried to persuade her to give in?

"What—what did you say?" She looked up into his mesmerizing blue eyes and fervently wished she were alone with him in their bedroom.

"I asked if you thought Trey might be behind the problems here at McNamara Industries and if he could have been the person who tried to shoot you."

"Oh. I don't want to think Trey is capable of either, especially not of trying to kill me. But I suppose it's possible." Cleo found that she could not stop herself from leaning forward toward Roarke. "We used to be close, when we were younger. Trey even occasionally took my side against Daphne. But once I started moving up the corporate ladder here at McNamara's faster than he did, he began to resent me."

"When Sam Dundee hired Dane Carmichael to run the Dundee agency for him, Dane extended the agency's services to include private investigation as well as private security."

Roarke wanted to take Cleo right this minute. Right there on her big desk. He wanted to spread her legs, strip off her stockings and panties, grab her lush little behind and thrust into her welcoming warmth.

"Morgan Kane is one of our top investigators," Roarke said. "I want to bring him over from Atlanta to train your new security force and to give your guard and night watchman refresher courses."

"If you want to bring in someone from the Dundee agency, then bring him in." Cleo's feminine instincts told her to open her legs, to stretch out her arms, to enfold Simon Roarke, to take him into her body and accept all that he could give her. If only he would take her. Not even ask her permission. Just know that she wanted him and act on that knowledge. "I'll cooperate fully with you in whatever steps you think necessary."

"I want every employee to know that I'm heading up a security force to investigate McNamara's problems," he said. "It's possible that whoever is creating havoc here at the plant will think twice about doing anything else if he or she knows."

"Whatever you want," Cleo told him.

Roarke could feel her heat, could sense her desire. What the hell was she trying to do—drive him crazy? Or was she, in her own inexperienced way, trying to seduce him? Dammit, why didn't she just come right out and tell him that she'd changed her mind, that she wanted to have sex with him and she wanted it now?

Or was she trying to push him over the edge so that he'd make the first move? No way. He wasn't going to make it that easy for her. She was the one who had set up the ground rules for their marriage. She'd have to be the one to change them. No matter how much he wanted her—and he wanted her bad—he wasn't going to take her until she asked for it. Maybe not even until she begged for it.

Lifting his hands off the desk, Roarke stood and took a step backward, stopping less than a foot away from Cleo. He didn't break eye contact as he distanced himself from her.

Come get me if you want me, honey. His hardened sex strained against his slacks. *You've got to know I want you. All you have to do is say the word and I'm yours.*

Cleo crossed her ankles. Her heels rested on the side of the desk. She had thought Roarke wanted to kiss her, but just as she was about to reach up and put her arms around his neck, he pulled back, moving away from her.

"I think tomorrow will be soon enough to bring in Mr. Kane and start hiring people for the security force," Cleo said. "This afternoon, I'd like to continue our tour of the plant. By the end of the week, I want you acquainted with all our employees and them with you."

"You really care about these people, don't you?" he asked.

"McNamara Industries wouldn't exist without our loyal, hardworking employees. Uncle George taught me how important it is to take care of this company, and that means taking care of the people who make it run."

"Come on, Boss Lady. Lead the way." Roarke willed his body under control.

When he took her arm and draped it through his, Cleo hesitated momentarily, allowing herself time to adjust to the feel of him, his warmth and strength. "We'll end our tour in shipping and receiving, at the loading platforms."

Roarke followed Cleo out of her office and into the elevator leading three stories down to the plant level. He watched her closely as she led him through the laboratory. She stopped to speak to every technician, introducing each by name just as she'd done in the plant yesterday. Running three shifts, seven days a week, McNamara Industries employed nearly three hundred people, and there wasn't a one Cleo didn't know.

McNamara's was a small chemical plant, as plants go, but it was the life's blood of River Bend. And those nearly three hundred employees and their families depended on this little family-owned business.

Cleo carried a heavy burden on her shoulders—the fate of hundreds of McNamara employees and their families as well as the responsibility of a group of ungrateful, manipulative, dependent relatives. Roarke decided his wife was one of the strongest, most in-control women he'd ever known. She was the total opposite of Hope, who had been weak and dangerously emotional. As long as he lived, he would never forgive himself for not realizing sooner how mentally unstable Hope had been.

But Cleo was as different from Hope as sunlight is from

darkness. In one short week, Roarke had learned to admire Cleo greatly. His speculation about her nobility had been correct. She was a woman with a mission, and that mission was to save the livelihood of her treasured employees and keep McNamara's a family-owned and -operated business.

"We have people working here now whose grandfathers once worked here for Uncle George and my grandfather, before World War II." Cleo led Roarke into the shipping and receiving department, where raw materials needed to produce McNamara fertilizer were brought in and the finished product sent out.

"Hey, Blake." Cleo waved at an attractive man with black curly hair. "Come meet my husband."

A tall, lanky man in his midthirties turned around and smiled. "Ms. McNa—I mean Mrs. Roarke."

Carrying a clipboard in his hand, he limped toward them. That's when Roarke noticed the heavy brace on the man's leg.

Cleo and Blake exchanged a hearty handshake, then Cleo turned to Roarke. "Simon, this is Blake Saunders, our shipping and receiving foreman. He's the man who keeps everything moving in and out of McNamara Industries. Blake, this is my husband, Simon Roarke. Simon is going to head up a small security force here at the plant to investigate the accidents we've had and to look into some recent computer tampering."

"Rumors have been spreading like wildfire," Blake told them. "An accident-free plant with a top-notch maintenance crew doesn't suddenly start having accidents. At least not two in ten days."

"What are people saying?" Cleo asked.

"They're saying there's something fishy going on." Blake nodded toward the crew of workmen, each man busy at his job. "We know Mr. Sutton and his folks want you to sell McNamara's. And...well...some of us have been wondering just how far a person would go to try to persuade you to sell. Not saying anything against Mr. Sutton and certainly not accusing him of anything."

"It's all right, Blake. I understand. I have my own doubts. That's why Simon—Mr. Roarke—is going to begin an investigation and hire a small security force."

"May I tell the men?" Blake laughed self-consciously, then corrected himself. "I mean the crew. I keep forgetting that we've got Margie. She's so much like one of the boys, most of the time I forget she's female."

Roarke scanned the crew, trying to figure out which one was Margie. Then he saw her. Big, rawboned, with linebacker shoulders, Margie drove one of the forklift trucks that the crew used to stack the pallets of fertilizer sacks and to load those pallets onto trucks for shipping. When Margie lifted a stack of pallets and turned the forklift, Roarke noticed that she was young and not bad-looking. But there was a hardness in that face, a strength and determination that warned off intruders.

"I have an even better idea," Cleo said. "Why don't we let Roarke introduce himself to the crew and explain things."

Blake glanced at Roarke, the two men's gazes meeting squarely. In that one moment, Roarke sized up the other man and made an instant judgment call. Blake Saunders was an okay kind of guy.

"Listen up," Blake said loudly, getting the attention of several crewmen. Then slowly, one by one, the workers paused to listen.

"Why don't we go over to your desk so you can show me your new pictures of Michael," Cleo suggested. "I think Simon can handle this without any help from me."

"How'd you know I have new pictures of Michael on my desk?" Laughing, Blake followed Cleo across to the partition in the corner that created his work nook.

Cleo listened while Roarke introduced himself and explained about the problems McNamara Industries had been having and the steps he intended to take to investigate those problems and to prevent any future incidents.

Cleo lifted a gold-framed photo of an adorable one-year-old boy with his father's curly black hair. "How's Michael doing since the doctors put the tubes in his ears?"

"Great. We sure did appreciate those balloons you sent to the hospital, and the toys," Blake said.

Cleo and Blake chatted while Roarke spoke to the crew, then when Roarke finished speaking, he glanced around, looking for Cleo. When he saw her, he motioned to her. She nodded and smiled. Although the employees talked among themselves, they went back to work quickly.

"I forgot to congratulate you on your marriage, Mrs. Roarke," Blake said. "I hope you and Mr. Roarke will be as happy as Kristy and I are."

"Thank you." Cleo wished everyone would stop congratulating her on a marriage that was as phony as a three-dollar bill. She felt like a fraud. Dammit, she was a fraud. She'd been married over a week and still hadn't consummated her marriage. What difference did it really make how well acquainted she and Roarke were before they made love? The end result would be the same—divorce.

The telephone on Blake's desk rang. When he reached out to answer it, Cleo mouthed "Goodbye" and started walking toward Roarke, who had just stepped out onto one of the loading platforms.

Under different circumstances, she would be proud to be married to Simon Roarke. He'd certainly acquired the respect of all the McNamara employees. She'd seen it in their eyes when they'd met him, noted it on their faces when they listened to him speak. He was a commanding presence. Strong. Self-assured. Emitting an aura of power.

Roarke watched Cleo as she walked toward him. She took quick, short steps, her black heels tapping on the concrete floor. Behind Cleo, Margie turned the loaded forklift around and headed it in the direction of the loading platform on which Roarke stood. A truck waited at the end.

The forklift lurched forward. Margie yelled. Cleo swirled around just in time to see the forklift barreling down on her. Margie jumped out of the vehicle. Her robust body hit the hard concrete floor. She cried out in pain.

Cleo froze to the spot for one brief instant, then realized she was in danger. Before she could move, Roarke shoved her out of the forklift's path, pushing her so hard that they both toppled to the floor. As they hit the concrete, he lifted her so that his body took the brunt of the fall.

She clung to him, her heart in her throat. Gasping for air, she gazed into his eyes and saw genuine fear. He'd been afraid for her.

"I—I'm all right," she told him. "Are you hurt?"

He lifted her to her feet, steadying her with his strong arm around her waist. "I'm okay, but we're both probably bruised and we'll be awfully sore by morning."

The forklift rolled out onto the loading platform. Without a driver to guide its path, the vehicle veered to one side and dove headlong off the side of the platform, crashing onto the pavement below. Several pallets filled with sacks of fertilizer hit the concrete and broke apart.

"What happened?" Cleo caught a glimpse of the crew as several rushed toward her, while some hurried to help their injured co-worker and others went to inspect the wrecked forklift. "Is Margie all right?"

"I'm not sure what happened," Roarke said. "Margie seemed to lose control of the forklift and you just happened to be right in the way."

"I didn't lose control," Margie said as Blake and another man helped her to her feet. "The damn brakes wouldn't work. I tried using the emergency brake, but I couldn't get it to work, either."

Jerking her head around, Cleo stared at Roarke. "Another unexplained accident?"

"Blake, have one of your men take Margie to the emergency room," Cleo ordered.

"I'll be okay," Margie said.

"Let's make sure of that," Cleo told her. "Regardless of what the ER doctor tells you, take tomorrow off."

"And Blake," Roarke called out to the foreman, "get maintenance down here, pronto. I want that forklift gone over with a fine-tooth comb. I want a full report on my desk first thing in the morning."

Blake issued orders to a crewman to drive Margie to the hospital, then rushed over to his desk and called maintenance.

"The rest of you guys get back to work," Blake said once he'd hung up the phone. "Morton, get that mess cleaned up. Use another forklift and get any of the undamaged pallets loaded."

Leaning against Roarke, Cleo glanced down at his big hand lying across her waist. Blood pooled across his knuckles.

"You've hurt your hand." Turning in his arms, she lifted his hand and inspected it.

"It's nothing. I skinned it when we fell."

"We should go to first aid and let the nurse clean it," Cleo said, holding his hand tenderly.

"You can clean it for me when we get home." He jerked his hand away from her, placed it in the center of her back and nudged her forward. "We were planning on leaving straight from here, weren't we?"

"Yes, but—"

Blake walked up beside them. "Do you think the forklift was sabotaged?"

"I think it's likely," Roarke said.

"You believe someone intended for me to be run down?" Cleo asked.

"No." Roarke slipped his arm around her waist and pulled her up against him. "There's no way anyone would have known exactly when you'd be in shipping and receiving, and if this person tampered with the brakes, there would be no way of timing precisely how long it would take them to malfunction."

"So this was set up as another plant 'accident,'" Cleo said. "And another McNamara employee has been injured."

"Should I call the sheriff, Mr. Roarke?" Blake asked.

"Let's hold off on that until I see the maintenance foreman's report. If the brakes on the forklift were tampered with, then I'll notify the local authorities."

"Yes, sir." Blake looked at Cleo. "Are you sure you're all right? Is there anything I can do for you?"

Cleo held her trembling hands out in front of her. "Whew. I guess I'm still a little shaky, but I'll be fine. I need to get out of these dirty clothes—" she glanced down at her soiled linen suit, scuffed heels and shredded panty hose "—and maybe take a hot bath before my muscles start screaming."

"I'll handle things here," Blake said. "And, Mr. Roarke, I'll make sure that report is on your desk first thing in the morning."

"Fine." Roarke grasped Blake's hand and shook it firmly. Once Blake walked away, Roarke said in a low voice, for Cleo's ears only, "I'll have Kane fly in tomorrow, and we'll get an internal investigation under way as soon as possible."

Roarke didn't like the smell of this accident—it stank to

high heaven. It made perfect sense to sabotage equipment in the plant and to create computer problems if all the assailant wanted was to pressure Cleo into selling McNamara Industries. But then if the person's motive was to kill Cleo, things didn't quite add up. The only incident that might have been an attempt on her life had been the rifle shots, which hadn't come close to hitting her. There was definitely more going on here than met the eye. He just hadn't quite figured out what. Not yet. But he would. Then heaven help the person or persons causing trouble for Cleo.

"If you need another Dundee man, that's fine with me," Cleo said. "But with you already here, why do we really need someone else to investigate and to hire and train a security force?"

Roarke dropped his hand to her hip and squeezed gently. "Are you sore from the fall?" he asked.

"Not much. But I do feel a bit battered," she admitted. "I'm okay, Roarke. Now, answer my question."

"Because, Mrs. Roarke, I can't be in more than one place at a time."

"Meaning?"

"Meaning that I can't be with you twenty-four hours a day, protecting you, and handle all the details of a complete investigation, while hiring and training a security team."

"Oh. Yes, I suppose you're right."

With his hand on her back, Roarke guided her down the side steps, off the loading platform and into the private executive parking lot. When they reached her Jaguar, Cleo's steps faltered. Roarke steadied her instantly, one arm going around her waist as one hand clamped down on her shoulder.

"I thought you said you weren't injured." Roarke growled the words as he gazed down at the blood seeping through her scuffed jacket sleeve, staining the lavender linen.

The pavement beneath her feet swirled around and around. Moaning quietly, Cleo grabbed Roarke's arm and leaned against him. "I'm just a little dizzy."

Roarke swept her up in his arms, unlocked the Jag and deposited Cleo on the passenger side, then rounded the car and slid into the driver's seat.

"I'm taking you to the hospital!" He revved the motor,

shifted into Reverse and zoomed the Jag backward, out of the parking place.

"No, please. I'm all right. Really. I'm not dizzy anymore. I think maybe it was just a tiny bout of delayed shock or something."

"If you don't want to go to the emergency room, then as soon as we get home, I'm going to check you over thoroughly myself. And if I think you need to see a doctor, you won't argue with me."

"Thanks." She reached over and clasped his forearm. "I agree to your terms."

Roarke shifted gears. Second. Third. Fourth. Fifth. He flew the Jag out of the parking lot and onto the highway.

"Roarke?"

"What, Boss Lady?" He hazarded a glance at her. Her face was too pale. Even if she wouldn't admit it to herself, Cleo was badly shaken.

"When we get home, if we run into Aunt Beatrice before we can clean up, would you please help me downplay the accident?"

"I'll do what I can to reassure her, but your aunt is no fool. She's bound to suspect the truth."

"Exactly what is the truth?" Releasing Roarke's arm, Cleo lay back in the seat and rested her head on the soft leather.

"The truth is that someone's damned and determined to get you to sell McNamara Industries," Roarke told her as he maneuvered her Jag along the highway, heading west toward home. "I think the shooting right after your uncle's funeral was only an attempt to frighten you, and I believe these problems at the plant are designed to wreak havoc and convince you that the safest course of action is to sell."

"I will not be intimidated into selling McNamara's!"

"Once this person realizes that the scare tactics aren't working, that's when your life will be in real danger."

He hated the very thought that someone might try to kill Cleo. Already, without meaning to, he'd become emotionally involved with his client. It was something he'd never done before. In the past he'd been too smart to let his personal feelings get in the way of performing his duty.

It wasn't as if he loved Cleo. But he did like her. And he

respected and admired her. And he wanted her almost to the point of madness. Once he'd had her, everything would be all right. He could handle liking her, respecting her and admiring her and still do his job. But when it came to keeping her safe, he had to have his mind one hundred percent on protecting her. As long as he felt like a mongrel chasing a bitch in heat, he risked making a mistake. And one mistake on his part could cost Cleo her life.

She glanced at him. He saw her in his peripheral vision.

"I'm glad I married you," she said. "Having you at my side makes me stronger. I know I'm not alone. You'll help me save McNamara's."

"I'll do my best," Roarke said.

"Thank you...Simon."

Her use of his Christian name created a hard knot of apprehension in his belly. He preferred for her to call him "Roarke"—it kept their relationship on a business level—and despite their discussion about it on their wedding night, she usually used the less intimate name. But when she called him "Simon" in that sexy, raspy voice of hers, it made him want to hear her cry out his name in the throes of passion. Every time she called him "Simon," he knew it meant something to her—that she was beginning to care for him. And that could be dangerous. For both of them.

Chapter 6

Roarke opened the bedroom door for the housekeeper and took the first-aid kit she handed him. "Thanks, Pearl."

She glanced down at Roarke's skinned and bloody knuckles, then peered across the room, where Cleo sat on the edge of the chaise longue. "Do you need any help?"

"No, thanks." Cleo removed her scuffed heels, then inspected her ripped panty hose, and realized that beneath the ruined nylon her left leg was badly scraped. "I'll make sure Simon's wounds are tended."

Pearl gave Cleo a once-over, pausing when their eyes met. "What about your wounds, Cleo Belle? You look pretty battered up to me."

"I'll take care of my wife," Roarke said. "She refused to go to the hospital, so she has no choice but to let me examine her and make sure she has no serious injuries."

"She's always been stubborn," Pearl told him. "Ever since she was no higher than my knee. Always wanted her own way. Knew what she wanted and figured out how to get it. I've discovered that the only way to handle her when she's being stubborn is with brute force." Pearl chuckled, apparently remembering times when, as a child, nothing short of physical restraint had saved Cleo from harm.

"I'll keep that in mind." Glancing at Cleo, Roarke grinned. "If you hear her hollering, you'll know I've had to resort to letting her know who's boss."

Cleo stuck out her tongue at him. His grin widened. "Don't listen to Pearl," Cleo said. "I was an angelic child. I never gave anyone a moment's trouble."

"Well, now, Mr. Roarke, if you believe that one, I've got some swampland in Florida I'll sell you real cheap." Pearl laid her pudgy hand on Roarke's arm. "She's as stubborn as the day is long. She might well have the soul of an angel, but as a child she had a mean, stubborn streak. And though she's learned to control it some since she grew up, it still rears its ugly head from time to time. You just watch out for it."

"I'll do that," Roarke said.

When Pearl started to leave, Cleo called out to her. "Wait."

Stopping immediately, the housekeeper glanced over her shoulder at Cleo. "When Aunt Beatrice returns from the bridge party at Mrs. Madden's, tell her that I'll see her at breakfast. There's no point in worrying her about what happened at the plant. I'll tell her in the morning. That way she'll be able to get a good night's sleep tonight."

"What if, during dinner this evening, Trey mentions the accident at the plant?" Pearl asked.

"Trey had a trip planned to Huntsville this afternoon, so I doubt he'll learn about the accident before I tell him in the morning," Cleo said.

"I'll do my best to handle things below." Pearl looked directly at Roarke. "You handle *things* up here."

"I'll certainly try," Roarke said, then closed the door behind Pearl when she walked out into the hall.

With the first-aid supplies in his hands, Roarke turned around and watched while Cleo removed her ripped jacket and tossed it on the floor. He clenched his teeth when he saw the two large bruises on her left arm.

He had to find a way to keep Cleo safe from any more plant "accidents." Although this one hadn't been planned to injure her, it had. And whoever was creating havoc at McNamara

Industries was probably either the same person who had taken a shot at Cleo or was a cohort.

"I'll have to throw this suit away. I'm afraid it's ruined." Gripping her elbow, she lifted her arm, turning it slightly to get a better look at the darkening bruises. "Oh, they look awful, don't they? Like someone hit me really hard a couple of times."

Slowly, silently, Roarke crossed the room, laid the first-aid supplies at the foot of the chaise longue and removed his sport coat. He tossed the coat onto a nearby chair and reached out for Cleo. Without making a comment or asking permission, he began unbuttoning her blouse. She stared down at his big fingers working the buttons loose. The side of his hand brushed against her breast. Her nipple beaded instantly. She sucked in her breath and looked up at him. Their gazes met and held.

"I—I can unbutton my own blouse," she told him. But by the time she spoke, he was already pushing her short-sleeved, purple silk blouse off her shoulders.

His big hands felt like fine sandpaper, the palms callused from the physical workouts that keep his body in fighting form. Lifting her arm in one hand, he ran his fingers gently over the bruising, then up to her shoulder and across to her neck.

Her aching body tingled with awareness. She hadn't allowed a man to touch her this intimately since Paine Emerson had seduced her. And not even the girlish love she'd felt for her former fiancé had induced such a strong, physical need.

"If we'd gotten an ice pack on this, it would have helped," he told her as he ran his hand over her right shoulder and down her arm, inspecting it for damage. "Is it already sore?"

"Yes," Cleo admitted. "To be honest, I'm sore all over."

And I'm aching inside, she thought. I can't bear for you to touch me like this, and yet I don't want you to stop.

"It might be even worse in the morning," he said.

She nodded in agreement, knowing that by morning not only would her body be sore, but after another night of lying next to Roarke, she would be aching with longing.

He undid the closure on her skirt, then eased down the zipper. "Lift your hips up just a little, so we can get your skirt off."

Her heartbeat roared in her ears as the deafening flood of blood raced through her body. Obeying his command without a word of protest, she lifted her hips. He slipped off her skirt, then pushed up her silk slip. When his fingers slid beneath the waistband of her panty hose, she gasped and looked up at him.

Staring directly into her eyes, he said, "We've got to take these panty hose off so I can take a good look at your leg."

He took his time removing the hose, all the while stroking her hips and legs with his fingers as he maneuvered the tattered material downward. She closed her eyes, savoring the sensation of his gentle touch, while at the same time she tried to control her body's reaction. But she could no more stop her breasts from tightening and throbbing and her femininity from moistening and clenching than she could stop the sun from rising in the morning.

Blood had dried and stuck to the nylon along her lower thigh and upper calf, so he took extra precaution, being as gentle as possible. She winced and opened her mouth on a silent cry when he loosened the soiled and shredded panty hose from her scraped flesh.

After throwing the ruined hose on top of her discarded clothing, Roarke lifted her leg and examined the injury. Without any warning, he scooped her up in his arms, picked up the first-aid kit and headed toward the bathroom.

"What—" She grabbed him around the neck. "I can walk!"

The scent of sweat and dried blood clung to him. Breathing in those warrior odors, Cleo shivered and fought the urge to rest her head on his shoulder.

"Quicker this way," he said as he sat her down on the vanity stool in the bathroom. "Doesn't look like anything serious. I'll clean these scratches and scraps." He laid the kit on the vanity and popped open the lid. "Other than having some ugly bruises and being sore for a while, you should be fine."

"What about you?" Cleo asked, looking at the dried blood on his knuckles. "You must have done that when you rolled me over on top of you and your hands skidded along the concrete floor.''

"I'll make a deal with you, Boss Lady. You be a good girl and let me tend to your wounds, and when I finish, you can tend to mine."

"You're used to getting your way, aren't you?"

"I'd say that was something we have in common."

Turning his back to her, he rummaged in the first-aid kit and removed a small bottle of peroxide. Glancing up at him, she immediately saw bloodstains on the back of his shirt. Stains that had darkened a large circle across his shoulder blade and dotted a trail of droplets down to his waist. Her gaze focused momentarily on the hip holster that housed his sleek, deadly Beretta.

"Roarke?"

He turned around, peroxide and cotton balls in his hands. "Yeah?"

"Your back has been bleeding."

"I figured it had." He poured the peroxide on her scraped leg. "You can take a look at it for me." Once the peroxide bubbled on her wounds, he blotted the residue off with the cotton swabs. "I don't think this needs to be covered, but I'll check it again in a few hours and see."

Suddenly she felt quite vulnerable sitting there in her slip, with Roarke hovering over her. He played the role of protective and caring husband to perfection, but Cleo's instincts told her that his attentive actions went far beyond mere acting.

"Thank you," she said.

"You're welcome. It was my pleasure, Boss Lady."

Cleo stood on weak, trembly legs, wanting nothing more than to fall into Roarke's strong arms. "Now it's my turn to play nursemaid and see to your injuries."

He unbuttoned his soiled shirt, revealing his broad, hairy chest. Cleo watched, tantalized, as he removed the shirt and tossed it on the floor. He turned his back to her and waited. She grimaced when she saw the raw, red scrape across his right shoulder blade.

"Well, what does it look like?" He glanced over his shoulder and grinned when he saw the dismay on her face. "That bad, huh?"

"Oh, no, not bad at all. Just bloody." Forcing herself to concentrate on the task at hand and not on Roarke's incredible physique, Cleo picked up the peroxide bottle and doused his wounds. The excess liquid ran down his back, dribbling onto his slacks. "Damn!" Grabbing several cotton balls, Cleo swabbed at the trickling peroxide dampening his waist.

"What were you trying to do—give me a bath in that stuff?" he asked jokingly, then turned around and held up his scuffed knuckles. "Just dab these with a little peroxide."

He had to know how nervous she was, and had probably guessed the reason. She felt foolish overreacting to a man's gentle touch and the sight of his partial nudity. It wasn't as if this was the first time he'd touched her or the first time she'd seen him without his shirt. He slept in nothing but his pajama bottoms every night. But this was the first time she had given herself over to the pure sensual pleasure of sight and touch.

Cleo cleaned his knuckles quickly, then recapped the peroxide bottle and closed the first-aid kit. "There. I think we'll both live."

She whirled around, prepared to leave the bathroom and escape Roarke's nearness. In her haste, she didn't notice that he had eased toward her, and when she turned, she brushed against his bare chest. Throwing up her hands in surprise, she froze to the spot. Roarke grasped her hands and laid them on his chest.

She felt the steady beat of his heart. Her hands quivered. Her stomach fluttered. She swallowed hard.

His gaze traveled from her flushed face, down her throat and over the rise of her breasts, which pressed up above the lace on the bodice of her lavender slip.

"You're a lovely woman, Cleo Belle." He slipped his hand behind her head and grasped her neck.

She stared at him, hypnotized by the look in his piercing blue eyes. Of their volition, her fingers threaded through the thick, dark hair curling over the center of his muscular chest. She opened her mouth to speak. To tell him that he was a handsome man. That it was a pleasure just to look at him. But before she could utter one word, Roarke tightened his hold around the back of her neck, pressed her face upward and swooped his head down, capturing her mouth in a hot, wet kiss.

She gave in to the slow, damp, heated desire spreading through her like sweet honey over warm bread. As he deepened the kiss, she responded wildly, gripping his shoulders and pressing her body intimately to his. His sex pulsed against her. Her femininity tightened and released, then tightened again in greater awareness and stronger need.

Just when she thought she couldn't bear another moment of this tortured arousal, Roarke clutched her buttocks in his big hands and lifted her up and into his hardness. She cried out from the sheer agonized pleasure, the sound muffled by his lips on hers, his mouth devouring hers.

On the precipice, ready to plunge headlong into mindless sensuality, Cleo mumbled a complaint when Roarke ended their kiss and released her. When she continued clinging to him, he stepped backward. Her fingertips grazed his chest, then she retreated, lowering her arms and gazing up at him questioningly.

"Six days isn't long," he said, his deep voice calm and controlled.

"Six days?" Her mind couldn't seem to focus, refusing to comprehend the meaning of his words.

"We were married eight days ago today. In six days we will be married two weeks."

"Oh." Realization dawned.

"Have you changed your mind about waiting the full two weeks?" he asked.

"I...I don't..."

"You're in charge of this marriage, Boss Lady. I follow your orders."

"Yes, I know. I'm just not sure if we should—"

"Think about it and let me know," he told her. "I'm going to go change into a pair of jeans, then make a call to Morgan Kane at Dundee's."

"You're going to call Mr. Kane this evening?"

"Yes. After the incident today, I don't want to delay bringing him in. If I can get in touch with him now, he can be here by breakfast in the morning."

"I see. Well…yes, of course. By all means, go call Mr. Kane."

For some odd reason she felt as if Roarke had deliberately thrown a bucket of ice water on her. Was he toying with her? Tempting her?

Had he taken Pearl's suggestions to heart and used *brute force?* Had the kiss been intended to show her that he, and not she, was really the boss of their marriage? Damn the man! She'd show him who was boss. If he thought she couldn't last six more days without his lovemaking, then he was wrong. She'd lived through a week of sleeping beside him, longing for him to reach out and take her, dreaming of what it would be like to belong to him. She could wait another six days. But while they were waiting, she was going to make him suffer as much as she did.

While making arrangements with Kane to fly from Atlanta to River Bend on the first available flight, Roarke watched his wife. She entered the closet, leaving the door ajar just enough to allow him a glimpse. Not once did she glance his way or acknowledge that she knew he could see her. Slowly, provocatively, she pulled her slip up over her head and discarded it. For a couple of minutes Roarke couldn't think, couldn't remember what he was saying to Kane. Actually, for about half a second, he didn't even realize he was on the phone.

Wearing nothing but a pair of lavender silk panties and matching bra, Cleo searched through her clothes. She removed an item off the rack, looked at it and replaced it; then she repeated the procedure several times. Roarke's sex, which he'd just gotten under control, grew hot and heavy again. What the hell was she doing? If he didn't know better, he'd swear she was putting on a show for his benefit. To drive him crazy!

Cleo's petite body was slender, but not lacking in all the right curves. Her hips flared nicely and her butt was full and tight. And her breasts—ah her breasts. High, round and firm. And larger than anyone would suspect hidden there beneath her simple little suits.

"Huh?" Roarke hadn't heard what Kane had said.

"I said I'll be on your doorstep at the crack of dawn,"

Morgan Kane told Roarke. "Hey, buddy, what's wrong with you? You seem distracted."

"Sorry, I let my mind wander." Yeah, his mind, his libido and his sanity had all wandered into dangerous territory. "I'll work with you, but I'm going to need you to take charge of the investigation. My main function is protecting Cleo." What was she doing now? he wondered. No, she isn't going to. She wouldn't. She would! His body tightened painfully. Cleo unhooked her bra, removed it slowly and tossed it on top of her slip. He was going to kill her! "Huh? I didn't get that?"

"Dammit, man, if I didn't know better, I'd swear you were right in the middle of having sex," Kane said. "Where's your mind?"

My mind is on my wife's bare breasts, Roarke thought. Hell, she had to know what she was doing. Didn't she? Maybe not. Maybe she didn't realize she'd left the door cracked enough to put her body on display.

"Look, I've got to run. I'll see you first thing in the morning." Not certain whether Kane made any reply, Roarke hung up the phone.

He crossed his arms over his chest and stared at Cleo's breasts. All he had to do was close his eyes or just turn away to end his torment. But he did neither. His gaze caressed her. His thoughts tasted her pink nipples. Instantly, as if she knew what he was thinking, her nipples puckered.

Holding his hands at his sides, he balled them into fists and silently cursed his own male weakness. Why was he punishing himself like this, visually devouring a woman he couldn't bed for six more days? If things continued this way, he'd be a raving lunatic by the end of the week. If he wasn't married to Cleo, if he hadn't made a bargain with her, he'd sure as hell go out and find himself a willing woman as soon as possible.

Cleo pulled a pair of soft, yellow cotton slacks off a hanger. Her breasts swayed when she bent over to drag the pants up her legs. Roarke closed his eyes then, as his mind flooded with thoughts of those luscious breasts dangling over him, of his mouth reaching up to taste their sweetness. When he opened his eyes a few minutes later, she had slipped a baggy yellow T-shirt over her head.

Find something to do, he told himself. Get your mind off

having sex with Cleo. Looking around the room, he noticed the bookcase. That's it. He'd read awhile.

Cleo walked out of the closet and over to Roarke, who stood in front of the open bookcase. She placed her hand on his shoulder. He tensed instantly.

"Looking for something in particular?" she asked.

"No. Just anything to pass the time until Ezra brings up dinner." If she didn't remove her hand, he was going to either slap it away or jerk her into his arms. He knew she wasn't wearing a bra, and that if he pulled her up against him, he'd be able to feel her nipples pressing into his chest.

"I've got Stephen King's latest, if you like horror, and a couple of other bestsellers. And several archaeology books, if you're interested." Cleo reached inside the bookcase and pulled out a leather-bound volume. "This book belonged to my grandfather. It's a history of River Bend from the early 1800s to the mid 1930s."

When she held the book out to him, he accepted it, their hands just barely touching. He looked into her eyes and knew she'd felt the jolt of awareness that passed between them just as surely as he had.

"Thanks." *Get the hell away from her, man, before you're the one doing the begging!*

"Sure."

Cleo crossed the room, lifted her briefcase off the desk at the foot of her bed and removed a file folder. She slumped onto the floral chaise longue, then brought her knees up to use as a prop for her folder. Once she had it open, she flipped through the contents, stopping at the section she needed to study. If McNamara Industries' orders were being deleted from the computer, the person responsible might have left some evidence of the tampering.

She glanced over at Roarke, who had sat down on the bed and braced his back against the headboard. Why didn't the man button his shirt? Was he deliberately tempting her by giving her a partial view of his magnificent chest? Marvelously muscled. Gloriously hairy. And brutally scarred. She had to ignore him, to pretend he didn't arouse her.

She smiled secretly, remembering the nerve it had taken for her to undress down to her panties in front of him. He had no way of being sure she'd done it on purpose. She'd closed the closet door more than halfway. She had never in her entire life set out to purposely arouse a man. But she'd rather enjoyed putting on a striptease show for her husband. By the time he'd hung up the phone and she'd come out of the closet to find him by the bookcase, he'd gained some control over his body. But his nostrils had been flared, his sex semierect, and a fine sheen of perspiration glistened over his upper lip.

She loved knowing that he was attracted to her, that he wanted her as she wanted him. But just as she knew how he felt, he knew the same about her. It was as if they were in a game of wills, to see who would give in first—before the appointed two weeks were up. In retrospect, she realized she'd been foolish to make such a decree, considering how sexually aware she'd been of him since the moment they'd met. But in fairness to herself, her reasoning had been sensible. She'd wanted to give them both time—admittedly, especially herself—to adjust to being married, before they consummated their union. Although her sexual experience was limited to a brief relationship with Paine Emerson, she had dated over the years and been attracted to several men. But never—ever—had she felt anything to compare with the way she felt every time she looked at Simon Roarke.

For the next few hours, they gave each other plenty of space, keeping to themselves except when they shared dinner in the sitting room. While eating, they limited their conversation to business, discussing the forklift accident, the computer tampering and Morgan Kane's expected arrival the next day. Cleo spoke briefly to Blake and relayed the messages to Roarke. Margie Evans had been released from the emergency room with a sprained wrist and minor bruising. And maintenance's initial finding was that someone had definitely tampered with the brakes on the forklift.

Roarke remained in the sitting room while Cleo returned to the paperwork waiting on her desk. He opened the armoire that hid a thirty-five-inch television. Slumping onto the sofa, he clicked the remote to ESPN and lowered the sound to just barely audible.

Cleo studied the information on McNamara Industries' orders for the past month until her vision began blurring. Pinch-

ing the bridge of her nose, she braced her elbow on the desk
and rested her head.

A piercing scream shook Cleo from her restful meditation.
Then she heard a second scream, followed quickly by a third.
My God, who was screaming? And why?

Cleo rose so quickly that she knocked her briefcase onto
the floor. Roarke flew out of the sitting room, dashed over to
the nightstand and removed his Beretta. He met Cleo at the
bedroom door and pushed her behind him as he eased the door
open.

"I'll go find out what happened," he told her. "You close
this door and lock it. And don't open it to anyone you
wouldn't trust with your life. Is that understood?"

She nodded her agreement. The moment Roarke stepped
into the hallway, she closed and locked the door. Waiting impatiently, she paced the floor. She heard voices in the hallway,
but couldn't distinguish the speakers.

Someone tapped softly on her door. Gasping, she jumped,
then shivered. "Who is it?"

"It's me, dear, Aunt Beatrice."

Cleo unlocked the door. Hurrying inside, Beatrice threw her
arms around her niece and held her close. Cleo returned her
aunt's hug, then grasped Beatrice's hands. "What's going on?
Who was doing all that screaming?"

"Oralie," Beatrice said. "She swears she saw a man peeping in the windows."

"Downstairs?"

"Yes, in the front-parlor windows. And the hysterical fool
wouldn't stop screaming." Beatrice huffed disgustedly.
"Perry and I didn't see a thing. Oralie was working on her
needlepoint and Perry and I were listening to a Mozart con-
certo."

"Where's the rest of the family?"

"They're all downstairs," Beatrice said. "Or they were a
few minutes ago. They followed Simon down the stairs.
Daphne and Trey are trying to comfort their mother. I think
Marla poured Oralie some sherry."

"Where's Roarke?"

"Simon went outside to check the grounds. He asked me
to come up and explain to you what happened and stay with

you until he returned.'' Beatrice walked over and closed the bedroom door, then locked it. ''I told him that Oralie had a delicate disposition and was prone to hysteria. But he said he wasn't going to take any chances where your safety was concerned.'' Beatrice patted Cleo's arm. ''My dear, you are most fortunate in your choice of a husband. Considering the unusual circumstances, he is the perfect man for you.''

''Yes, I believe he is.'' Cleo walked into the sitting room and looked out the row of windows. She had planned to wait until morning to tell her aunt about McNamara Industries' problems, but since it was unlikely anyone would get a good night's sleep after Oralie's outburst, Cleo decided there was no point in delaying. ''We're having trouble at the plant.''

''What sort of trouble?'' Beatrice joined her niece, draped her arm around her shoulders and pulled her away from the window. ''Simon said not to show yourself in front of the windows. Your silhouette would make a perfect target.''

''He thinks of everything, doesn't he?''

''He's been trained for it, you know.'' Beatrice led Cleo over to the sofa and they sat side by side. ''What's going on at the plant?''

''Someone tampered with the computer and deleted several big orders. Those orders were never shipped.''

''How long has this been going on?''

''Only since Uncle George died.''

''I see.'' Beatrice sighed loudly. ''Daddy had no idea what a hornet's nest his will would stir, did he? Since Trey is an executive with access to the computers, I assume he's the chief suspect.''

''One of the suspects, anyway,'' Cleo said. ''But it's possible that whoever's behind the problem is paying an employee to delete the orders.''

''What about Hugh and Daphne? He's weak enough to be influenced by her greed.''

''There's more going on than computer tampering.''

Sitting very still, her sharp green eyes studying Cleo's face, Beatrice laid her hand over her niece's. ''Something more dangerous?''

''There have been three accidents at the plant since Uncle George's funeral. One today.'' Cleo hesitated, not wanting to upset her aunt. But she knew she couldn't keep the truth from Beatrice. "We're fairly certain that someone tampered with the brakes on a forklift. Margie Evans was injured. A sprained wrist and some bruising. And…well, when the forklift went out of control, I was directly in its path."

Beatrice grasped Cleo's wrist and looked anxiously into her eyes. "You weren't hurt, were you?"

"Roarke shoved me out of the way. I got a few scrapes from the fall on the concrete floor, but that's all."

"What does Simon intend to do about these problems?"

"He called another Dundee Security employee tonight and the man will be here by morning," Cleo said. "Mr. Morgan Kane will train a small security force for McNamara's and, under Simon's supervision, he will head up an investigation into the computer tampering and the accidents."

"While Simon guards you."

"That's right." Cleo shivered. "I hate this being suspicious and afraid, this second-guessing everyone and everything."

Beatrice wrapped her arms around Cleo and drew her niece's head down into her lap. She stroked Cleo's shiny red hair, so like her own. "I have every confidence in your husband. He'll protect you."

Lying contentedly with her head in her aunt's lap, as she had done so often when she was a child, Cleo wished that she could spare Beatrice the truth. But they both had to face reality. And the sooner, the better. "What makes this whole thing so difficult is knowing that someone in the family has to be behind everything—the problems at the plant and the attempt on my life."

A loud knock on the bedroom door brought Cleo and Beatrice up off the sofa. Side by side, the two walked into the bedroom.

"Yes?" Cleo called out.

"It's me, Roarke."

Cleo rushed to open the door. The moment her husband appeared, she let out a sigh of relief. "Did you find anyone?"

"Not a soul," he said. "I don't think there was ever anyone peeping in the windows. Mrs. Sutton's imagination must have gotten the best of her."

"That's happened before," Beatrice said. "Besides, she's

been a nervous wreck ever since Daddy died. She made a nasty scene at the reading of the will.''

''Well, Mr. Sutton said he'd given his wife a sedative and put her to bed. And Trey sent Marla to their room. The rest of them are downstairs waiting for us. They're demanding a family meeting.''

''They're what?'' Beatrice screeched.

''For what reason?'' Cleo asked.

''They want to hire a night watchman for the grounds,'' Roarke said. ''Daphne told me that she's felt uneasy ever since someone took a shot at you, and now that her mother has seen someone lurking about outside, the sensible thing to do is hire protection for the family.''

''They're trying to throw suspicion off themselves,'' Beatrice said. ''I wouldn't put it past Daphne to be at the root of all our problems.''

''I think we should meet with them,'' Roarke said. ''Cleo, you tell them that you think hiring a night watchman for the grounds is an excellent idea and you'll see to it immediately. Then we'll have Kane put one of his security people on the job.''

''Do you think that's necessary?'' Beatrice asked.

''If they're bluffing, we'll call their bluff,'' Cleo said.

''And we'll be putting one of our own men in place and not someone they hire.'' Holding the door open, Roarke nodded. ''Shall we join the family powwow?''

''By all means.'' Cleo marched into the hallway, her head held high.

An hour later, Roarke and Cleo returned to her suite, the immediate family emergency settled, if not to everyone's satisfaction, at least to Roarke's. As long as Cleo continued allowing him the power to make all security decisions, he felt relatively certain that he could keep her safe. And her safety was his top priority.

Daphne and Trey had protested Roarke's hiring the night watchman for the grounds, telling him plainly that he was a newcomer to the McNamara-Sutton family and had no right to take charge. Cleo backed Roarke a hundred percent, and since she held the purse strings, the others begrudgingly acquiesced to her wishes.

Daphne had pursed her red lips in a little-girl pout and huffed loudly. Roarke suspected he was the first man she'd been unable to twist around her little finger, and so was frustrated at not being able to get her way and seduce him into her bed.

"It doesn't matter to me who hires this security person," Perry Sutton had told them. "Oralie insisted that I speak to y'all about hiring someone and I promised her that I would. She refused to take her sleeping pill until I agreed."

Roarke locked the bedroom door as he did every night. Cleo retrieved her gown and robe from the closet, then headed toward the bathroom.

"I'm tired. This has been a long, difficult day," she said. "I'm going to take my bath and go to bed."

"Go ahead," Roarke told her. "I think I'll watch a little TV. I'll keep it low so it won't disturb you."

She paused in the bathroom doorway. "Simon?"

"Yeah?" Dammit, he wished she wouldn't call him "Simon" when they were alone. But he could hardly demand that she call him "Roarke." What could he tell her? That her using his first name aroused him?

"Thank you for taking this job. For marrying me," Cleo said.

Before he could reply, she hurried into the bathroom and closed the door. Every time she said something sweet and sentimental like that, the hairs on the back of his neck stood up. A warning? He was beginning to worry that Cleo just might possess the power to get through his defenses and make him feel something more than sexual desire. He couldn't let that happen.

Roarke picked up the remote and stretched out on the loveseat, hanging his feet over the edge. He found a special on A&E about World War II.

No matter how tired he was, he intended waiting until Cleo was sound asleep before he took his shower and joined her in bed. It was difficult enough lying there beside her when she was asleep, but he couldn't bear it when he knew she was awake and could possibly turn to him and ask him to make love to her.

While one part of his brain registered the events on the television special, another part went over the entire day's events. As the minutes ticked by, he wondered how long it would be before she emerged from the bathroom, fresh, clean and warm from her bath. She'd taken a dark green silk teddy and robe into the bathroom with her. Did she intend to sleep in nothing but a lace teddy?

"Roarke!" Cleo's overly calm voice called out from the bathroom.

He jumped to his feet. "Is something wrong?" He rushed into the bedroom, stopping outside the closed bathroom door.

"I—I can't get out of the bathtub. There are spiders crawling around on the floor. And—and I'm pretty sure that they're brown recluse spiders."

"Stay right where you are," he told her.

"Please, Simon. Help me!"

Chapter 7

Not even as a child had Cleo been the type of female who was afraid of insects. Much to Aunt Beatrice's dismay, as a preschooler Cleo had been fascinated by grasshoppers and ladybugs and had often handled them with great delight. But spiders were something else altogether. She'd been taught that black widows and brown recluses could be deadly. Pearl had told horror stories about how her own little brother had almost died from a severe reaction to a brown recluse bite.

Cleo stood in the middle of the huge whirlpool tub, her wet, naked body shivering, her nerves jangling. She hadn't noticed anything unusual when she'd entered the bathroom earlier. Nothing out of place.

How could half a dozen spiders have crawled into the bathroom? They couldn't have. One? Unlikely, but possible. Six? Out of the question. Someone had to have placed them inside the large, fluffy towels stacked on the white-wicker shelves at one end of the tub.

Cleo shuddered, remembering how she'd reached out and picked up one of those towels and seen a brown recluse clinging to the terry-cloth surface. The tiny, brown spider had wriggled its eight legs. Cleo had gasped and dropped the towel, but not before she'd noticed the dark, violin-shaped mark on its back near the head. Pearl had been the one who'd taught her how to instantly recognize the poisonous creature.

Within minutes she had noticed other identical spiders crawling over the stack of towels. That's when she had called for help.

Roarke opened the bathroom door, stepped inside and closed the door behind him. Cleo crossed her arms over her breasts, but felt rather silly thinking about modesty at a time like this.

"Be careful," she cautioned him. "They're crawling all over the floor. I've counted six of them."

His gaze traveled the length and breadth of the twelve-by-twelve-foot bathroom, noting the location of all six spiders. "Stay in the tub. I'll get you out."

He had thought of little else but Cleo's naked body lying beneath his. And her little striptease in the closet earlier had certainly added fuel to the fire. For half a second, he looked at her, absorbing the fine lines of her body, the delicate, slender beauty of her feminine curves.

His sex grew hard and heavy. Dammit, he couldn't help how his body reacted, could he? After all he was a man, and Cleo was a lovely, desirable woman.

He crossed the bathroom and stopped at the edge of the tub. Deciding to do the gentlemanly thing, Roarke reached toward the wicker shelves, intending to pull out a towel and wrap it around Cleo.

"Don't," she screamed. He glared at her, his expression questioning her sanity. "The spiders crawled out of the towels. There could be more inside them."

He nodded his understanding, then glanced down at where a spider inched close to his right foot. Without hesitation, he raised his foot and smashed the thing.

"Let me get you out of here, honey," he said. "Then I'll come back in here and take care of these little pests."

Roarke lifted her out of the water and into his arms, bringing her naked body up against his chest. In his walk to the door, he ground another spider beneath his feet. Cleo clung to him, shivering, as much from fear as from the chill. After closing the bathroom door behind them, Roarke dashed over to the bed and set Cleo on the edge, then lifted the quilt coverlet and draped it around her shoulders.

When she looked up at him with her big, trusting green eyes, he could not resist the urge to kiss her. He brushed his lips quickly across hers.

"Stay put. I'll be right back." He headed toward the bathroom.

"Please be careful." She clutched the quilt in both hands, savoring the warmth and protection it provided.

He rewarded her concerned plea with that self-confident little grin of his that she had grown accustomed to over the past week. Then he disappeared into the bathroom.

Fidgeting nervously as she sat on the edge of the bed, Cleo wondered if she shouldn't do something. Call the exterminator? Phone the police? Warn the rest of the family that their home had been invaded by poisonous spiders?

No, there wasn't any need to alarm the rest of the household when she felt certain the spider infestation was limited to her private bath. And if she called the police, what would she tell them? One of my relatives is trying to kill me and I think they planted half a dozen potentially deadly spiders in my bathroom? And she'd wait for Roarke's assessment of the situation before she made a call to the exterminator this late at night.

Maybe she should put on some clothes. The lace teddy and robe that she'd intended wearing to torment Roarke lay on the vanity stool in the bathroom. She had other teddies. She could slip into one of them. No, Roarke had said for her to stay put. When he emerged from his spider annihilation mission, she would be right here, waiting for him.

In retrospect, things didn't seem as scary as they had just a few minutes ago when she'd been totally naked and surrounded by a troop of three-eighths-of-an-inch assassins. Odd, she thought, how completely she'd come to count on Simon Roarke, how totally she trusted him to protect her.

Even though she'd been fortunate enough to have been nurtured, loved and adored by Aunt Beatrice and Pearl and trained for success by a loving Uncle George, Cleo had always possessed an independent streak. A need to take care of herself. A determination to do things without assistance, and to do them her own way. And yet here she was, relying on someone else—a man who, although he was her husband, was practically a stranger. But he didn't seem like a stranger. After less than two weeks' acquaintance, she had no doubts that she could trust Roarke with her life. And not simply because he was her employee, but because he was the kind of man who instinctively took care of his own.

"Mission accomplished." Roarke emerged from the bathroom like a conquering hero, having vanquished the foe. "We'll get an exterminator in first thing tomorrow, strictly as a safety precaution. I'm certain there's not a spider left alive. And Pearl's going to have a job straightening up the mess I made in there."

Cleo found that she'd lost her voice when she tried to speak, to verbally respond to Roarke. He stood there, his hair slightly mussed and damp, and grinned at her. His shirt was partially unbuttoned, enough so she could see his moist, curling chest hair. And his sex bulged against his jeans.

She rose up off the bed, mesmerized by the power radiating from Roarke and urged into action by her own feminine needs. With the quilt draped around her shoulders, she clutched the edges together across her chest. She stared at him, wanting to ask him to make love to her, but her voice was mute. Only her eyes spoke for her.

Roarke halted, stopped dead in his tracks by the look in Cleo's warm green eyes. Was he reading her right? Was she asking for what he thought she was? Or had he let his own desperate need for her influence his perception?

"Cleo?" *Tell me, dammit! Say the words, honey. I want to hear you ask.*

With her gaze fixed on Roarke, she took several tentative steps toward him. The sound of her rapidly pumping heart roared in her ears. She felt hot and moist, and ached unbearably. All she knew was that she wanted Roarke. No, she needed him. Now.

Boldly, she released her grip on the quilt and allowed it to drop from her shoulders and slide down her body, forming a cotton mound on the floor. She stood before him, naked, unashamed and painfully aroused. Being a wanton seductress was something new for her. But then, wanting a man the way she wanted Roarke was also a new experience.

"Ah, Cleo Belle." Roarke tensed, every muscle tightening, every nerve fully alert. His sex grew hard and heavy. "Come here." He didn't open his arms, he simply stood unmoving, waiting for her to obey his command.

They kept their eyes focused on each other, their gazes locked. Cleo walked toward him, slowly, surely. And all the while she wondered if her weak legs could make the short journey. When she reached him, she broke eye contact, lowering her head shyly, needing for Roarke to make the next move. She had come this far, done this much. Now it was time for him to take charge.

"Let me look at you," he said.

Cleo shivered. Her breasts ached, needing his touch to bring them relief.

His gaze traveled over her, from the cap of red silk covering her head to the triangle of red fluff at the apex between her thighs. Small and delicately made, her skin like porcelain, Cleo possessed a perfect, petite body.

His instincts told him that she'd never done anything like this before, never served herself up on a silver platter, her body an offering to a man's desire.

"You're lovely," he told her. "The loveliest thing I've ever seen."

Throbbing, tingling, aching sensations created turmoil inside her. She didn't know how much longer she could stand here without crumbling, without crying out, without begging him to end her agony.

"Undress me," he said, and lifted her hands to his chest.

With unsteady fingers she finished unbuttoning his shirt and spread it apart. Gasping, she shut her eyes. The sight of his hairy, muscled chest took her breath away. She ran her hand over his chest, loving the feel. Tangling her fingers in the thatch of hair, she pressed her cheek against his chest and breathed in the rich, earthy aroma of an aroused man. Her man. Her husband.

She traced the thick scar tissue on the right side of his chest with her fingertips. "How did you get these?"

"Bullets. It happened on an assignment last year. I almost died."

"Oh." Lowering her head, she kissed his scars.

Threading his fingers through her hair, he grasped her head. "Finish the job, honey." Roarke's voice was thick with desire. "Undress me."

Opening her eyes and lifting her head, Cleo stared up at him. He was so tall he towered over her. He released her hair. She slipped the shirt down his shoulders, over his arms and let it drop to the floor. She stared at his belt buckle. She could do this. She had to do this. Roarke wasn't going to help her. He intended to make her strip him.

Struggling several minutes with the buckle, she finally undid it. Then she unsnapped and unzipped his jeans. His sex bulged against the exposed vee of his cotton underwear. She gripped his hips and tugged on his jeans, pulling them down. When they reached his ankles, the jeans hung on his feet. Kneeling before him, Cleo unlaced his athletic shoes. Roarke kicked them off one at a time, then held up his left foot. She removed his sock, then the other when he lifted his right foot.

She glanced up the long length of his legs. Powerful, hairy legs. When she swayed forward, resting her head against him, Roarke reached down and lifted her hands to the elastic waistband of his briefs. Staying on her knees, she tugged his underwear over his hips, over his straining sex and down his legs. Roarke stepped out of his briefs and stood there before her, totally naked, fully erect and powerfully male.

Placing his hands under her armpits, he lifted her until her mouth was almost touching him intimately. Her warm breath felt like flames against his engorged shaft. She placed her lips on him, the first kiss hesitant, the next and then the next more eager, as she kissed him from root to tip and back again.

When he could no longer bear her moist, hot caresses, he grasped her head in both hands and drew her sweet mouth away from him. Groaning, the sound a ravaged statement of need, he threaded his fingers through her hair. When she looked up at him, her face flushed, her eyes glazed with passion and her damp lips slightly parted, Roarke thought he would explode.

He lifted her to her feet, his breath ragged, his heart thundering like a wild, racing stallion. Pulling her up to him and off her feet, he pressed his sex against her belly, her breasts against his chest. Then he devoured her mouth in a kiss that robbed her of her breath and of what little sense she had left.

She flung her arms around him, taking his kisses and returning them full measure. Clutching her buttocks in his big hands, he crushed her mound against his sex. She cried out. He moaned.

"Tell me, Cleo. Tell me and I'll put us both out of our misery."

"I want you," she said breathlessly. "Make love to me. Please."

Gathering her up and into his arms, he carried her to the bed and laid her in the center, then came down on top of her. He was hard and heavy and big. So very big. He made her feel tiny and helpless against his strength.

He kissed her savagely, conquering her mouth with his thrusting tongue. Moving hastily on to new territory, he attacked her breasts with tender fierceness, squeezing them gently as he lifted them. He pinched one puckered point, then the other. She moaned and writhed beneath him. Lowering his mouth, he sucked greedily, moving from one begging nipple to the other.

While his mouth ravaged her breasts, he stroked her belly, then moved his hand downward, probing the notch of her legs. When he touched her intimately, her hips rose off the bed. He slipped his hand between her thighs, parting them, then inserted his fingers into the damp, hot tightness. She buckled, her body undulating, pleading for his possession.

"Now, Simon. Now!" She gripped his buttocks, forcing him closer.

"Yes, Cleo. Now." His tongue plunged into her mouth the exact moment he removed his hand and thrust into her waiting warmth with his hardness.

Her body sheathed his, surrounding him snugly within a hot, fluid grip. She was as ready for this mating as he. As mindless with passion. As desperate with need.

He knew he couldn't make it last, for either of them. They were both too hungry, too starved for satisfaction. He moved in and out, increasing the pace with each lunge.

She gasped loudly. Her swollen femininity clenched him

tightly. And then she cried out her release. Furious. Overwhelming. Earth-shattering. The spasms shook her body.

Roarke moved faster, his thrusts harder and deeper. And while she still quivered with the aftershocks of her release, he spilled himself into her. He shuddered, then his body jerked several times as it emptied the last drops of completion. Groaning with satisfaction, he stared down at Cleo, and the sight of her lying beneath him, so blissfully fulfilled, stirred his body.

Damn, he barely had the energy to breathe. He sure as hell wasn't ready for another wild ride. Not this soon. But his body was telling him that it wanted more. *Hey, you horny bastard, don't you know how old we are?* he asked the part of his anatomy over which he had no control. *We're nearly forty. So act your age, will you?*

Sliding off Cleo and onto his side, he brought her into his embrace and placed soft kisses all over her face.

"You've just proven an old adage," Roarke said.

"What old adage is that?" Snuggling against him, she laid her hand over his belly and caressed the line of dark hair leading down to his manhood.

Easing his hand between her legs, he petted her intimately and savored her small, breathless gasp. "The old adage that dynamite comes in small packages," he told her. "You, my little darling, are pure dynamite."

"Oh, that old adage," she said, moving her hand slowly downward until she encountered his renewed arousal. "I don't disagree entirely, but—" circling him, she stroked him intimately and grinned when he drew in a sharp breath "—I happen to know, firsthand, that a certain type of dynamite comes in a big package."

The combination of her seductive words and her talented hand brought Roarke's manhood to full readiness. He delved his fingers into her, manipulating her feminine core. She moaned her pleasure.

"You know I want you again, don't you?" he asked.

"Yes, I know."

"And you want me, too."

"Yes," she said.

"You aren't too sore from the first time, are you?"

"No, Simon, I'm not too sore."

Without saying another word, he lifted her on top of him, placing her gently, allowing her to make the final plunge that would completely unite them. She straddled him as if he were that untamed stallion Pearl had compared him to. And the moment she brought him totally inside, he lifted his hips and hoisted himself to the hilt. With his hands guiding her and his lips feasting on her breasts, Roarke encouraged her wild ride. Her tempestuous release hurled him over the edge into savage fulfillment.

She fell on top of him, their bodies bonded with perspiration and satiation. He stroked her hair, her neck, her back and her buttocks. They fell asleep with his big, dark hand cupping her hip as his body cushioned hers.

Roarke awoke suddenly, his heart racing at breakneck speed. Damn, he'd been dreaming. Just dreaming. Cleo was all right. She lay snuggled against him, her head on his shoulder, her hand resting on his belly. He breathed a sigh of relief. She was safe. Thank God. Easing his arms around her gently, trying not to wake her, he pulled her into his embrace. Her naked body was warm and compliant, and the very feel of her skin against his aroused him. He longed to make love to her again. She had been as hot and wild as he'd hoped she would be, giving herself completely, holding nothing back. And she had tempted him beyond all reason to give equally to her. But both times, in the end, he had held back, afraid to allow himself the freedom to experience the emotions clamoring for release.

No matter how much he wanted Cleo and she him, their time together was limited. Theirs was not a love match, not a lifetime commitment. She might cling to him passionately, giving herself to him as he knew she'd never given herself to anyone else, but nothing could change the fact that he was her employee. She'd hired him for three reasons—to protect her, to keep McNamara Industries a family-run operation...and to impregnate her. Once he'd served his purpose, his job would end and they'd both go their separate ways.

Being Cleo's husband had certain benefits, the least of

which was being her lover, and he might be tempted to hang around after the job ended, if the circumstances were different. But they weren't. Once she told him she was pregnant, he'd make plans to leave. Surely by that time they would have discovered who was trying to harm Cleo and sabotage McNamara's.

But what if he'd gotten her pregnant tonight? They had made passionate love twice. Pregnancy was a possibility.

Shimmery moonlight shone in through the French doors and floor-to-ceiling windows, illuminating the room with a soft, pale light. He looked at the woman in his arms, the strands of her short hair shiny cinnamon threads against his hard, leather-brown shoulder.

If she was pregnant—this soon—he couldn't leave her and her baby unprotected. But that didn't mean he would have to stay. It wasn't as if he was indispensable. He could easily turn his bodyguard duties over to Morgan Kane, or keep Kane on the investigation and bring in Gabriel Hawk. But could he really leave Cleo's protection to another man, no matter how well-trained that man was? No, of course he couldn't. Not after tonight. Tonight Cleo had become his, in every sense of the word. He'd just have to hope that he hadn't impregnated her already. Hanging around to watch her grow bigger with his child every day hadn't been part of their bargain. He'd made it perfectly clear that this child would be hers and hers alone.

He'd already been given one chance at fatherhood and he'd screwed up royally. Cleo's child deserved better. And so did Cleo. She deserved a man capable of loving her and committing himself to her for the rest of their lives. He wasn't that man. He knew himself too well. Inside, where it really counted, he was a burned-out shell. The fire of guilt and remorse and self-hatred had gutted his soul years ago. That fire had begun the day he'd received the news that Laurie had died. It had blazed inside him at his little girl's funeral. And the day he'd said goodbye to Hope at the private mental hospital where she'd been committed, that internal fire had raged. Day by day, week by week, year by year, the inferno had slowly destroyed him, destroyed any ability he'd ever had to love.

Cleo roused, opening her eyes and looking up at Roarke with tenderness. She smiled.

"You're awake," she said. "Couldn't you sleep?"

"I slept like the dead for several hours after..." Pausing, he stroked her cheek. "I'm not going to let anything happen to you. Whoever is playing these deadly games is going to lose. I'll see to it."

Stretching far enough for her lips to reach his, she kissed him, then pulled away. "I know you will." Bracing her elbow on the bed, she supported the side of her face with her hand and gazed adoringly at Roarke. "We both know that someone deliberately planted those spiders in the bathroom."

"Yeah. And tomorrow I'll have to call the local authorities. We'll have to bring them in on this and on the problems at McNamara Industries." He liked the way she looked at him, her eyes filled with tenderness and just a hint of passion. He supposed a lot of women got mellow after sex, and some, like Cleo, would get sentimental. He usually didn't hang around long enough to find out. He hadn't slept the night through in a woman's bed in a long, long time.

"This is just the beginning, isn't it? If I continue refusing to sell McNamara's, my life will remain in danger and the problems at the plant will only escalate."

"If you're having second thoughts, Boss Lady, now's the time to say so."

"No second thoughts," she said. "No second thoughts about any of my decisions."

He understood her meaning. She was telling him that she wasn't sorry she'd hired him as her bodyguard and her husband. Right now, he was glad Cleo McNamara had walked into his office and made him a proposition he couldn't refuse. But he knew that in a few months, when this job ended and he left River Bend, he *would* have second thoughts. For the rest of his life, he would wonder if he'd done the right thing, fathering a child and then deserting it.

He had deserted a child once before, giving his military career greater precedence in his life than he'd given his daughter's welfare. But this time, he was thinking of the child first, knowing that the best thing he could do for Cleo's future baby was to get out of its life and stay out.

"What's wrong?" Cleo asked. "You seem to be a million miles away."

"Fifteen years in the past." He'd spoken before he'd thought, but covered his slip by saying, "I was just considering how much my life has changed over the years. I've gone from a gung-ho young soldier to a middle-aged warhorse who wants to retire to a farm somewhere."

"And the money I'm paying you will buy you that farm."

"Yeah."

The sheet that had barely covered Cleo's breasts slipped downward. When she reached out to grab it, Roarke jerked her hand away. The sheet drifted slowly to her waist, leaving her breasts exposed to the cool air and Roarke's hot appraisal. Her nipples puckered. He ran the tip of his finger over one jutting point and then the other. Cleo held her breath as shivers of awareness rippled through her.

"I didn't know it would be this way," he admitted, lifting himself up and over her, bracing his body with his hands planted, palms down, on the bed.

"What way?" she asked, her breathing quickening, her body straining upward pleadingly.

"I didn't know that once we made love, we wouldn't be able to keep our hands off each other."

"It's crazy, isn't it?" Cleo placed her arms around his neck and brought his head downward, his lips closer to hers. "I didn't realize that I could ever feel like this. It's a raging hunger, isn't it?"

"Yeah, that's exactly what it is." He parted her thighs and slid between them. "And I want to feed that raging hunger again right now."

"So do I." Spreading her thighs, she opened herself up fully to his invasion. The moment he entered her, she lifted her hips and draped her legs around his waist.

Roarke took control of their mating until the final moments when Cleo's body dictated the rules of release for both of them. She moved against him, taking his thrusts and returning them, bringing them both closer and closer to completion. When she tightened around him and cried out in earth-shattering pleasure, his body took its cue from hers and spiraled out of control into a jetting explosion.

Chapter 8

"**W**ake up, sleepyhead."

Cleo opened her eyes and stared up into Roarke's handsome face. Smiling, she stretched like a contented cat, then reached up and draped her arms around his neck, bringing his mouth down to hers for a morning kiss.

Roarke took charge of the kiss immediately, knowing how easily it could get out of control if he didn't end it quickly. He wasn't sure he liked the way Cleo could turn him inside out, the way she could make him want her so desperately. He wasn't used to a woman having that much power over him.

He removed her arms from around his neck and sat down on the edge of the bed. She snuggled against him.

"Good morning, Simon."

"Good morning, Cleo."

She eased away from him and sat up straight. Allowing the sheet to slide down to her waist, she stared at him and smiled. "You've already showered and dressed. How long have you been up?"

He tried not to look at her full, round breasts that beckoned to him, pleading for his touch. Damn, if she didn't cover herself, he'd be lost. And this morning wasn't the right time to fall back into bed and make love to Cleo. This morning was the time for business—serious business.

He shot up off the bed, crossed the room and went into the closet. Emerging with a blue satin robe, he tossed it to her. "Put that on. You're far too tempting the way you are right now, Cleo Belle."

Lifting the robe from where it had fallen over her lap, Cleo grinned at her husband, then slowly slipped into the robe. "There, is that better?"

"Much." Roarke sat back down on the edge of the bed. "We have a lot to accomplish today. I've been up a couple of hours."

Scooting to the edge of the bed beside Roarke, she laid her hand on his arm. "What have you been doing during the two hours you've been up?"

"I made some phone calls—" he nodded toward the sitting room "—from in there. I didn't want to disturb you. You were sleeping so soundly."

"I was exhausted. Your wore me out," she said teasingly as she stroked the inside of his wrist with the tip of her index finger.

He grinned, but quickly forced his mouth into a sober line and grasped Cleo's shoulders. "There's nothing I'd like more than to make love to you again right now, honey. But we're expected downstairs for breakfast in about twenty minutes, so unless you want to greet your family looking the way you do right now—"

"Why are we having breakfast with my family this morning?"

"Because it's time."

Standing, Roarke dragged Cleo up and out of bed, then gave her a gentle shove toward the bathroom. When she halted, turned around and gave him a questioning stare, he shook his head.

"Hey, do you believe I'd send you in there if I thought there was any danger? I checked the bathroom out thoroughly before I took my shower." Gently clamping his hands down over her shoulders again, he guided her forward. "Just ignore the mess."

She hesitated at the closed door. "Why is it time for us to

have breakfast downstairs? And who did you call this morning?''

"I called the police and spoke to a Sheriff Bacon. He was very accommodating. Seems he knew your uncle George and thought highly of him. He's going to check into a few things for me.''

"I see.'' When he gave her another shove, she balked. "Who else did you call?''

"I phoned the exterminator who regularly services the house. Someone named Roy Bendall. He'll be out this morning.''

"Neither phone call explains why we're eating breakfast with the family,'' Cleo said.

"I remembered something from when I read over the information about the members of your family that I asked you to compile for me.''

"What did you remember?''

"That your uncle Perry is a retired college professor, whose background was in entomology. He'd know everything there is to know about the brown recluse, wouldn't he?''

"You're planning to tell my family what happened last night and then watch how they react, aren't you? You're going to cross-examine Uncle Perry and see if you can make him sweat.''

"Something like that.''

"Do you think Uncle Perry is behind the threats on my life and the problems at the plant?'' Cleo asked.

"It's possible, isn't it? He and his entire family would benefit if you were out of the way.''

"Yes, I suppose you're right. Uncle Perry and I have never been close. He's always seemed to resent me.''

When Roarke gave her another nudge, she opened the bathroom door and disappeared inside, closing the door behind her. She stood perfectly still for several minutes as she surveyed the area, noting the total disarray. There didn't appear to be an inch of her private bath that Roarke hadn't examined. She shivered as she remembered that there wasn't an inch of her own body that Roarke hadn't examined. Shutting her eyes, she leaned her head back against the door and sighed deeply. The moment she thought about their passionate lovemaking, Cleo's body responded to the memory. Her nipples puckered; her femininity throbbed. How was it possible to want him again so soon?

Making her way carefully across the cluttered tile floor, Cleo watched for any movement, the slightest sign that even one spider might have escaped annihilation. With an unsteady hand, she reached down and picked up one of the scattered clean towels from the floor. Reaching inside the glass-enclosed shower, she turned on the brass faucets and started the water flow.

Taking one final look around the room, she stepped inside the shower enclosure. Filling the net body scrub with scented liquid soap, Cleo washed her arms and shoulders, then hesitated at her breasts. They were a little tender, her nipples sore from Roarke's diligent attention. As she rubbed the lather over her breasts, she sucked in her breath as a tingling sensation spiraled outward and downward, reaching her feminine core.

She had never known that making love could be so all-consuming, so totally, completely, earth-shattering. Paine Emerson had been her first and only lover, but he'd been a boy of twenty-two, and she now realized that he'd been an inexperienced, inept lover. If she hadn't been so infatuated, so youthfully, foolishly in love with him, her intimate moments with him would have been a great disappointment.

Having had Simon Roarke as a lover, Cleo now understood how sexual desire could dominate a person's life. And if that desire was combined with other equally strong emotions, the results could be explosive. And that's exactly what her feelings for Roarke were—explosive. With each passing day she grew to like and respect her husband more and more. He was, as Pearl had told her, a fine man.

Yes, that's exactly what Simon was. A fine man. A man she not only needed in her life, but very much wanted.

As rivulets of water cascaded over her, Cleo circled her belly with the nylon net scrub. Was she already pregnant? Had her husband given her a child during their hours of hot, passionate lovemaking?

The thought of being pregnant, of carrying Roarke's baby inside her, created a warm happiness deep in her heart. Someday she could tell their child what a good man his father had been, could honestly say that their union had meant more to her than a business deal. But how could she ever explain why Roarke wasn't a part of his life? Why the child's own father hadn't wanted anything to do with him?

Stilling the circling motion of her hand, Cleo clutched the net scrub, then tossed it onto the floor. While she rinsed the foam from her body, she tried to stop thinking about being pregnant, about the possibility that Roarke's son—or daughter—could have taken root in her womb.

The longer it took her to become pregnant, the longer Roarke would remain a part of her life. He couldn't leave her until he fulfilled all his obligations. As much as she longed to be pregnant, she hoped that she wasn't. Not yet. Not until she found a way to persuade Roarke to stay with her during her pregnancy and afterward help her bring up their child.

"They're eating out on the patio, by the pool," Pearl said. "I'll bring your plates out directly. We're having blueberry pancakes this morning. Coffee and juice are on the serving cart out there, Mr. Roarke."

"Has everyone come down?" Cleo asked.

"Everyone," Pearl said. "Y'all are the last ones, but folks understand your being late, since y'all are still honeymooners."

Cleo willed herself not to blush. Before this morning there had been no truth to the charade they'd been enacting as happy newlyweds. But after last night, she felt quite a bit like a deflowered virgin bride, and was afraid the aftereffects of sexual pleasure hung over her like a bright, shiny halo, proclaiming her wedded bliss to the whole world.

"Pearl, I'm expecting several visitors this morning," Roarke told the housekeeper. "I believe all three of them will arrive while Cleo and I are at breakfast. I want you to be sure to announce each gentleman and bring him directly out to the patio."

"Three visitors this morning?" Narrowing her gaze, Pearl stared quizzically at Roarke. "Just what's going on?"

"Cleo had some unexpected guests in her bathroom last

night." Roarke took Cleo's hand in his. "Someone planted half a dozen brown recluse spiders in her bath towels."

"Oh, my dear Lord!" Reaching out, Pearl patted Cleo's cheek. "Them little creatures are dangerous. My baby brother nearly died from one of 'em's bite. Are you all right, Cleo Belle? Why didn't—"

"I'm fine. Roarke killed all of them," Cleo said.

"One of our visitors this morning will be the exterminator," Roarke said.

"Good. You called Roy Bendall. We don't want to come across one of them spiders that might have escaped." Pearl grabbed Roarke's arm. "If somebody planted the brown recluses in Cleo's bath towels, then my guess is one of your other visitors will be a lawman."

"Sheriff Bacon," Roarke said. "I understand he was on friendly terms with the late Mr. McNamara."

"Phil Bacon's daddy used to be sheriff before him," Pearl said. "The McNamaras have always taken a friendly interest in local politics, if you know what I mean."

"Pearl, you make it sound as if Uncle George had the local law in his hip pocket." Cleo shook her head. "And you know that isn't true. Phil Bacon is as honest as the day is long."

"I suppose he's as honest as a politician gets, and that's what a sheriff is. Part lawman and part politician," Pearl said.

"You've got an opinion on everything and everyone, haven't you, Pearl?" Roarke squeezed Cleo's hand, then lifted it to his lips.

Pleased with her husband's genuine affection, Cleo shivered inside and the tiny shivers radiated pleasure through her whole body.

Pearl fixed her gaze on Cleo and Roarke's clasped hands. "You're right about that. I'm an opinionated old woman. And with every passing day, my opinion of you gets better and better." She stepped directly in front of Roarke and looked up at him. "Who's this third visitor we're expecting this morning?"

"Morgan Kane," Roarke said. "He flew into Huntsville from Atlanta and is driving here. He's a private security agent and an investigator."

"Looks like it's going to be a busy morning around here."

Pearl planted her hands on her hips. "I'm sure going to be close by so I can see how the Suttons deal with all the excitement."

Hand in hand, Roarke and Cleo walked through the double French doors and outside onto the patio area, near the pool. The entire clan quieted instantly when he and Cleo approached. Only Aunt Beatrice seemed pleased to see them. Cleo leaned over and kissed her aunt on the cheek. Roarke seated her at the far end of the table, then poured two glasses of juice and placed them side by side. After filling two cups with hot coffee, he put one in front of Cleo and the other next to her, then seated himself beside his wife.

He had deliberately placed himself where he could watch the others. Even the cleverest person sometimes gave himself away with a word or a look, a reaction to something unexpected. Three unexpected visitors might trigger a suspicious response in one of the Suttons. But which one? Roarke wondered as he surveyed the length of the heavy glass-and-metal table and he paused briefly to study each person.

Even though he automatically excluded Beatrice McNamara from his list of suspects, he let his gaze linger on her. Looking at this woman gave him a preview of what Cleo would probably look like thirty years from now. There was a strong family resemblance. From their red hair and green eyes to their petite bodies and small, delicate bone structure. Cleo could have easily been the child Beatrice never had.

"We're simply delighted that y'all decided to finally join the family for a meal," Oralie said as she lifted the Haviland china cup to her lips.

"I can't say that I blame Cleo for wanting to keep her new husband all to herself." Daphne licked a drop of syrup from the side of her mouth. "I know if I had a husband like Roarke, I'd keep him locked in my bedroom for a month."

"Daphne!" Oralie scolded. "I will not tolerate such disgraceful talk at my breakfast table."

"Don't upset yourself, Mother." Trey folded the newspaper behind which he'd been buried and laid it on the table between his plate and Marla's. "You know as well as I do that Daffie loves to shock you almost as much as she loves to needle Cleo."

"What a thing to say." Oralie smiled faintly. "You'll give Mr. Roarke the wrong impression of our family, dear."

"I imagine Mr. Roarke has already formed an opinion of us, and our pretending to be anything other than what we are won't fool him," Daphne told her mother, then stared directly at Roarke. "Aren't I right about that, Simon?" She spoke his name in a sultry drawl, turning the pronunciation of his name into an invitation. "You've got us all sized up, haven't you? I'll bet you've even narrowed down the suspects, eliminating Aunt Beatrice because she adores Cleo so, and Pearl and Ezra for the same reason. And of course, no one would suspect sweet, mousy little Marla."

"Daphne, you're a bitch!" Trey snarled.

Marla Sutton's pale cheeks flushed. Dropping her chin to her chest, she gazed down into her lap. Roarke tended to agree with Daphne's assessment. It would be difficult to picture the quiet, shy, sweet young woman in the role of a potential murderess. Even the woman's sedate, old-fashioned page-boy haircut and expensive but plain attire added to her overall Jane Eyre appearance.

But appearances could be deceiving. Roarke had seen too much evil and cruelty, often disguised as sweet innocence, to disregard the possibility that behind Marla Sutton's gentle facade a killer existed.

Pearl breezed outside, carrying two plates stacked high with blueberry pancakes. Roarke marveled at how easily the elderly, overweight housekeeper maneuvered. She set one plate in front of Cleo, the other in front of Roarke.

"Roy Bendall is here," Pearl announced.

"Ask him to come on out," Roarke said. "I want to speak to him, give him some specific instructions before he begins."

"Roy Bendall?" Perry Sutton looked at Roarke for the first time. The fork he held quivered in his unsteady hand. "Why is the exterminator here? He's already been here this month, hasn't he?"

Roarke thought that Perry must have once been a very handsome man. Remnants of that youthful beauty still lingered on his lined face, in his large, dark eyes and in the sturdy build of his body. But something had beaten this man, whipped him into a shadow of what he'd once been. Roarke had seen men like that before. Men who had allowed the spark of life to die inside them. Men who had given away their strength and dignity to some carnivorous force whose hunger could never be appeased. He had come close to becoming one of those men. If he'd stayed married to Hope, it could have happened to him.

"I called Roy Bendall earlier," Roarke said. "I want him to give Cleo's suite a going-over."

"Why would Cleo's rooms need inspecting?" Oralie asked.

"Here he is." Pearl showed the auburn-haired, freckle-faced Mr. Bendall out onto the patio.

"Believe me, I don't know how any spiders could have gotten in Ms. McNamara's suite," Roy said. "I can promise you that they didn't crawl into the house by themselves. Just ask Pearl. I do good work. There's not so much as an ant in the kitchen."

"No one is blaming you, Roy," Cleo said.

The short, stocky Roy relaxed his tense stance. "Why anybody would want to harm Ms. McNamara, I don't know, but I'd stake my reputation on the fact that those brown recluses were deliberately brought into this house."

"Brown recluse spiders!" Aunt Beatrice gasped. "In the house? In your rooms?" She turned her concerned gaze on Cleo. "When? How?"

Cleo reached across the table and laid her hand reassuringly over Beatrice's. "Last night Roarke killed half a dozen spiders that someone had placed inside one of my bath towels."

"Who on earth would have done something so despicable?" Oralie rested her hand over her heart.

"I think Mr. Roarke is accusing one of us, Mother," Trey said. "Isn't that right? You believe that planting the spiders was another scare tactic to try to frighten Cleo into selling McNamara Industries."

"Mr. Bendall, I want every inch of Mrs. Roarke's suite inspected and then sprayed," Roarke said. "Pearl will clean up when you're finished and air out the rooms."

Before Pearl could escort Roy Bendall back inside the house, Ezra appeared in the doorway.

"The sheriff's here," Ezra told them. "Said he's here to see Cleo Belle...er...that is, he's here to see Mrs. Roarke."

"Please ask Phil to join us for breakfast," Cleo said.

"You've called in Phil Bacon?" Perry Sutton set his cup down on the saucer so hard that coffee splashed over the sides.

"Someone is trying to harm my wife," Roarke said. "When I spoke to Sheriff Bacon, he assured me that his department has been involved since the day someone took a shot at Cleo. He wants to get to the bottom of this and arrest the person responsible."

As Roy Bendall exited, Sheriff Phil Bacon entered. Pearl poured the tall, robust young man a cup of coffee and handed it to him. Accepting the coffee with a gracious nod, the sheriff sat down beside Cleo.

"'Morning, folks." Phil greeted the entire family with one of his wide, toothy grins, then focused his attention on Cleo. "Your husband tells me that there was an accident at the plant yesterday and you nearly got run over by a forklift. And this wasn't the first 'accident' McNamara Industries has had since your uncle died."

"This is simply awful." Beatrice halfway rose out of her seat. "Cleo could have been killed."

Cleo eased her aunt down, petting her as she did so. "I told you that I wasn't hurt. I'm fine. Just a few scratches and bruises."

"And I understand that last night, you had a scare when you found a bunch of spiders in your towel," Phil said.

"Where do you suppose someone could get hold of half a dozen brown recluse spiders?" Roarke asked.

"I don't have any idea," the sheriff said. "But I sure as hel—heck, intend to find out. Whoever's causing trouble for Ms. McNa—that is, Mrs. Roarke isn't going to get away with it. Not in my county. I'll have a couple of my deputies look into those plant accidents."

"Thank you, Phil," Cleo said. "We'd appreciate all the help you can give us. You know how many jobs depend on my keeping McNamara Industries a family-run business. If anything happens to me, Aunt Beatrice won't have enough voting power to block a sale."

"Believe me, I understand." Phil gave Trey Sutton a hard stare, then turned his displeased look on Daphne.

"As soon as you have something to report on those spiders, I expect to hear from you," Roarke said. "Knowing where they might have been acquired could give us a clue to the culprit's identity.''

"Oh, my.'' Sighing loudly, Oralie rubbed the sides of her forehead, pressing her fingertips into the edges of her salt-and-pepper hair. "Pearl, would you please bring me my stomach medicine? All this talk about spiders and accidents at the plant and suspects and culprits has made me quite nauseated.''

Pursing her lips in a pout, Pearl tapped her fingers on the serving cart and gave Oralie a disgusted glare. "You want the liquid stuff or the little tablets?''

"The tablets, please. And do hurry.'' Holding her hand out to Perry, she looked at him, her expression pleading. "You know what a weak disposition I have. My greatest regret is that I've always been rather delicate.''

Perry patted his wife's hand as if it were some inanimate object, his touch gentle and yet emotionally detached. "Yes, my dear.''

Roarke wondered how many times Perry Sutton had spoken those three words. Hundreds? Thousands? How many times during his three-year marriage to Hope had he said, "Yes, honey,'' trying to comfort and pacify a woman who could not be consoled?

Pearl took her time leaving, her slow departure proclaiming her opinion on the true state of Oralie's health.

"I'm sorry if our discussing this nasty mess in front of you has upset you, Miss Oralie,'' Sheriff Bacon said. "I sometimes forget that there are still ladies around with delicate sensibilities. My daddy would never have made such an error. Please accept my apologies.''

"Certainly, Phillip.'' Oralie lifted a trembling hand, then let it fall helplessly to her side. "I quite understand that a man in your position is exposed to all sorts of people.''

"Unfortunately, that's true,'' the sheriff said.

Opening the French doors, Pearl stepped outside, then cleared her throat. All eyes focused on the housekeeper's face, everyone noting her closed-mouth smile.

"Where is my medicine?'' Oralie demanded.

"I'll get it in a minute,'' Pearl said. "Just thought Mr. Roarke would want to know that there's a Mr. Morgan Kane here to see him.''

"Who?" Beatrice asked.

"What the hell is this—Grand Central Station?" Trey shoved back his chair and stood. "What's going on, Roarke? Have you called in the damn marines now?"

"Not the marines," Roarke said. "The navy. To be specific, a former SEAL." He motioned to Pearl. "Tell Kane to come on out and meet the family. After all, he'll be staying here at the house and working at the plant. So there's no time like the present to introduce him."

"I'm afraid that I, for one, don't understand what's going on." Perry Sutton stiffened his spine and sat straight up in the padded patio chair.

"I think it's perfectly clear." Trey gripped the back of his wife's chair, his fingers biting into the cushion with white-knuckled intensity. "Cleo's husband is bringing in a professional."

"A professional what?" Oralie asked naively.

"Yes, Roarke, do tell us exactly what Mr. Kane does for a living." Daphne glanced at the doorway, where Pearl stood, a large shadow looming behind her inside the house.

"Kane." Roarke's command thundered in the sudden eerie quiet.

Everyone looked toward the French doors. The moment Morgan Kane appeared, Cleo's mouth fell open and Daphne gasped, then purred. Cleo thought that Morgan Kane was probably one of the most devastatingly handsome men she'd ever seen. Almost beautiful, in a totally masculine way. Younger than Roarke by a few years, perhaps somewhere around thirty-five, the tall, broad-shouldered blond filled out his Armani suit like an athletic cover model.

He strutted out onto the patio with a military-trained bearing, his body honed to perfection. He stopped at the far end of the table, directly behind Perry Sutton, removed his dark sunglasses and stared at Roarke with cold, intense gray eyes.

"Morgan Kane, meet my wife's family. Everyone seated at this table is a suspect, with the exception of Aunt Beatrice."

Beatrice smiled shyly and nodded. "Are you from the Dundee agency, Mr. Kane?"

"Yes, ma'am," Kane said, his voice a deep baritone, his accent decidedly Southern.

"Just what is the Dundee agency?" Daphne slid back her chair and stood, giving their visitor a full view of her long, bare legs and her large, braless breasts. Her orange terry-cloth short-shorts and matching halter top only enhanced her dark, exotic beauty.

"Private security and investigation, ma'am," Kane said.

"I'm Daphne Sutton." She rounded the table slowly, making her way toward Kane and giving him ample time to appreciate the view.

"I've hired Kane to find out who's behind the accidents at McNamara Industries and to prevent any future problems," Roarke informed them.

"I resent the way you've taken over," Trey said. "At the plant and now here at home. Just who the hell do you think you are, running roughshod over all of us?"

"I'm—" Roarke said.

"He is my husband," Cleo told them, her voice deadly calm. "He has every right to go to whatever lengths he feels necessary in order to protect me and to protect McNamara Industries."

"For God's sake, Cleo, if you'd just sell the damn plant, none of this would be necessary." Trey's hazel-brown eyes glittered with fury. A dark, angry flush colored his cheeks. "Your stubbornness is putting your life in danger and destroying this family."

Daphne sauntered close to Morgan Kane, inspecting him as if he were a prized piece of horseflesh. "I would just love for you to personally investigate me."

"I intend to *personally* investigate every member of your family," Kane said. "When I get through, I'll know who flosses his teeth and who doesn't."

"Cleo, I object to this man's presence here. It's bad enough that your husband is a trained killer. Now, with Mr. Kane's arrival, we'll have two in the house," Oralie said, then glared at Pearl. "For goodness' sake, will you please go get my medication!"

Pearl hesitated momentarily, then slowly walked into the house.

"I'm sorry if my husband's and Mr. Kane's backgrounds

bother you, Aunt Oralie," Cleo said. "But Mr. Kane isn't leaving until he completes his assignment."

"You're determined to make this situation as difficult for everyone as possible, aren't you, Cleo?" Perry Sutton asked.

"I don't want to make anything difficult, Uncle Perry, but I'm not going to let y'all have your way. Not this time." Jumping to her feet, Cleo flung her napkin down on the table. "There's a lot more at stake here than my getting my way on this issue. There are hundreds of jobs on the line. Doesn't anyone else care about these people? Are all of you so selfish that you aren't capable of seeing past your own needs?"

"Daddy cared about his workers," Beatrice said. "And that's why he left you in control. Because he knew you'd take care of his company and all his employees."

"Uncle George was getting senile," Trey said.

"He was not!" Beatrice screamed.

"Cleo was always Uncle George's favorite," Daphne said. "Senile or not, he would have left her in control. I just think it's amusing that he made sure she found herself a husband before he turned over all the power to her."

"I'm afraid Cleo would never have married otherwise." Oralie sighed dramatically. "Most men abhor aggressive, domineering women." She cast her sorrowful gaze at her niece. "I tried to guide you the way I did Daphne, instilling in you both all the ladylike virtues, but I'm afraid I failed."

"You did the best you could, my dear." Perry patted Oralie's hand.

"Good God, Mother, I believe you're getting senile yourself." Trey balled his hands into fists and pressed them against the sides of his thighs. "Don't you realize what the issue is? Unless Cleo sells the damn company, we're going to lose millions and wind up stuck with an unprofitable business."

"That's it!" Cleo marched around the table, halting directly in front of Trey. "McNamara Industries is not an unprofitable business! And no one is going to lose millions. Not in the long run." Cleo whirled around and glared at Oralie. "And I never married before now because I chose not to." Turning slowly, she smiled at Daphne. "Mr. Kane is staying to do his job. And if you get in his way or try to interfere in what he has to do, I'll kick your butt out of this house. Do I make myself clear?''

"Jealous, Cousin? Are you staking a claim on Mr. Kane?" Daphne grinned. "Isn't your husband enough for you?"

Cleo closed her eyes and counted to ten. She would not allow Daphne or anyone else in this family to push her over the edge. Uncle George had kept an uneven peace for as long as she could remember, his powerful personality as strong a deterrent as the threat of cutting someone out of his will. Since his death, the family had begun falling apart. The bitterness, anger and hatred that had been simmering just below the surface had finally bubbled to the top and boiled over onto everyone's lives.

"Phil, I apologize for my family," Cleo said. "Please let me know when you have any information on those spiders." She looked directly at Trey. "Mr. Kane will be leaving here shortly to go to the plant. I want you to give him your full cooperation and assist him in any way you can. Do I make myself clear?"

"Perfectly clear." Scowling, Trey clenched his jaw tightly shut.

"You're enjoying finally getting to play Lady of the Manor, aren't you?" Daphne brushed by Cleo, deliberately shoving her.

Temporarily losing her balance, Cleo swayed dangerously close to the pool's edge. She fought the unnatural fear, reclaiming her senses at the last moment.

"Grab her, Perry," Beatrice cried out. "Don't let her fall into the water!"

Perry Sutton, who was the closest to Cleo, knocked over his chair as he stood and reached out for his niece. He grabbed her arm, pulling her toward him and steadying her.

Roarke flew across the patio and jerked Cleo into his arms. Her breath came in gasping swallows. She grasped the front of Roarke's shirt, then laid her head on his chest.

"What's wrong, honey?" Why had his wife gone suddenly white? Why had the prospect of Cleo falling into the pool struck fear in Beatrice's heart and frightened Cleo senseless?

"You must be careful, Cleo, dear," Oralie said. "It was

unwise of you to stand so close to the edge of the pool. Anything could have happened.''

Lifting her head from Roarke's chest, Cleo looked toward the French doors, where Daphne stood watching, a slightly wicked smile on her face.

''Nothing would have happened, except Cleo would have gotten wet and ruined her neat little blue suit,'' Daphne said. ''Her husband would have saved her from drowning.''

Cleo whispered to Roarke, ''I'm going upstairs to change, and then I'm going to the plant.''

Roarke followed Cleo as she walked across the patio, her leather heels clipping loudly on the stone surface. The moment they entered the house, Roarke grabbed her and whirled her around to face him.

''Want to tell me what that was all about?'' he asked.

''It was about Daphne playing childish games,'' Cleo told him. ''I embarrassed her in front of Phil Bacon and Mr. Kane, so she felt compelled to embarrass me in return.''

''I understand that, but what I don't understand is your reaction to almost falling in the pool.''

''I used to be terrified of falling into the pool.'' She lifted her chin defiantly, her gaze meeting his head-on. ''A few months after I came here to live, when I was a very small child, I almost drowned in that pool.''

''You were allowed to play in the pool all alone? No one was watching you?''

''I—I don't know. I have no memory of even getting into the pool. Pearl found me and saved my life. I'd still be scared of the water if Uncle George hadn't forced me to learn how to swim. But everyone in the family knows about what happened years ago and that occasionally, I'm still wary of the swimming pool.''

''Is it possible that someone tried to kill you all those years ago?'' Roarke hated to ask, but he couldn't shake the feeling that someone in this household had wanted to see Cleo dead long before George McNamara had left her in control of his fortune.

''No. No. I—I...'' Cleo slumped against Roarke. He wrapped her safely in his arms and stroked her back lovingly.

"If that's possible, then there's more to the threats on my life than someone wanting me to sell McNamara's. Someone hates me. Truly hates me."

Chapter 9

Cleo rubbed the bridge of her nose, then ran her hand over her face and down her neck. Her back hurt, her shoulders ached and she felt the beginnings of a headache. Laying aside the file folder Roarke had given her less than fifteen minutes ago, she shoved back her chair and stood. Things were worse at McNamara Industries than she'd thought. The sabotage was more widespread, and the damage far more extensive. Someone had truly created havoc with the company's computer system. And it had all happened since Uncle George's death.

It had taken Morgan Kane less than forty-eight hours to discover the extent of the damage. He'd handed Roarke a complete report when he'd come in from the plant thirty minutes ago. And after reading the report immediately, Roarke had turned it over to Cleo and left her alone to absorb the information. He'd assured her that since Kane was now on the job and had already assembled a security force of two men and one woman, no one would have the opportunity to tamper with the computer system again. Right now, their main objective was to straighten out the present mess.

At moments like this, Cleo wished she could escape from her own life, from the burdens of being CEO of McNamara

Industries, from the responsibility of caring for others. If she could escape to some deserted tropical island, she would want Roarke to go with her. They could frolic in the ocean, bask in the sunshine and make love under the stars. No past. No future. No worries. Just endless happiness.

But she couldn't escape, couldn't run away from the danger that threatened her and her company. She had little choice but to stay and face whatever lay ahead, to confront the person who wanted to destroy her life and ruin the family business. She had to fight and win this battle.

There was another battle she wanted to win. But in her heart, she feared it was a lost cause. She wanted to win Simon Roarke, and she was willing to fight whatever demons plagued him, whatever tormenting memories held him prisoner. He stayed at her side during the day, guarding her diligently, and at night he held her in his arms and made mad, passionate love to her. But there was a part of himself that he held back, a private, tortured part of his soul that he would not share. He protected her and possessed her with equal fervor, but where she was unable to control her emotional response to him, he never relinquished complete control. Only in the throes of passion did she possess him as surely as he possessed her. And those moments were fleeting—an ephemeral ecstasy soon ended.

Roarke knocked on the door, opened it and walked into the study. He saw her standing in front of the empty fireplace, her red hair glimmering in the honeyed glow of the pewter chandelier that hung from the vaulted ceiling. A spiral metal staircase led from the ground level up to a mezzanine library level lined with rows of bookshelves.

"Have you read Kane's report?" He closed the double pocket doors behind him.

"Yes, I've read it." Turning slowly, she picked up the file folder from the enormous Jacobean desk that dominated Uncle George's private study. "Where's Kane now?"

"He's in the kitchen. Pearl's serving him a late dinner."

"Pearl approves of Kane," Cleo said. "She constantly amazes me. At first she objected strenuously to our marriage, but you won her over quickly. Then I was certain she'd disapprove of Kane, and now here she is, clucking over him like a mother hen.''

''He doesn't know how to handle her mothering.'' Roarke chuckled. ''Kane's a cold, solitary son of a bitch. I've never known him to succumb to any type of emotion or let any woman get to him, whether she was trying to mother him or trying to seduce him.''

''Have you known him long?''

''Long enough to know that I can trust him, and that he's one of the best at what he does.'' Roarke glanced at the manila folder Cleo held in her hand.

She lifted the files, shaking the folder. ''Well, your Mr. Kane certainly pinpointed all of our computer problems.''

''All the security codes are being changed and Kane is working with the computer expert he brought in. They're putting safeguards in place to make sure this doesn't happen again.''

''We've already lost thousands of dollars, maybe tens of thousands, if I can't make things right with several of the companies who do business with us.'' Cleo dropped the file on the nineteen-century silver tray that topped the coffee table. Sitting down on the tufted, oxblood leather sofa, she crossed her legs at the ankles, rested her head on the plush back and laid her hands in her lap.

Roarke watched her, noting the worry lines across her forehead and the slightly drooped corners of her mouth. She pinched the bridge of her nose, then spread her hand across her forehead and rubbed her temples with thumb and forefinger.

''Do you have a headache?'' He crossed the room, stopping directly behind Cleo. Reaching down, he ran his fingers into her hair and massaged her head. She sighed. ''You'll find a way to straighten things out. Just don't make yourself sick worrying,'' he said.

''I am on the verge of a bad headache, but you're helping prevent it. Thanks.'' She loved the feel of Roarke's strong yet gentle hands easing the tension from her head and neck. In a relatively short period of time, she had come to depend on him, to rely on his strength, his protection and his understanding. She could not allow this dependency on her husband to become a weakness. If she found that she couldn't live without him, she would be lost. Simon hadn't said or done anything to indicate that their relationship had become anything more than what it was meant to be—a business arrangement. But it had become more to Cleo—much more. If she wasn't very careful, she'd find herself in love with a man who didn't love her.

"At least Kane caught the payroll inaccuracies before this week's checks were printed," Roarke said. "That's one disaster you can avoid."

"I shudder to think what would have happened if he hadn't discovered the problem before checks went out."

Releasing Cleo's head, Roarke rounded the sofa and sat down beside her. "Luckily, all the lab data are on backup disks. Without those disks, months of research would have been lost."

"Who's doing this? Dammit, who?" Knotting her hands into tight fists, Cleo lifted them into the air. "The payroll messed up, lab files deleted and a rash of orders either erased or altered where the wrong amounts were sent out or were sent to the wrong companies or not delivered at all. Whoever is doing this doesn't care anything about the company, and is willing to do anything, cause any amount of chaos to force me to sell."

Taking her fists into his hands, he drew them to his lips and kissed her knuckles. "We'll find out who did this. Trey is the most obvious suspect. On the other hand, Hugh Winfield, who as a company lawyer has access to all the computer files, minored in computer science in college."

"Don't narrow it down to Hugh or Trey," Cleo said, pulling her hands out of Roarke's grasp. "Anyone could have hired someone within the company to sabotage the computer system."

"That's true, but—"

"Marla!"

"What?"

Cleo shifted her body around to face Roarke, bracing her back against the sofa arm. "Marla worked at McNamara Industries as a secretary. That's how she and Trey met. Marla is very knowledgeable about computers and she'd know our system inside out.''

"I'll be sure Kane knows that. He's got the situation under control," Roarke assured Cleo, "and whoever was behind the problems won't be able to do any more damage. And if he...or she...is foolhardy enough to try anything again, they'll be caught in a trap, just like that.'' Roarke snapped his fingers.

"I almost wish whoever it is would try something.'' Cleo rested her head on Roarke's shoulder. "I want this person caught and stopped. I want this nightmare to end.''

Roarke slipped his arm around her waist and lifted her onto his lap. Circling her neck with one arm, she laid her head back down on his shoulder.

"Cleo? Honey?''

"What?'' She lifted her head and stared into his troubled blue eyes.

"There's a possibility that whoever's behind the problems at the plant isn't the same person who's threatening your life.''

"You really believe there are two members of my family out to destroy McNamara Industries and me?''

"It's possible. And they could be working together or separately.''

"So catching the saboteur at McNamara's won't necessarily end the danger to me, will it?''

"We'll have to wait and see.'' Roarke encompassed Cleo in his big arms, holding her possessively. "In the meantime, I'm going to do everything in my power to keep you safe. Just don't take any chances and don't trust anyone in your family, except—''

"Aunt Beatrice.''

"Sooner or later, they're going to make another move. We have to be very careful because we don't know what form the next attack will take or when it will come.''

A knock on the door thundered through the room. Cleo jumped. Roarke's body tensed. Cleo sucked in a deep breath.

"Oh, God, I'm jittery,'' she said.

"It's all right, honey. My nerves are pretty frayed, too.''

The knock sounded again. Cleo looked at Roarke and smiled. He eased her off his lap and back onto the sofa.

"Yes?'' Cleo said.

"Cleo, it's Uncle Perry. May I have a word with you?"

She exchanged a curious stare with Roarke and when her husband nodded affirmatively, she sighed.

"Yes, of course, Uncle Perry. Please come in."

As her uncle spread apart the double pocket doors, he hesitated momentarily when he saw Roarke. "I was hoping to speak to you in private."

Roarke rose from the sofa. "Whatever you have to say—"

"I think that can be arranged," Cleo said. "Simon, darling, I don't think Uncle Perry would be foolish enough to try to harm me with you just outside in the hall."

Roarke grumbled. He didn't trust Perry Sutton any more than he trusted the man's hotheaded son. But Cleo was right. The man was no fool.

"I'll be right outside." Roarke glared at Perry as he slowly exited the room. Pulling the doors together, he didn't quite close them completely.

Scanning the hallway, he found it empty. Trey and Marla had excused themselves and gone straight to their suite after dinner. Daphne was out on the town with Hugh. And the last he'd seen of them, Beatrice and Oralie were in the parlor together, Beatrice reading and Oralie doing some sort of needlework.

He couldn't put his finger on the problem, but his instincts warned him that something wasn't quite right, that trouble was brewing. He hated getting these gut feelings. Nine times out of ten, they were right on the money. He always seemed to have a sixth sense for danger.

When this assignment ended, he was going to quit this business and put the past behind him. He wasn't going to second-guess a person's every action, wasn't going to question everything other people said and did. He was going to buy the farm he'd always wanted and live a peaceful, solitary life. No danger. No suspicions. No constantly watching his back. He'd had enough—more than enough. And he wanted out.

But every day he spent with Cleo made him question his great plan for the future. The sooner he wound up this assignment and left River Bend, the better off he'd be. He'd already let Cleo get under his skin—something he should never have allowed to happen. Every time he took her in his arms, she melted against him. Every time he kissed her, she surrendered. And every time he made love to her, she gave him all she had to give. The problem was that she expected the same from him and knew he was holding back. And each time, it became a little more difficult not to give in completely, a little harder to regain absolute control.

No matter how much he wanted Cleo and enjoyed their physical relationship, he could not—would not—allow her complete power over him. And he would never allow himself to care for her, not in a way that would endanger his emotions. He could not survive loving another woman and child and losing them forever. And if there was one thing Simon Roarke was, it was a survivor.

"What did you want to talk to me about, Uncle Perry?" Cleo faced Trey and Daphne's father, a man she'd known all her life and yet really didn't know at all. In all the years that they'd lived under the same roof, Perry Sutton had never made any effort to be a real uncle to Cleo. Other than the times when he'd staunchly supported his wife and children whenever Uncle George had taken Cleo's part in any disagreement, Perry had pretty much ignored Cleo. Of course, he hadn't paid a great deal of attention to his own children, either. Before his retirement, he'd practically lived at the local college where he taught, and when he was at home, he'd spent most of his time in his greenhouse, tending to his precious flowers.

"I did not place those spiders in your bath towels," he said, a slight tremor in his deep voice.

"Has someone accused you, Uncle Perry?" Cleo asked. Eyeing him speculatively, she noted that sweat dotted his upper lip. He stuck his hands into his jacket pockets. Were his hands trembling? she wondered.

"Since Sheriff Bacon reported to your husband that he's convinced the brown recluses that were put in your bathroom came from an experiment in Covenant College's science lab, Mr. Roarke has all but accused me." Perry took a tentative step toward Cleo. "He's questioned me repeatedly. He says things like 'As a retired professor, you stop by the campus fairly often, don't you?' and 'No one would think anything

about your visiting the science lab, would they?' He thinks
I'm the one trying to harm you, doesn't he?''

"Uncle Perry, if you are innocent...if you have nothing to
hide, then there's nothing for you to worry about.''

"If I'm innocent?'' His voice rose to a loud, vibrating pitch.
"My God, Cleo, do you think I'd actually harm you?''

"I don't know,'' she said honestly. "Your entire family has
a great deal to gain if I die.''

"George McNamara is somewhere down in hell right this
minute, laughing his head off.'' Perry removed his hands from
his pockets and rubbed them together nervously. "He's enjoying seeing me suffer. He always did like to see me sweat.
And I'm sweating now, Cleo. Does that give you pleasure,
too?''

"No, Uncle Perry, seeing you sweat gives me no pleasure.
And I'm sorry that your relationship with Uncle George was
so detrimental to you. What I don't understand is that if you
and Uncle George hated each other so much, why did you stay
here? Why didn't you leave years ago?''

Removing his hands from his pockets, Perry wrung his
hands repeatedly and paced the room. He stopped abruptly by
the Palladian windows. "If I'd been more of a man, I would
have left. I'd have taken my wife and children and gotten as
far away from River Bend as I could have. If I had, maybe
Trey and Daphne wouldn't be... Maybe Oralie and I...''

"Did you stay for the money?'' Cleo asked. "Did you think
Uncle George would disinherit Aunt Oralie and Trey and
Daphne if y'all weren't living here in his home?''

"The money didn't have a damn thing to do with my staying.'' He glared at Cleo, his eyes overly bright, a fine mist of
tears coating their dark surface. "I had...personal reasons for
wanting to stay. And Oralie never would have left. You know
how much her social position here in River Bend means to
her. Being a McNamara is what her life is all about.''

"Yes, I'm well aware of how much being a McNamara
means to Aunt Oralie,'' Cleo said. "She wanted desperately
to be Uncle George's favorite and resented him and Aunt Beatrice because they both adored my father so. But she thought
she'd finally won Uncle George over when she saw how he
loved her twins. Then when my father died and my mother

deserted me and I came to River Bend to live permanently, Aunt Oralie resented my intrusion into her perfect little world."

"Oralie can't help being the way she is." Perry hung his head, sadness and defeat overcoming him.

"You've always resented me, too, haven't you, Uncle Perry? You dislike me a great deal. I've always felt it, but pretended otherwise. My existence has made life much more difficult for you, hasn't it?"

Lifting his head just a fraction, he moved his eyes upward and glared at Cleo over the rim of his glasses, which were perched on his nose. "Yes. Yes. Anything that creates a problem for Oralie makes my life more difficult." He tilted his chin up and stared directly at Cleo. "But I haven't tried to harm you. You must believe me. Beatrice loves you so dearly. Despite everything, I would never... Please, Cleo, ask your husband to stop tormenting me. I am guilty of many things—foolishness, stupidity, cowardliness—but not of trying to kill you."

"I'll speak to Simon, but—"

Roarke opened the pocket doors. "Sorry to interrupt," he said.

Aunt Beatrice stood in front of Roarke, a small silver tray in her hands. "It's my fault, I'm afraid. I insisted on bringing you your evening tea, my dear."

"It's all right," Cleo said. "Come on in. Maybe you can persuade Uncle Perry that no one has accused him of trying to harm me."

Roarke looked over Beatrice's head, his stare questioning Cleo. Her return gaze reassured him that everything was under control. He stepped back into the hall, but left the double doors open.

"Why on earth would anyone accuse Perry, of all people?" Beatrice set the silver tray down on the Jacobean desk, lifted the small china teapot and poured the hot liquid into a matching Lennox cup. "Perry wouldn't hurt a fly."

Beatrice glanced at Perry and the warm smile disappeared suddenly. He gazed at her, the look melancholy and wistful. She returned his gaze with the same tender longing. Tears gathered in the corners of her sad, green eyes. Cleo felt like a voyeur witnessing this bittersweet moment between two people who had once been in love. She remembered the first time she'd noticed this type of heartbreaking exchange between them. She'd been thirteen and had asked Pearl what it meant. Now she often wished that Pearl had never told her about Aunt Beatrice and Uncle Perry's past relationship.

"Mr. Roarke has been harassing me ever since Sheriff Bacon reported to him about the brown recluses being taken from the science lab at Covenant College," Perry told Beatrice. "I've been pleading with Cleo for understanding. Bea, you know I'd never do anything to harm her. You know I wouldn't."

Beatrice set the teapot down and turned to her niece. "You must put a stop to this immediately!" Tilting her head, she looked out into the hallway, where Roarke stood guard, his back to them. Snapping her head around, she faced Cleo. "I can't believe you could possibly think that Perry is capable of attempted murder."

"Aunt Beatrice, no one has accused Uncle Perry of anything. Roarke has simply been asking him questions in an effort to get to the truth and find out who put those spiders in my bathroom."

"Well, Perry most certainly didn't do it!"

"Beatrice, don't upset yourself this way." Perry took a hesitant step toward her, then stopped abruptly. "There's no need for you to fight my battles with Cleo the way you always tried to do with your father."

"I—I simply can't bear to…" Beatrice breathed deeply. Tears trickled down her cheeks. "I can't bear to see you suffer."

Perry cleared his throat loudly. He blinked away the mist covering his eyes, nodded to Beatrice and hurried out of the room. Roarke stepped inside the study and closed the pocket doors.

"Aunt Beatrice, I know that you believe Uncle Perry is incapable of harming me, but—"

"There are no buts! He knows you're like my own child, that I love you more than my own life. He'd never…never…" Tears streamed down Beatrice's face. Her small, delicate hands trembled.

"Oh, please don't do this to yourself." Cleo rushed to her aunt's side, slipped her arm around her waist and led her to the wingback chair opposite the sofa. "Sit down."

Beatrice eased down into the huge chair. Cleo knelt in front of Beatrice and took her aunt's quivering hands into hers.

"I'm sorry, dear," Beatrice said, squeezing Cleo's hands. "I didn't mean to act so silly. It's just that I know the kind of person Perry really is and the thought of... No, no, you must never suspect Perry." Beatrice pulled her hands free and clasped Cleo's face. "Life has been so unkind to him, you know."

"Yes, I know." Cleo rose to her feet, glanced across at Roarke, who stood silently at the closed doors. She smiled sadly at him. He nodded.

She walked over, picked up the cup of tea her aunt had poured for her and brought it to Beatrice. "Here, drink this. Tea always soothes my nerves. That's why you fix it and bring it to me when I've had a difficult day."

Beatrice accepted the tea. The saucer shook in her unsteady hands. She lifted the cup to her lips and sipped.

"Better?" Cleo asked.

"Yes, dear." Beatrice continued sipping the tea.

Cleo sat down on the sofa. "Don't worry about Uncle Perry anymore. I promise Roarke won't harass him."

Cleo felt Roarke tense. She glanced up instantly and saw the disapproving look in his eyes. If only she could explain her promise to Aunt Beatrice. *Take me on faith,* she tried to convey to him. *Believe that I know what I'm doing.* As she stared at Roarke, she saw his big body gradually relax and she knew that on some level, she had reached him with her thoughts.

When Beatrice finished the tea, Cleo jumped up, took the cup from her and placed it on the tray. "Everything's all right now. Right?"

"Yes—" Beatrice gasped for air. "Oh, dear. I'm afraid I—" Her face twitched. She laid her hand on her cheek. "My—my cheek is numb."

"What's wrong?" Cleo rushed to her aunt's side. "Roarke, come here—quickly! Something's wrong with Aunt Beatrice."

When he reached Beatrice, she was breathing erratically. Checking her pulse, he found it irregular. His mind sorted through his past experiences. Erratic breathing. Irregular pulse. Facial twitching and numbness.

Beatrice grabbed Cleo's hand. "I'm going to be sick." She tried to get out of the chair, but before she could rise to her feet, she swayed backward, then promptly threw up.

"Oh, my. My," Beatrice moaned.

"I'm calling 911." Cleo dashed toward the telephone on the Jacobean desk.

"No!" Roarke said.

Cleo stopped, her hand hovering over the telephone.

He'd seen this sort of thing before. Men. Women. Children. Animals. Poisoned. The symptoms varied, depending upon the type of poison used, but the results were usually the same. Death.

Roarke stripped off Beatrice's soiled blouse, then lifted her into his arms. "Get that afghan." He nodded at the cream knit shawl lying across the back of the leather sofa. "We don't have any time to waste. We've got to get her to the hospital immediately."

"Why?" Cleo jerked the afghan off the sofa and followed Roarke out of the study. "What do you think's wrong with her?"

Roarke carried Beatrice down the hallway and into the foyer. "Open the door and go get a car. Any car. Just hurry."

"What's wrong with her?" Cleo demanded.

"I'm pretty sure she's ingested some kind of fast-acting poison," Roarke said. "Every minute counts. Do you understand?"

Cleo flung open the door and ran outside. Trey's silver Mercedes was in the driveway. She opened the door and said a silent prayer of thanks that, as he often did, Trey had left the keys in the ignition.

Roarke laid Beatrice in the back seat. Cleo crawled in beside her, putting her aunt's head in her lap. Beatrice groaned, then gasped for air.

Roarke got in on the driver's side, reached inside his pocket and pulled out his cellular phone. He tossed it to Cleo.

"Call 911 and have them notify the hospital to expect us," Roarke said. "The hospital's on Madison Street, isn't it?"

"Yes, two blocks off Main," Cleo replied.

Roarke started the engine, shifted the gears into Drive and raced around the circular driveway and down the private road leading to the highway.

"After you contact 911, call the house and speak to Kane," Roarke told her. "Have him go into the study and get the cup Beatrice drank from, along with the teapot. Tell him to ask Pearl where the loose tea is kept. Then have him call Sheriff Bacon."

"The tea?" Cleo trembled as realization dawned.

"Yeah, honey. That'd be my guess."

The tea had been poisoned! The tea Aunt Beatrice had brought to her. The tea she'd given her aunt to drink. Cleo's private blend. No one else in the house drank that special blend. Of course! That had to be what had happened. Whoever doctored the tea hadn't meant to harm Aunt Beatrice. They'd meant to kill Cleo!

Chapter 10

Cleo paced back and forth in the emergency room waiting area, her soft leather sandals silent against the tiled floor. What were the doctors doing for Aunt Beatrice? Would they be able to save her life? Dear God, if she didn't find out something soon, she'd lose her mind!

How could this have happened? It wasn't fair. Aunt Beatrice had never done anything to harm another living soul. Why was she being punished this way?

Roarke draped his arm around Cleo's shoulder, bringing her frantic pacing to a halt. "Come on, honey. Let's sit down. You're not doing yourself or your aunt any good working yourself into a frenzy like this."

Turning into Roarke's embrace, she buried her face against his chest. He encompassed her in his arms. "Oh, Simon, why did I give her that damned cup of tea to drink? If only I'd gotten her a glass of water, instead."

Roarke cupped Cleo's chin in his hand and tilted her chin. She looked up at him. "This isn't your fault. You didn't poison the tea."

"You're sure, aren't you, that the tea was poisoned?"

"Yeah, I'm pretty sure. I've seen the symptoms before. My

guess would be cyanide or something related to it. That's what
I told Dr. Iverson.'' Roarke led Cleo over to a green vinyl
sofa in a corner of the room, away from the other people
waiting for emergency care. "Whatever was used had to be
water soluble. My guess is a powder of some kind.''

Resting her head against Roarke's shoulder, Cleo relaxed.
Roarke took her hand in his. "Who were you talking to on
your cellular phone when the nurses forced me to come back
out here?'' she asked.

"Kane.''

Her whole body tensed. Cleo lifted her head and stared directly at Roarke. "What did he tell you?''

"He and Sheriff Bacon are waiting at McNamara Industries
lab while Dave Hibbett runs some tests on the tea,'' Roarke
said. "Bacon agreed with Kane that your lab and technicians
could get results quickly, whereas waiting on the police lab
could waste time that we simply don't have.''

"Knowing what type of poison it was could save Aunt Beatrice's life, couldn't it?''

"Yeah, honey, it could.''

Cleo relaxed against her husband again, and together they
waited. Time stood still for Cleo. The minutes seemed like
hours. Just as Dr. Iverson emerged from the cubicle where
nurses and another doctor still worked with Beatrice, the emergency doors parted and the entire Sutton clan stormed in like
a threatening tornado.

"Where's Beatrice?'' Perry Sutton demanded. "That Kane
fellow said y'all had rushed her to the hospital.''

"What happened?'' Oralie asked. "She was perfectly fine
earlier this evening.''

"Was it a heart attack?'' Trey asked.

"A stroke?'' Daphne slipped her arm around her mother's
waist. "Is she still alive?''

Leaving Trey's side, Marla approached Cleo. "Is there anything we can do? The minute Mr. Kane told us that Aunt
Beatrice was ill and y'all were en route to the emergency
room, we rushed here as quickly as we could.''

"Thank you, Marla,'' Cleo said. "But there's nothing any
of us can do, except wait and pray.'' Cleo stood, brushed past
Marla and walked slowly over to Dr. Iverson.

Following Cleo, Roarke waited behind her, his hands on her shoulders when she faced the doctor. She trembled. He tightened his hold on her shoulders, giving them a reassuring squeeze.

"How is Aunt Beatrice?" Cleo asked, a slight tremor in her voice.

"We need to find out exactly what type of poison she ingested. I've begun some preliminary treatment, but—" Dr. Iverson hesitated briefly. "She's having great difficulty breathing, and I'm afraid she could go into respiratory failure at any time. Until we know what kind of poison she ingested, all we can do is treat the symptoms."

"We have Dr. Hibbett, from the company lab, running tests on the tea Aunt Beatrice drank shortly before she became ill," Cleo said.

"Sheriff Bacon is at the lab and he'll phone the hospital as soon as they have the results." Roarke watched Dr. Iverson, wondering if he had told them everything. But Roarke didn't have to be told that time was of the essence. Proper treatment could save Beatrice's life, but at this point, the doctor would be playing a guessing game.

"What are you talking about?" Oralie nudged Daphne in the ribs and loosened her daughter's hold about her waist. She pushed past Trey and Perry. "Are you saying that Beatrice drank some sort of poisoned tea?"

"Yes," Roarke said, without glancing at Oralie. "Beatrice drank the tea she'd prepared for Cleo."

"But no one ever drinks that stuff except Cleo." All eyes turned to Daphne when she spoke. Her cheeks colored slightly. "Well, it's no secret. Everyone knows that Pearl buys that special brand for Cleo."

Dr. Iverson reached out and took Cleo's hands. "We're moving Miss McNamara up to ICU, Cleo. I promise you that we'll do everything possible to save her."

"Dear God, you're saying that Beatrice could die." Perry's voice quivered. His eyes filled with tears.

Cleo glanced at her uncle and saw genuine fear and great sorrow on his lined face. Quickly she turned back to the doctor. "Thank you."

Dr. Iverson disappeared behind the private emergency room door. A nurse emerged and came directly toward the family.

"Mrs. Roarke?"

"Yes," Cleo replied.

"Y'all can go on upstairs to the ICU waiting room. We'll be transferring Miss McNamara immediately."

"May I see her?" Cleo asked.

"Not until we have her in ICU, and then only if... Well, we'll just have to wait and see."

Roarke draped his arm around Cleo's shoulder as she turned to face the Suttons. Surveying the group, he wondered which one of them had deliberately poisoned Cleo's tea.

Perry Sutton looked as if he might crumble at any moment. His tall, slender body suddenly seemed haggard and his handsome face appeared pale and gaunt. Apparently, he was genuinely distraught over Beatrice's condition, but his concern did not rule him out as a suspect.

Cleo had been the target, not Beatrice. Only a chance happening had prevented Cleo from drinking the tea.

"Why on earth would Aunt Beatrice drink your tea?" Daphne asked. "She has always preferred coffee, even in the evenings."

"She had brought the tea to me, as she often does when I'm working in the study," Cleo said. "But tonight, she was upset and I thought...I thought a sip or two of my tea might help calm her."

"You gave her the tea after I left?" Perry asked.

"What do you mean, after you left?" Oralie grabbed her husband's arm. Her neatly manicured nails bit into the sleeve of his jacket.

Roarke had never seen Oralie looking less than perfect. Her curly salt-and-pepper hair was cut stylishly short and fluffed into a soft halo around her square face. Diamonds, rubies and sapphires glistened on her fingers and two heavy gold bracelets jangled on her wrist.

Her hazel eyes glimmered as she glared at Perry, who tightened his jaw, grasped her hand and lifted it from his arm.

"I was speaking privately with Cleo when Beatrice came in with the tea," Perry said.

His explanation obviously satisfied Oralie, who turned her

full attention on Daphne. "Where is Hugh? Did he come with you?"

"Hugh loaned me his car, but he simply couldn't leave the Andersons' dinner party," Daphne said. "I've promised to call him and let him know how Aunt Beatrice is doing."

Roarke glanced at Daphne. She still wore a silver satin tealength dress. Amethyst teardrops dangled from her ears and a matching bracelet circled her wrist. She was a beautiful woman, but there was something cold and hard about her. He'd known her type. The kind who made a man pay with his life's blood for her favors. Like mother, like daughter? he wondered.

Cleo slipped her hand into Roarke's. When he looked at her, a tight knot of pain formed in his stomach. The very thought that it could have been Cleo on her way to ICU, that it could have been Cleo hovering between life and death right now, unnerved him far more than it should. As much as he liked and respected Cleo, the possibility of her dying shouldn't scare the hell out of him.

But she was his responsibility. His job was to protect her, to keep her from all harm. How could he have prevented the poisoning? Not even he would have suspected a cup of tea made by Aunt Beatrice's loving hand could prove deadly.

"Let's go upstairs," Cleo said. "I want to be there, just in case they'll let me in to see her."

"Come on."

Together they walked out of the emergency room and down the hallway to the elevators. The Suttons followed closely behind. Trey and Marla whispered to each other, while Daphne and Oralie openly discussed the possibility that Beatrice might be dying. Perry remained quiet. Roarke noticed that his eyes were filled with tears.

When the elevator doors opened, Roarke rushed Cleo inside and punched the close button quickly, shutting out the rest of the family. As the doors fastened, they heard Trey shouting at them.

"Thank you," Cleo gripped Roarke's hand. "I'd had about all I could take of them."

"They'll be right behind us," Roarke said. "I just gained

us a few minutes of solitude. You'll have to face them all again once we get upstairs.''

"One of them poisoned the tea. One of them is responsible for what happened to Aunt Beatrice.''

"Yeah. At least one member of your family is capable of murder. But which one?''

"I wish it were anyone except a member of my own family, even Hugh,'' Cleo said.

The elevator stopped at the third floor. The doors opened automatically. Cleo closed her eyes, took a deep breath and said a quick, silent prayer for her aunt Beatrice.

A young blond nurse whose name tag read K. Mullins met them the moment they entered the ICU waiting room. "Are you Mrs. Roarke?''

"Yes.'' Cleo's heartbeat roared in her ears like a jet engine. "Has something happened to my aunt?''

"It's good news, Mrs. Roarke,'' the nurse said. "Dr. Iverson said to tell you and your husband—'' she glanced up at Roarke and smiled "—that Sheriff Bacon called. The lab identified the poison.''

"Oh, thank God.'' Cleo swayed unsteadily on her feet.

Roarke grabbed her, putting his arm around her waist and lifting her against him. "Did Dr. Iverson say what it was?''

"Yes. It was some sort of fluoroacetate. Dr. Iverson mentioned something about it being a rodenticide, I believe. But he said the stuff was banned years ago.''

"What was banned?'' Oralie asked, as she and her troupe descended upon the ICU waiting room. "Is there news about Beatrice?''

"Dr. Iverson will be out shortly,'' Ms. Mullins told Cleo, then excused herself and returned to the intensive care unit.

"What was that all about?'' Trey asked.

"The lab identified the poison,'' Roarke said.

"So quickly?'' Perry stood behind his wife and children, his shoulders slumped, his face moist with tears. "Does that mean they'll be able to save Beatrice?''

"It means that Dr. Iverson will be better able to administer whatever treatment is available for that type of poison, even though many poisons are similar.'' Roarke answered Perry's question, but his gaze never left Cleo. She was his main concern. Hell, she was his only concern.

He guided her farther into the waiting room, eased her down onto a brown vinyl cushion and then joined her on the row of backless seats attached to the wall.

Oralie and her brood chattered among themselves, occasionally throwing out a question or comment to Roarke or Cleo. Neither of them responded, and when Roarke finally gave them his killer stare, they stopped speaking to him altogether.

Perry Sutton stood by the windows facing the back parking lot. He didn't say a word and never once turned to reply to anything his wife or children said to him. Several times Roarke noticed the man's shoulders shaking.

Cleo held Roarke's hand, finding strength and comfort in his nearness. This man had been a part of her life for only a couple of weeks and yet she could not imagine turning to anyone else at a time like this. Simon Roarke was a solid, immovable rock. Powerful. Dependable. Trustworthy.

Over the next hour, Cleo watched the clock. Wondering. Waiting. Praying. She had ignored Aunt Oralie and her cousins entirely, tuning out their incessant jabber. But occasionally she glanced over at her uncle, who had sat down at the far end of the waiting room, physically separating himself from his family. He sat with his eyes closed, but Cleo suspected that he wasn't asleep.

"Mrs. Roarke?" Ms. Mullins appeared in the doorway.

Cleo jumped. "Yes?"

Roarke helped her to stand. "Easy, honey," he said.

"Dr. Iverson said that you may come in and see your aunt for a few minutes."

"Thank you." Cleo hugged Roarke, then pulled away from him and followed the nurse into the ICU.

"What's happened?" Perry opened his bloodshot eyes.

"They're letting Cleo go in to see Aunt Beatrice," Daphne told her father.

Dr. Iverson met Cleo at the foot of Beatrice's bed. He patted Cleo on the back, a comforting, fatherly gesture.

"It was touch and go there for a while. She went into convulsions and I was afraid she'd slip into a coma, but since giving her an injection of calcium gluconate, the convulsions have stopped. It's possible that the symptoms will reappear later, but we'll treat them if and when that happens."

"Is she going to be all right?" Cleo glanced at her aunt. Beatrice looked so small and pale lying there, her petite body connected to an endless assortment of wires and tubes. Lifesaving devices. Dear Lord, please let them be just that.

"I can't guarantee her recovery," the doctor said. "But Beatrice is a fighter, and with God's help she should pull through."

Cleo eased around to the side of her aunt's bed. Hesitantly, she touched Beatrice's slender arm, then stroked her hand tenderly.

"I'm here, Aunt Beatrice. Right here at your side. You're going to be all right. Do you hear me? You're going to be just fine." Tears filled Cleo's eyes. When they spilled over onto her cheeks, she swatted at them with her fingertips.

Dr. Iverson laid his hand on Cleo's shoulder. "Stay only a few minutes, then when you go out one other family member may come in for a brief visit."

Nodding agreement, she slipped her hand beneath her aunt's and squeezed softly. She swallowed the sobs trapped in her throat. "I love you, Aunt Beatrice. You know that, don't you? You've been more of a mother to me than my own mother ever was. You hang in there, do you hear me? You fight hard to get better. I can't do without you."

Cleo knew she'd stayed longer than she should have when the nurse tapped her on the shoulder. She turned to face Ms. Mullins.

"I'm sorry, Mrs. Roarke, but if another family member wants to see Miss McNamara, you'll have to let him or her come in now," the nurse told her.

"Yes, of course. Thank you."

When Cleo exited the ICU, she found Roarke with a coffee cup in his hand, waiting just outside the door. He encircled her shoulders and pulled her against him.

"Dr. Iverson thinks she has a chance of surviving." Cleo's knees suddenly felt wobbly, her head light.

Tightening his hold on her, Roarke guided her to a seat, then knelt in front of her and handed her the cup of coffee. "Here. Cream. No sugar. Drink it, honey."

Clasping the foam cup in her hands, Cleo lifted it to her lips and took a sip of the warm, creamy liquid. After slowly downing half the cup, she looked across the room at her uncle, who sat on the edge of his seat, his head bowed. He held his hands between his legs in a prayerful gesture.

"Uncle Perry, you can go in and see Aunt Beatrice for a few minutes," Cleo said.

Perry shot to his feet, fatigue and anxiety falling miraculously from his shoulders. He ran across the room, totally oblivious to everyone and everything around him.

Before he reached the waiting room doorway, Oralie cried out, "Why is Perry being allowed to see Beatrice? Why not me?"

Perry walked out of the waiting room and straight into the ICU, as if Oralie had never spoken.

"It's all right, Mother. We'll all get a chance to see Aunt Beatrice." Daphne petted her mother's arm.

"No, I'm sorry," Cleo said. "No one else is going to see Aunt Beatrice tonight."

"On whose orders?" Trey asked.

"Dr. Iverson said only one visitor after me," Cleo told her cousin.

"Then why Perry?" Oralie asked sharply, bitterness in her voice.

"Because he truly cares about Aunt Beatrice, which is more than I can say for any of you." Cleo ignored Oralie's outraged gasp and Trey's angry curse.

Cleo calmly finished her coffee, then set the cup down on a side table to her right. She turned to Roarke. "If Uncle Perry is the one who poisoned the tea, he'll break under the strain of knowing he almost killed Aunt Beatrice."

"Exactly what is there between Perry and Beatrice? I've noticed some sort of invisible bond between them."

"That's a perfect way to describe it," Cleo said. "An invisible bond."

Oralie glared at Cleo. "What are you two talking about over there? I heard you mention Perry's name."

"Don't upset yourself, Mother," Daphne said.

"It's ridiculous for you to assume that my husband cares more about Beatrice than I do," Oralie said. "She's my own dear first cousin, isn't she? And she's only related to Perry by marriage."

Cleo looked directly at Oralie. "You know why I told Uncle Perry he could go in to see Aunt Beatrice."

"What does she mean by that remark, Mother?" Trey stirred from his seat beside Marla, who had fallen asleep and was awakened by her mother-in-law's outburst.

"I want you to march right in there and bring your father out!" Oralie said. "He has no business in there with Beatrice."

"What the hell's going on?" Trey looked quizzically from his mother to Cleo.

Before either could reply, Perry Sutton returned from the ICU, his face damp with tears. On some instinctive level, Cleo wanted to go to her uncle and put her arms around him. But she didn't.

"There you are," Oralie said. "I'm ready to leave, Perry. This has all been too much for me. I'm completely exhausted. You know what a nervous disposition I have."

Perry glanced at his wife, his face void of emotion. "Yes, my dear, I know."

"There's nothing we can do for Beatrice by staying," Oralie told him.

"You're quite right. There's nothing any of you can do for Beatrice by staying here." Perry looked at his son. "Trey, you and Marla take your mother home. Daphne, you go with them and see to your mother's comfort."

"Aren't you coming?" Daphne asked.

"You are not staying here!" Oralie rose to her feet. Glaring at her husband, she walked slowly toward him.

When Oralie stood directly in front of Perry, her cheeks bright with anger and her eyes wild with rage, he smiled. And that odd little smile on her uncle's face sent cold chills up Cleo's spine.

"Yes, my dear, I am staying." Perry's voice was deadly calm.

Oralie whirled around so quickly she almost lost her balance. Daphne grabbed her mother's arm. "Take me home immediately," she demanded. "I can't bear another minute of this."

Daphne guided Oralie out into the hallway. Trey and Marla followed. Trey hesitated, then turned around and said, "Please call us if Aunt Beatrice's condition worsens."

"Yes, I'll call," Cleo said, and breathed a sigh of relief when her aunt and cousins boarded the nearby elevator.

Perry slumped into a chair by the door, crossed his arms over his chest and closed his eyes. Cleo watched him for several minutes, wondering if she should go over and talk to him, try to comfort him. She didn't.

"Do you want to tell me what that was all about?" Roarke asked.

"I asked Pearl a similar question when I was about thirteen," Cleo said.

"And what did Pearl tell you?"

"Years ago, when Aunt Beatrice and Uncle Perry were young, they fell in love and planned to marry."

"What happened?"

"Aunt Beatrice grew up in an age when nice girls didn't have sex before marriage, so she wanted to wait until after their wedding."

"And?"

"Aunt Oralie was jealous of Aunt Beatrice. She wanted Perry for herself and didn't have any qualms about seducing him in a weak moment." Cleo glanced across the room at Perry Sutton and her heart ached for him. "Aunt Beatrice would have forgiven him and married him anyway, except... Oralie was pregnant. With twins."

"Trey and Daphne."

"Of course Uncle Perry married Aunt Oralie and the rest, as they say, is history."

Roarke groaned. "God, what messes we make of our lives. We human beings find a way to screw up everything and destroy ourselves in the process."

Cleo touched Roarke's face, stroking his stubble-roughened cheek. "I'm glad that you're here with me. That I'm not having to go through this alone."

He took her in his arms. She went willingly. An overwhelming sense of belonging came over her. This felt so right. Being with Simon. Her husband.

Roarke nudged Cleo. She purred in his arms like a sleepy kitten. He lifted her off his lap, where she'd slept most of the night, set her beside him on the vinyl sofa and shook her gently.

"Wake up, Cleo Belle. It's visiting hours. You can go in and see Aunt Beatrice in a few minutes."

Cleo opened her eyes slowly. The first thing she saw was Roarke's face. That wonderful, strong, handsome face. Smiling, she sat up straight and stretched.

"The last thing I remember is your lifting me into your lap and telling me to take a nap."

"That was around midnight last night," Roarke said. "It's nearly six o'clock."

"Did you get any rest?" Unable to resist touching him, she laid her hand on his chest. "You must have been uncomfortable with me lying on you all night."

"I got plenty of rest," he told her. "You're as light as a feather." He leaned down and whispered in her ear, "Besides, that's not the first time you've slept on top of me most of the night."

She made a funny little sound deep in her throat, a mixture of moan and laughter. "I probably look a fright." She stood, then reached down and picked up her shoulder bag. "I need to go to the bathroom." She glanced around the waiting area. "Where's Uncle Perry?"

"He's already gone in to see Beatrice."

"Oh. Okay. Could you rustle us up some coffee while I go freshen up?"

"I'll see what I can do."

Roarke walked down the hall to a small alcove where a row of vending machines stood. He removed a couple of dollars from his wallet and inserted one into the coffee machine, then punched a button. He repeated the process, then returned to the waiting room.

He set Cleo's coffee on the side table, then walked over to

the windows and looked out at the parking lot. Lifting the cup to his lips, he sipped the hot, black brew.

Since Beatrice had lived through the night, her chances of recovery had improved. He was grateful that Cleo's aunt hadn't died. Cleo loved Beatrice deeply and was devoted to her. How different would his own life have been if his aunt Margaret had shown him the affection Cleo had received from Beatrice? His father's sister had been a cold, harsh woman who'd never once said a kind word to him. Not even when he'd first come to live with Margaret and Eddie Bullock, and had been a scared, lonely boy of nine whose father had just died and left him an orphan.

Roarke's life had been without love, without any human warmth and kindness, until he'd met Hope. She was beautiful, bright, bubbly, and he'd fallen for her so hard he hadn't had a chance of escaping. Hell, he hadn't wanted to escape. He'd thought she was everything he'd ever dreamed of, everything he'd ever wanted. He'd been wrong.

She'd wanted him to leave the army. He'd tried to explain what being a member of the Special Forces meant to him. She didn't understand. She didn't even try.

A year into their marriage, he'd known what a mistake he'd made. But Hope clung to him, begging him not to leave her, not to stop loving her. She was so needy, so desperately needy, and no matter how much he gave, it was never enough.

"Do I look better?" Cleo asked as she emerged from the bathroom. "I cleaned up a bit. Washed my face and combed my hair." She spied the coffee cup on the table. "Oh, good. Coffee."

"You look fine, honey. A little tired, maybe."

A tall, bony, middle-aged nurse appeared in the doorway. "Mrs. Roarke, your aunt is awake and asking for you and your husband."

"She's awake." Cleo laughed nervously. "Oh, she'll fuss at me for staying here all night." She smiled at the nurse. "Is my uncle still in with her?"

"Yes. He's waiting until y'all come in before leaving. I must say, your uncle is quite devoted to her, isn't he? Just watching the way he looks at her, you can see how much he loves her."

"Yes, I know exactly what you mean," Cleo said.

They followed the nurse into ICU. Perry sat beside Beatrice's bed, holding her hand. Beatrice glanced up and smiled when she saw Cleo.

"You gave us quite a scare last night." Cleo leaned over and hugged her aunt. Gazing into Beatrice's weak eyes, Cleo clenched her teeth to keep from crying.

Perry released Beatrice's hand, then bent over and kissed her forehead. "I'll be right outside."

"No, wait, Perry," Beatrice said. "I want all of you to go on home. I'm out of danger now, aren't I, Ms. Danton?" She glanced at the skinny nurse. "I'm going to be just fine."

"You've certainly come through the night with flying colors," Nurse Danton said. "We're hoping you'll be fully recovered and able to go home in a few days. If you continue to improve, Dr. Iverson will put you in a private room sometime late tomorrow."

"See," Beatrice told them. "Go home. Take baths. Eat something. Tend to business. You can come back and see me this afternoon."

"I'll be back." Perry waved at Beatrice, then turned and left the ICU.

"I didn't want to say anything while Perry was here." Beatrice lifted her hand, reaching for Roarke. "Come here."

Roarke took her hand in his. "I'm right here, Aunt Beatrice."

Smiling, she sighed deeply. "I'm so glad that Cleo has you at her side. She's in real danger. If we had any doubts about how far this person will go, I think this incident should erase those doubts."

"Do you know what happened?" Cleo asked.

"I heard Rob Iverson and the nurses talking," Beatrice said. "Of course they didn't know I could hear them. I was poisoned, wasn't I? Or rather, the tea I prepared for Cleo had been poisoned."

"Yes, dear." Cleo stroked her aunt's forehead, brushing back a strand of silver-streaked red hair.

Beatrice clutched Roarke's hand. "You must find this person and stop him before he kills Cleo!"

"Don't upset yourself, Aunt Beatrice." Roarke turned her

hand over and gave it several reassuring pats. "I'll take care of Cleo."

"Whoever did this must hate Cleo a great deal." Beatrice's eyes filled with tears. "Find the person who hates Cleo, before it's too late. It's not Perry, but it could easily be Oralie. Or Daphne. Or even Trey."

"I'm sorry," Nurse Danton said. "I'm afraid y'all are going to have to leave and let Miss McNamara get her rest. If you'd like to speak to Dr. Iverson, I'll have him call you at home, Mrs. Roarke, after he's seen your aunt later this morning."

"Yes, have him call her later," Beatrice said. "Now, Simon, take her home and see that she eats and gets some rest before you let her come back to this hospital."

Neither Simon nor Cleo said a word on the elevator ride down to the ground level of the hospital. When the doors opened, Cleo gasped. Sheriff Phil Bacon stood there, waiting for an elevator.

"I was on my way up to talk to y'all," he said.

"Why don't we go into the coffee bar over there." Roarke pointed to his left.

The three of them sat down at a small table in the corner. Cleo reached under the table and clutched Roarke's hand.

"Cleo, your private stock of tea was laced with a poisonous substance that your people at McNamara labs tell us was odorless and tasteless, and very deadly."

She gripped Roarke's hand even more tightly. "How would someone get such a poison?"

"Well, that type of poison, according to your Dr. Hibbett, used to be in rodenticides and stuff like that, but the government banned it years ago."

"Then how—" Cleo asked.

"There's still some of it around," Phil Bacon said.

"Do you have any idea where the amount put in Cleo's tea came from?" Roarke squeezed Cleo's hand.

"As a matter of fact, we do. And that's why I needed to talk to you."

"You found the source of the poison?" Cleo sucked in her breath. "So soon?"

"We did a search of your house and the grounds," the sheriff told her. "I've had my men out there all night."

"You found the poison at my house?"

"No, ma'am, we found it in your uncle's greenhouse."

"What?" Cleo bit down on her bottom lip.

"There was about a fourth of a bag of the stuff in the bottom of the trash. It was an old bag. Someone had wrapped it in a separate plastic bag and covered it with all sorts of debris."

"Uncle Perry's greenhouse." Cleo spoke slowly, trying to absorb the meaning of what she'd been told and praying, for Aunt Beatrice's sake, that the most likely suspect wouldn't turn out to be guilty.

Chapter 11

May had exploded into fragrant bloom. Springtime flowers and shrubs littered the countryside. Nourished by several days of scattered thundershowers, the lawns were a vibrant green. Cleo hugged herself when she stepped out onto the screened back porch. "'God's in his heaven and all's right with the world,'" she quoted Browning. A shiver of apprehension quivered along her nerve endings. Despite the fact that Aunt Beatrice was home from the hospital and recuperating nicely, and despite the fact that for the past week absolutely nothing had gone wrong, either at home or at the plant, all was most definitely not right with the world.

Despite the appearance of normalcy, her life was anything but normal. My God, her family's company had been sabotaged, her aunt had nearly died from poisoning and she was paying her hired husband a million dollars to get her pregnant.

And they still didn't know who was trying to kill her!

Regardless of the peace and tranquillity at the house and the smoothly running operations at the plant, Cleo feared that this was all simply the calm before the storm. Even with Morgan Kane and his security force monitoring McNamara Industries seven days a week, twenty-four hours a day, Cleo kept waiting for another accident or another computer problem. It was like waiting for the other shoe to drop.

And Cleo couldn't remember a time when the Suttons had been so eager to maintain family harmony. Trey had kept his temper under control and Daphne had refrained from her usual catty remarks. And even Aunt Oralie hadn't acted like a jealous harpy whenever Uncle Perry showed any kindness toward Aunt Beatrice. It seemed highly unnatural to Cleo, and she'd said so to Pearl, who had agreed with her wholeheartedly.

"There's something not right about all this sweetness and light coming from the likes of them," Pearl had said. "It's like a pit of vipers disguising themselves as a bunch of harmless grub worms."

Whether it was Aunt Beatrice's near death or the sheriff's questioning of Uncle Perry—which had fallen just short of his arresting him on suspicion of attempted murder—that caused the change in the Suttons, Cleo was uncertain. But one thing she knew for sure—it wouldn't last.

The Suttons were scared. The whole lot of them. And each for his or her own reason. Now that Hugh Winfield was at Daphne's side every moment he wasn't working, Cleo counted him as a Sutton, and equally suspect in the company sabotage and the failed attempts on her life. Six suspects. Three blood related, two relatives by marriage and another a family friend she'd known since childhood.

Coming up behind her, Roarke slipped his arms around his wife and drew her back up against his chest. Leaning into his body, she lapped her arms over his. He kissed the top of her head, then rested his chin in the softness of her hair.

"I'm ready for our ride," he said. "I haven't been on a horse in years. Not much opportunity in my line of business."

"You'll be just fine. Riding a horse is like riding a bicycle. Once you learn how, you never forget." Cleo breathed deeply, taking in the delicious aroma of the fresh early-morning air and the clean, manly scent of her husband.

"I still think there are better ways to spend a lazy Saturday morning than going horseback riding." He nuzzled the side of her face.

Giggling, Cleo squirmed out of his arms and turned to face him. Simon Roarke was the only man she'd ever known who could fill her stomach with fluttering butterflies just by looking at her. But then again, she'd never known a man like her husband. Standing here before her, the morning sunshine casting a golden glow on his thick, brown hair and richly tanned skin, Simon was a magnificent sight. His faded blue jeans hugged his lean hips and long legs. She shivered, remembering the feel of wrapping herself around his hips, the pleasure of having those long, hairy legs straddling her.

Lifting her chin, she looked up into his mischievous blue eyes. "I knew you'd wake up with lascivious thoughts on your mind this morning," she said. "That's why I got up and out of the bedroom before you awoke."

Roarke grasped her face, cradling her chin between his thumb and forefinger. "What's the matter, honey? Are you getting tired of me already?"

Knowing that he was joking, she tried to keep the smile on her face and think of some similarly jovial response. But her thoughts turned serious. Didn't he realize that she would never grow tired of him, of his passionate lovemaking, of the blissful moments she spent in his arms, possessing him and being possessed by him? Didn't he have any idea how much he'd come to mean to her, how much she wanted him to remain a part of her life, even after she was pregnant, even after she was no longer in danger?

"You're having to think that one over way too long, Cleo Belle. Does that mean—"

Standing on tiptoe, she flung her arms up and around his neck. "It means that I was trying to think of a response as equally silly and ridiculous." She rubbed against him like a sleek, sensuous cat. He cupped her buttocks and lifted her off her feet, pressing her into his arousal. "I might get tired of you, Mr. Roarke, in about a hundred years or so. But even then, I doubt it."

"So why didn't we spend the morning upstairs in our bed, making love?" He took her mouth in a hot, hungry kiss and acknowledged her fervent response by lifting her body up higher onto his and deepening the kiss, devouring her with his passion.

She draped her jean-covered legs around his hips, returning his passion in full measure. Her core throbbed against his pulsating sex. She knew, as he did, that only the barrier of their clothes kept them from mating there on the back porch, in broad daylight, where they could be interrupted at any moment.

Roarke reluctantly ended the kiss, realizing full well that this either had to stop or be taken to the limit. He brushed his lips over hers, then whispered against her mouth, "Either we go back upstairs and finish this…or we go riding."

"I want to do both," she said tauntingly.

When he began lowering her slowly, she loosened her legs from around his body and allowed him to set her on her feet. "You want to go back upstairs and then go riding later?"

"No, I want to go riding now and finish this out there—" she gazed toward the thickly wooded area to the east of the house "—in a very beautiful, secluded spot I know."

Roarke grinned. The bottom dropped out of Cleo's stomach. "You, my darling wife, can be a very diabolical lady."

"If you say so. But I prefer to think of myself as inventive and adventurous. We haven't made love anywhere except upstairs in our suite. I thought a little variety was called for today. In celebration of a noneventful week."

"We've had variety," he told her, his lips twitching in an almost grin. "We've made love in the bed. You on top. Me on top. Side by side. From the edge of the bed. From the front. From the rear. We've made love in the shower, in the tub, on the love seat, in the chairs and even on the desk."

Cleo smiled broadly. Recalling each and every moment they'd shared, Cleo sighed. Her cheeks flushed a soft, delicate pink. "Yes, I know. But we've never made love outside. Hidden under the trees. With the smell of honeysuckle and wild roses all around us."

He grabbed her hand. "Come on, woman. What are we waiting for? Let's get down to the stables and saddle up old Paint."

Hand in hand, Cleo giggling quietly and Roarke grinning from ear to ear, they hurried off the porch, out of the backyard and down the unpaved lane leading to the stables.

"When I was a teenager, Uncle George kept over half a dozen horses stabled here," she said. "He loved to ride and he enjoyed having mounts for visitors. Of course, I've had my own horse since I was a child, just as Aunt Beatrice has. But now there's only Valentino and Sweet Justice.''

"Let me guess. Valentino belongs to Beatrice and Sweet Justice is yours. Am I right?"

"Aunt Beatrice has had Valentino since he was two years old. He's fourteen now. You won't have any problem handling him. He's a gelding and has a sweet disposition.''

"And Sweet Justice? Don't tell me he's a stallion.''

"Sweet Justice is an Arabian filly. Uncle George gave her to me for my birthday last year. She's barely two years old. She replaced Candy Man, an Arabian I'd been riding most of my life.''

The well-kept stables stood a half mile behind the main house. Willie Ross, whom Cleo had introduced to Roarke the first week of their marriage, met them just as they started to enter the enclosure. The sandy-haired man, with his wide, toothy smile, came out to meet them, walking with a slight limp. Cleo had told Roarke that as a child, Willie had been injured in an automobile accident that had left him physically and mentally impaired. But he was a gentle, loyal man, who had a knack for caring for horses as well as a deep love for animals in general. George McNamara had given him a job when he'd been a teenager and had kept him on at full salary even after he'd sold all but two of the horses. Cleo's uncle had remembered his stable hand in his will, requesting that Willie receive his wages as long as he lived.

"I was expectin' you down this morning, Cleo.''

Willie spoke with a pronounced slur. When he said her name, it came out sounding like Clay-ee-o.

"Got Sweet Justice and old Valentino all saddled up and ready for you and Mr. Roarke.''

"Thank you, Willie.'' Cleo patted the thin, frail man's arm. "Mr. Roarke and I plan to be out most of the morning. I'm going to show him some of my secret places.''

"You going to take him over to the Great Mississippi?'' Willie's laughter sounded like a grunting chuckle.

When Cleo smiled at him, the stable hand's face came alive with warmth and gentle affection.

"I'm going to show him the Great Mississippi and Sherwood Forest,'' Cleo said.

"He'll like 'em both." Willie looked up at Roarke. "I used to take care of Cleo, watch out for her when she was a little girl and played in Sherwood Forest and swam in the Great Mississippi."

"Sometimes Willie would play with me," Cleo said. "He'd be Little John and I'd be Robin Hood. And we used to sail a boat up the Great Mississippi."

"Sometimes I was Huck and Cleo was Tom, then next time she'd be Huck and I'd be Tom."

"Sounds like you two had quite a few adventures together," Roarke said.

"Yes, sir. That we did. Cleo's always been my friend."

Willie went inside and led Valentino out of his stall and into the stable yard. Roarke noticed a fine mist covering Cleo's eyes. He knew she ached inside with love for Willie and a deep sadness that a man of nearly fifty would forever have a little boy's mind.

The gray gelding Willie led had small, curved ears and large, expressive eyes. Roarke stroked the horse's long, arched neck as he accepted the reins. Valentino was a handsome fellow and obviously pampered. He nudged Roarke's hand.

"What do you want, buddy?" Roarke looked to Willie.

Willie pulled out a small apple from his baggy jacket pocket. "Old Val likes a treat. Whenever Miss Bea rides him, she always gives him an apple."

Roarke accepted the apple and offered it to Valentino, who took it greedily. Roarke laughed.

Willie rushed back into the stables, soon emerging with Cleo's mount. Sweet Justice was a magnificent specimen, a chestnut filly with a broad, muscular chest and deep girth. With her tail set high, she pranced toward Cleo.

"Here's my girl." Cleo hugged the beautiful Arabian. "Have you missed me, Sweetie?" The filly nuzzled Cleo's arm. "Yes, well, I've missed you, too."

Roarke waited for Cleo to mount, watching her graceful ascent. In the morning sunlight her hair shimmered a bright, rich auburn and Sweet Justice's shining coat was almost an exact match. Woman and horse seemed made for each other. Both were noble creatures. Proud, beautiful females. Aristocratic purebreds.

Roarke mounted Valentino and motioned the gelding to follow the filly's lead. Sweet Justice broke into a trot, taking free, straight strides.

"When I called Willie yesterday and told him to have the horses ready this morning, I asked him to give you Uncle George's saddle," Cleo said. "I thought it only fitting. Since you wouldn't be here in River Bend, wouldn't be married to me, except for Uncle George's will. In a way, as my husband, you're what Uncle George would have called the 'head of the household' now, and my 'lord and master.'"

Roarke laughed, trying to imagine anyone being lord and master of Cleopatra Arabelle McNamara Roarke. And the last job on earth he wanted was as head of a household that, until the past week's good behavior, thrived on jealousy, greed and hatred.

When Sweet Justice broke into a gallop, Valentino followed suit. The two Arabians struck a natural pace, floating across the ground with fast, free strides.

During the next hour, Cleo gave Roarke a grand tour of the estate then led him to what she and Willie had always referred to as the "Great Mississippi." In reality, the body of water was a large creek that bisected the McNamara property in half. But as a child, it had seemed vast, and had posed a challenge for her and Willie as they had ridden downstream in their old wooden canoe.

Roarke and Cleo slowed the horses. Cleo dismounted. "Well, what do you think?" she asked.

"This is the Great Mississippi?" he asked.

"To an eight-year old it was," she told him. "And those woods over there—" she pointed behind them "—were Sherwood Forest."

"Why were you Robin Hood instead of Maid Marian?" Roarke dismounted.

"Because Robin Hood was the one in charge. He was the one who led the merry men. And as long as I can remember, I've always liked being the boss."

"Yeah, I can believe that. You're a real bossy butt, Cleo Belle. A lot of men wouldn't find that trait appealing."

She slowly unbuttoned her short-sleeved, turquoise-and-yellow-striped blouse. "But you do, don't you, Simon? You like the fact that I'm a take-charge kind of woman."

She removed her blouse and tossed it on the ground. Roarke didn't take his eyes off her, focusing for the moment on her yellow satin bra.

"Yeah, honey, I like it. As a matter of fact, your bossiness turns me on."

Her gaze focused on his broad, muscular chest. She sucked in a deep breath. "I brought you here so we could go skinny-dipping."

"Is that so?"

"I want you to take off all your clothes, and then I want you to undress me." She looked at him, unsmiling, a dead-serious gleam in her eyes. "Turnabout is fair play."

"Whatever you want, Boss Lady." He unbuttoned his blue cotton shirt and threw it on top of Cleo's blouse.

As he slowly took off his clothes, he watched her, and loved the reactions she couldn't hide. As soon as he stripped off his shirt, she clenched and unclenched her hands. He knew she wanted to touch him, to run her fingers over his chest.

He removed the leather hip holster and laid his Beretta on the ground. Cleo's gaze followed his every action.

He unbuckled his belt and unsnapped his jeans. Cleo swallowed hard. He lowered the zipper. Cleo's mouth opened to a soft oval. He sat down on the ground and removed his boots and socks, then rose to his feet. Cleo took a nervous step toward him. He dragged his jeans down his hips and over his long legs, then kicked them aside. Cleo sighed deeply. Turning around so that his back was to her, he bent over and eased off his briefs. Taking his time, he turned back around and faced her in all his gloriously naked splendor. Cleo licked her lips.

A fine film of moisture coated her upper lip and forehead. Roarke knew her perspiration had little to do with the warm sunshine and a great deal to do with sexual heat. Cleo's body was a low-burning fire, easily stoked to a full blaze by her desire for him.

He loved knowing how much she wanted him.

Roarke stood before her, unmoving, like some bronze statue, his body honed to perfection. He was tempting her, she realized, waiting for her to succumb, to give in to her own wanton longings. But this was her game, and they were damn well going to play by her rules.

If anyone begged for mercy, it was going to be Simon Alloway Roarke. She intended to make him as hot as she was. She wanted to see his big, hard body drenched with perspiration. And Cleo knew exactly what to do to make him sweat.

"Come here, Simon," she commanded, like a queen giving orders to a servant.

He strutted toward her, shoulders and back straight, head held high, his long legs moving with the same muscular grace with which the Arabians trotted. Proud. Strong. Magnificent.

Control, Cleo cautioned herself. Control. She could so easily lose herself in Roarke's overwhelming masculinity. Everything female within her was drawn to that powerful male aura. When they were alone together, nothing existed except the two of them. No marriage of convenience. No plotting, conniving relatives. No family and business responsibilities. No regrets about the past. No plans for the future. Only the here and now. Only this wild, free passion that drove them to madness—and beyond.

When he was within a few inches of bringing their bodies close enough to touch, he stopped and looked down at her. "Is this where you want me?"

"Yes." She looked up at him. "Now, take off my clothes."

His gaze met hers. Radiant blue and warm amber-flecked green clashed in a battle of wills. They spoke without words, each understanding the other perfectly. Physically, he was much larger and a great deal stronger, but she possessed strengths that neither he nor any man possessed. She was woman. Keeper of men's souls. Guardian of untold treasures. Loving angel and vengeful she-devil. Earth mother and fiery temptress.

He clenched and unclenched his shaky hands, then reached out and loosened her leather belt. She shivered. He unsnapped and unzipped her jeans, then slipped his hands beneath the waistband, cupping the upper sides of her hips. He glanced up at her yellow bra. Her chest rose and fell with labored breaths. He eased her jeans downward, letting them ride low on her hips. Spreading his hands across her stomach, he rotated them in a caressing circle. When she sighed with pleasure, he knelt before her.

"You'd better brace yourself, Boss Lady." Lifting her hands, he placed them on his bare shoulders.

He picked up her right foot, tugged on her boot and jerked it and her sock off, and pulled her jean-clad leg free, then repeated the process with her other foot. Cleo gripped his shoulders, loving the hot, hard strength of his body.

Leaning low, he kissed first one and then her other knee. She swayed. He kissed a damp, moist trail up her right thigh, over her yellow satin bikini panties, across her naked belly and upward to the vee of her bra. Reaching around her, he unhooked the scrap of yellow satin and slid the straps down her shoulders. Her high, firm breasts fell free, exposed to the sun's heat, the breeze's warm breath and Roarke's piercing stare. He threw the bra on the ground, then cupped her breasts.

Cleo's body tightened, then released. A purely feminine tingling radiated upward from her central core.

Using the pads of his thumbs, he played with her nipples until they peaked in hard, throbbing points and begged for his mouth. He answered their plea, tormenting one nipple with his tongue while his fingertips toyed with the other.

Cleo moaned, the painful pleasure was so intense. "Simon!"

Halting the sensual torture, he lifted his head and looked at her. "I'm sorry, Boss Lady. I got a little sidetracked by your beautiful breasts. Don't worry, I'm going to finish what I started." He slid his hands inside the back of her panties, kneading her buttocks.

He was killing her by slow degrees, but she knew, despite his iron-will performance, that he was getting closer and closer to losing control. He could not hide his aroused state. His manhood stood at attention, hard and pulsating, passionate moisture trickling from the tip.

He took his own sweet time removing her panties, his hands caressing their way downward, his fingertips giving off electrical energy that sent shock waves through her body.

When her panties fell down to her ankles, she kicked them aside and reached out for Roarke. When she touched him intimately, he growled like a beast in pain.

She smiled as she encompassed him, stroking him with her closed hand. He jerked. Running her thumb across the tip, she spread the juice around his shaft.

"Dammit, woman!" Roarke hauled her up against him, but when he tried to lift her, she pulled away, then quickly dropped to her knees. He gazed down at her, his vision slightly blurred from the raging desire boiling inside him. "Don't tease me, honey. Not about this."

And that was the last coherent thing Simon Roarke was able to say for quite some time. Cleo played with him, tormenting him with her tongue, promising but not fulfilling, until Roarke's big body trembled. He was a mighty oak ready to fall. All it would take was one tiny push. One sweet, sweet tiny little push.

He grabbed the back of her head, urging her to give what she had promised. Threading his fingers through her hair, he pressed her face toward his body.

She made love to him with her mouth, tenderly, thoroughly, learning from his grunts and sighs what he preferred and what he didn't want. She brought him to the very edge, then hesitated, her own body quivering with need. Then she pushed him over the edge, headlong into earth-shattering release.

When some measure of sanity returned to him, he lifted her off her feet and up into his arms. His mouth took hers in a frenzy, feeding off her passion. He tasted himself on her lips, on her tongue, and his body reawakened. How was it possible? he wondered. He was damn near forty years old. Maybe he should remind a certain part of his anatomy that men his age couldn't make such a quick recovery.

Roarke carried her to the edge of the creek and set her on the grassy bank, letting her feet and calves hang over into the water. He walked into the creek, then lifted her to straddle his hips and eased the two of them into the water. She cried out when he entered her, surprised that he was ready again so soon. He guided her movements, back and forth, splashing the water around them. With her legs wrapped around his hips and her arms draped loosely around his neck, Cleo allowed Roarke complete control. The sensations mounted inside her quickly. He plunged deeper and harder, pounding into her until she screamed her pleasure.

The aftershocks of her fulfillment pelted him. He drove into her repeatedly, with quick, hard lunges, then jetted his release into her receptive body.

They clung together, their bodies shaky, their breathing harsh. Roarke supported her weight with his strength, and she was glad because her bones had melted and offered no support.

Gradually their weakness diminished and Roarke carried her out of the creek and up onto the grass. The horses grazed contentedly nearby. Roarke looked around for a secluded spot and spied two weeping willows, their long, feathery branches overlapping where they touched the ground. He carried Cleo inside the verdant cocoon, placed her on the warm, soft grass and lay down beside her. She reached over and clasped his hand.

They lay there, side by side, for several minutes. Neither of them speaking. Each listening to the other one's breathing. They dozed off and slept until the sun was high in the sky.

Rousing from her nap, Cleo gently awakened Roarke. "Let's don't go back to the house," she said. "Let's stay out here all day. If anyone needs to find us, Willie knows where we are."

"I can't think of anything I'd rather do than lie here under this willow with you all day. Both of us naked." He stroked the underside of her wrist with his thumb. "But we can't hide out here forever. Sooner or later, we'll have to go back and face what's waiting for us."

"What's waiting for us is my family, who have suddenly started acting like a Stepford family. Like sweet, docile robots." Cleo shook her head. "And I dread the thought of Aunt Beatrice finding out that Uncle Perry is the sheriff's number-one suspect."

"She still loves him, doesn't she?" Roarke ran his fingers through his hair.

"Yes, I'm afraid she does."

"But you're not still in love with Paine Emerson and you were never in love with Hugh Winfield. Is that right?"

Cleo braced her elbow on the ground, placing her body in a half sitting, half lying position. She gazed directly into Roarke's questioning eyes. "That's right. Despite the strong family resemblance, I am not a carbon copy of my aunt Beatrice. I'm not the type to spend my whole life pining away for a man I could never have. Besides, I wouldn't have Paine Emerson now if he threw himself at my feet and begged me to forgive him.''

Roarke positioned himself on one elbow and turned toward Cleo, his body mimicking the way hers rested on the bed of grass beneath them. ''What about Hugh Winfield?''

''What about Hugh?''

''Any regrets where he's concerned?''

''Only that I ever dated him in the first place,'' she said. ''We've been friends since we were kids, but I never seriously considered going out with him. Not until Uncle George suggested it.''

''Uncle George wanted you to marry Hugh.'' Roarke broke off a blade of grass and put it in his mouth.

''Uncle George wanted to make sure I didn't make the same mistake his daughter made. He was damned and determined to see me married and a mother. He truly believed I'd never be happy otherwise.''

''He must have hated Perry Sutton for hurting Beatrice the way he did. What I can't understand is why your uncle George allowed Oralie and her family to live with him.'' Roarke removed the blade of grass from his mouth and ran the tip up and down between Cleo's breasts.

Her nipples hardened instantly. ''I'm sure Uncle George did hate Uncle Perry for years, but after time passed and he saw that Perry paid dearly for his mistake every day of his life, then Uncle George's attitude mellowed. He never forgave Uncle Perry, but I think, in the end, he pitied him.

''To understand the situation fully, you have to know that my father and Aunt Oralie had lived with Uncle George since their early teens, after their parents died. Uncle George was really a father to his brother's children as well as to his own daughter. Would you believe that at one time Aunt Beatrice and Aunt Oralie were like sisters? Uncle George allowed Oralie to continue living with him because Aunt Beatrice asked him not to kick her out. Uncle Perry had very little money at the time and Aunt Oralie has always had very expensive tastes.''

"Beatrice is a remarkable woman," Roarke said. "Not many in her position would have been so generous."

"That's the kind of person she is. Loving and forgiving to a fault."

"Let's keep our suspicions and Sheriff Bacon's from Beatrice as long as we possibly can." Roarke ran the blade of grass across Cleo's tight nipples.

She gasped as the tingling sensation in her nipples raced downward. "I agree, but sooner or later, she's bound to find out. Especially if Uncle Perry really is guilty."

"You know, Cleo, despite all the circumstantial evidence against him, my gut instincts tell me that Perry Sutton didn't place those spiders in your towels and he didn't poison your tea." Roarke repeatedly raked the grass blade across Cleo's nipples.

She grabbed his hand. He looked at her and grinned, then pulled free and threw away the blade of grass.

"Why would an intelligent man, who is an entomology expert, with free access to the science lab where the spiders were kept, be foolish enough to take such a risk?" Roarke reached out and lifted an unruly strand of hair off Cleo's cheek. "And why on earth would a man use an outdated rodenticide, which he kept in his own greenhouse, to poison your tea?"

"It's almost as if someone were trying to set him up. But who? Why would Trey or Daphne set up their own father? And Lord knows, Aunt Oralie wouldn't. She couldn't survive without Uncle Perry's constant attention."

"If you're right, that leaves only Hugh Winfield. And he'd have nothing to gain unless he can persuade Daphne to marry him. Of course, I'm not as generous in my estimation of Daphne as you are. I believe she'd use anyone to get what she wanted. It's possible that she's capable of setting up her own father. Could be that she and Winfield are working together."

"Anything's possible, isn't it?" Cleo lay flat on her back, looking up through a fluttering, feathery green curtain at the bright blue sky overhead. "We're really no closer to the truth than we were two weeks ago."

"Have I failed you, Cleo?" he asked. "Did you expect—"

She covered his lips with two fingers, silencing him. "Mc-

Namara Industries is secure and well policed by Mr. Kane and his security force. That was your doing.'' She traced the line of his jaw with her fingertip. ''I'm alive and well and happier than I've ever been in my life. And that, too, is your doing.''

''Ah, honey, you shouldn't say things like that to a naked man.''

''Then you'd better put on your clothes,'' she told him.

''Later.'' He reached for her, grasping her by the shoulders and drawing her into his embrace. ''I have something in mind that requires both of us to be naked.''

''Oh, is that right?'' She rubbed her breasts against his chest and smiled when he moaned. ''Just what do you have in mind?''

''It involves a little payback for my loving wife,'' he said, slipping his hand between her legs.

''Payback? Tit for tat?''

He massaged the tiny kernel hidden in the apex between her thighs. Cleo lifted her hips up off the ground. ''You've got the idea, honey,'' he said.

''You're going to give me what I gave you.'' Her body dampened against his fingers, surrounding them with moisture.

''Lick for lick.'' Roarke inserted his finger inside her welcoming warmth.

Cleo blew out a deep breath. ''No one has ever...I mean...well, it'll be a new experience.''

''What you did for me was a new experience, too, wasn't it?''

''Yes,'' she admitted.

''And afterward, we'll rest for a while, then later, I want us to go for a ride in your Sherwood Forest.'' Lowering his head, he kissed her belly. ''And you're going to experience another first once we enter Sherwood.''

''Another—'' she gasped when he kissed her triangle of fiery curls. ''Another first? When we ride into the woods?''

''When we ride into Sherwood Forest,'' he corrected her. ''Today you're going to be Maid Marian.''

''Oh, I am, am I?''

He spread her legs and lifted her hips. ''Yes, my Cleo Belle, you are.''

She swallowed hard. "I suppose that means you want to be Robin Hood."

"Yeah, I suppose so," he said.

He flicked her intimately with his tongue. She moaned, the sound reverberating in her throat.

"All right, just this once—" she gasped as his mouth moved over her "—I'll be Maid Marian and you'll be Robin Hood."

"Whatever you say, Boss Lady."

Roarke took her where she'd never been, into an erotic paradise of pleasure. His mouth worshipped her femininity, savoring the smell and taste of her body, reveling in the feel of her undulating against his tongue, loving the sound of her hot, ecstatic cries.

And when she fell apart, shattering into a million shards of pleasure, he lifted her on top of him and told her to ride him hard and fast, to pretend he was a wild stallion she had to tame.

And tame him she did.

Chapter 12

Roarke read the report Morgan Kane had given him, then glanced up over the edge of the manila folder, looking his fellow Dundee agent square in the eye.

"All this does is make me wonder if we're dealing with more than one person." Roarke flung the file on the desk. "And whether or not the attempts on Cleo's life and the problems at McNamara Industries have a common perpetrator or if we have two family members working independently of each other."

"My guess is that we're dealing with at least two individuals," Kane said. "And they have separate agendas. Whoever was behind the problems at the plant wanted to force Ms. McNa—that is, Mrs. Roarke..." Kane hesitated, but continued when Roarke smiled. "To sell her uncle's company. But I'd say the person threatening your wife wants to see her dead."

"Yeah, I'm afraid you're right." It had been a long time since an assignment had frustrated Roarke to such an extent. Hell, who was he kidding? Despite the failures and near failures he'd experienced, despite all the stress and frustration of his worst assignments, nothing compared with this one. But then, he'd never allowed himself to become so personally involved before.

It wasn't as if Cleo was nothing more than a client. Dammit, she was his wife, albeit only temporarily, but still she *was* his wife. She slept in his arms every night. He worked at her side every day. And in stolen moments out of time, like yesterday's swim in the Great Mississippi, the hours spent shaded beneath the willow trees and an unforgettable trip into Sherwood Forest, he could almost convince himself that he and Cleo belonged together. But he knew better. He couldn't allow great sex with an incredible lady to cloud his vision of reality or give him any delusions that life actually offered people happily ever afters.

"Unfortunately all the evidence I've collected and the sheriff's department has collected is nothing more than circumstantial," Kane said. "The rifle that fired the shot that barely missed Mrs. Roarke belonged to her great-uncle and everyone in the house had access to the gun case. Since the person didn't hit the target, we don't know whether they were a poor shot or just didn't intend to kill in the first place."

Pushing the oversize leather swivel chair back away from the Jacobean desk in the study, Roarke motioned toward a chair across from him. "Sit down."

Kane slumped into the chair, his big, hard body filling it completely. "The brown recluse incident and the tea poisoning both point the finger at Perry Sutton, but there's nothing to link him to any of the problems at the plant. According to the guards and the secretaries at McNamara Industries, Mr. Sutton seldom even visits the place."

"My gut instincts tell me that Sutton isn't our man." Roarke tapped his index finger on the manila folder he'd tossed on top of the desk. "What I hate most about this situation is that there's not much we can do about unearthing this would-be killer until he or she strikes again. And I'll be honest with you, Kane. I hate like hell that Cleo is the only bait we can use to catch this person."

"I wouldn't want to be in your shoes." Leaning slightly forward, Kane rested his arms on his thighs and allowed his hands to dangle between his legs. "Protecting a woman you're married to can't be easy. I mean, even if there's no love be tween y'all and the marriage is a business arrangement, the two of you having a relationship has to make it difficult for you to view things objectively.''

Roarke wanted to vehemently deny Kane's observation, but there was no way he could. The man was right. "I'm trying to handle things, not to let what's between Cleo and me get in the way of my judgment or interfere with doing my best to keep her safe."

"Maybe we can't catch the person trying to kill Mrs. Roarke until another attempt is made on her life, but we can do something about catching whoever wreaked havoc at Mc-Namara Industries.''

Roarke glanced down at the folder. "Trey Sutton was a prime suspect, until I read your report. Now I have to place Hugh Winfield and perhaps Daphne Sutton at the top of my list.''

"I know Ms. Sutton and Winfield are dating, but why suddenly, after her uncle's death, did she start stopping by the plant on the nights Winfield worked late, when she'd never done that before? Was she encouraging Winfield to tamper with McNamara's computer system? Were they planning the accidents that plagued the plant for weeks?''

"It's possible," Roarke admitted. "Very possible. But the fact that Marla Sutton started having lunch at the plant with her husband, in his office, a couple of times a week, is suspicious. According to Trey's secretary, his wife seldom if ever had lunch with him at the plant before George McNamara's death. And Trey wasn't known for eating in his office.''

"That means that during her lunch visits, Marla Sutton could have been using her computer knowledge to do some major damage. Since she was once a secretary at McNamara's, she'd be familiar with their computer system.''

"What do you suggest we do, short of eliminating all the security systems you've put into place, to catch our culprit?'' Roarke asked.

"I suggest we set a trap for our big rat," Kane said.

"Using what as bait?'' Leaning back in the enormous leather chair, Roarke narrowed his eyes and grinned. "Ellen Denby?''

"The fact that Ellen is a woman has worked to our advantage before when we've brought her in on a case. Men tend to make the mistake of believing that because she's an attractive female, she's not as smart or tough or capable as her fellow agents.''

Laughing robustly, Roarke shook his head. "That's why you brought her in and pretended to hire her as part of McNamara's new security team. You wanted her in place, just in case we needed her."

"She can play the dumb blonde around Trey Sutton and Hugh Winfield. And when we think the time is right, we'll put her on night duty. Alone. She'll tell each one of our boys in advance."

"Hell, who knows, it just might work," Roarke said.

"It's worked before. Ellen can be mighty convincing when she wants to be."

"Yeah, but woe be it to any who gets fooled by her. Behind that pretty face and gorgeous figure, our little Ellen is a pit bull.''

A knock at the closed door interrupted Roarke and Kane's private meeting. Both of them tensed instantly.

"Yes?" Roarke asked.

The pocket doors slid open. Daphne Sutton, dressed in a micromini, skintight, backless, red sundress, sauntered into the room. "I hate to disturb y'all, but Phil Bacon just called and said for Kane to call him right back. He's home from church, but he'll be leaving to go to his mother-in-law's for a late Sunday dinner in about thirty minutes."

"The sheriff wants to talk to Kane?" Roarke asked. "The phone in here didn't ring."

"I was walking by Kane's room and heard his phone ringing. Did you know you'd left your cellular phone lying on your bed?" Daphne asked. "The door was unlocked, so I went in and answered the phone for you."

"I'll go give Bacon a call," Kane said.

Daphne sashayed across the study, her slender hips shifting seductively. "When I asked Phil why he'd bother a body on a beautiful Sunday afternoon, he said he was just returning Kane's earlier telephone call. Something about his using the sheriff's department's firing range." Daphne sat down on the

edge of the Jacobean desk and looked back and forth from
Roarke to Kane.

"Yeah, I asked the sheriff if he'd set up a convenient sched-
ule for me to get in a little practice." Kane rose from the
chair, excused himself and exited the room, leaving the doors
open behind him.

"I take it that our Mr. Kane is a crack shot and doesn't
want his skills to get rusty while he's on an assignment."
Daphne draped her body across the top of the desk, lifting
herself in a semiupright position. "Are you a sharp shooter,
too, Roarke?" She slithered across the desk until she reached
him, then dangled her long, bare legs off the side.

"I'm not as good as Kane," Roarke said. "But I usually
hit whatever I aim at."

"I can't picture a man like you married to my little cousin
Cleo." Daphne lifted one leg and stretched it out toward
Roarke. The toe of her red sandal hit the edge of his chair.
She tapped her foot repeatedly against the chair.

"What sort of man do you think I am? And why can't you
picture me married to Cleo?"

"I'd say you're an adventurer, a man who's lived his life
on the edge. And my bet is you like your sex hot and wild
and as untamed as the life you've lived." Slipping her hips
off the desk, Daphne grasped the side with her hands to balance her body, then slid her foot between Roarke's thighs,
pressing him intimately when her foot hit its mark. "Cleo is
a tame little tabby, who's never done anything exciting in her
entire life. Business is the only thing that matters to her."

Roarke knocked Daphne's foot away so quickly that she
almost lost her balance. While she struggled to climb back on
top of the desk, he stood up and glared at her.

"That just goes to show how little you know your cousin,"
Roarke said. "My wife happens to be the most exciting
woman I've ever known."

"Is she paying you to say things like that, too?" Daphne
glowered at Roarke, her breathing harsh and her cheeks
slightly flushed. "We all know that she went off to Atlanta
on a shopping trip and bought herself a husband."

"Think what you want to," he told her. "The bottom line

is that I'm Cleo's husband and I intend to take good care of her and protect her from any and all harm.''

"Are you going to get her pregnant, too?" Daphne asked. "If she isn't pregnant within a year, she'll lose control of McNamara Industries, you know."

Roarke grinned. "Let's just say that we're doing everything we can at every available opportunity to make that happen."

Daphne's exotically beautiful face hardened. Her green eyes sizzled with a barely contained anger. Slithering off the desk, she walked over to Roarke.

"Cleo must be paying you plenty to screw her." Daphne eased her arms around Roarke's neck and rubbed herself against him. "You must be getting pretty bored with all that cool, controlled sweetness."

Just as Roarke reached out to remove himself from Daphne's clutches, she pressed her lips against his and tried to force his lips apart with her tongue.

"Oh, excuse me," Cleo said as she walked into the room. Roarke grabbed Daphne's arms and threw her away from him with such force that she almost fell. She caught the arm of the swivel chair and laughed, then turned around to face Cleo.

"We thought we were alone," Daphne said. "I'm afraid I don't know what to say. How to explain."

"Cleo, this wasn't what it looked like," Roarke told his wife.

"Oh, I think it was exactly what it looked like." Cleo walked across the study and rounded the desk. Opening a bottom side drawer, she withdrew a laptop computer. "I forgot and left this down here. I need to do a little work this evening." She took several steps toward the door.

"Cleo?" Roarke called out to her.

"Yes, dear?"

"Don't you want an explanation of what you saw?"

Hugging herself around the waist, Daphne nibbled on her bottom lip. "I'm really sorry, Cleo."

Cleo's loud laughter filled the room. She turned slowly and glared at her cousin. "Simon isn't Paine Emerson or Hugh Winfield. He's twice the man either of them ever was. And he's *my* man!"

"Well, your man is a wonderful kisser," Daphne said.

"How would you know?" Cleo smiled devilishly. "He didn't kiss you. You kissed him. Or you were trying to. And Simon was trying to push you away when you attacked him."

"You're deluding yourself if you think he didn't want me."

"No, Daffie, you're deluding yourself if you think he did."

Roarke stood there speechless as his wife turned around and walked out of the study. Daphne huffed loudly. Roarke chuckled. Well, he'd be damned. Cleo trusted him. She trusted him completely.

When he rushed past Daphne, she called out, "Where do you think you're going?"

"I'm going to find my wife so I can kiss her," he said.

He left Daphne in the study and raced up the stairs, catching up with Cleo in the upstairs hallway. Without saying a word, he scooped her up in his arms and carried her into their suite. He tossed her down on the bed, then came down on top of her, kissing her breathless.

They tore at each other's clothes, and when they had removed enough essential garments, Roarke took her hard and fast and wild. They reached their climaxes simultaneously, their bodies joined in ecstasy, their hearts beating in unison and their souls touching for one spellbinding moment.

They both treasured what they shared, but knew, despite the trust they had in each other, the magic couldn't last.

Cleo had difficulty concentrating. She couldn't seem to keep focused on the row of figures before her. Her mind kept wandering off in a decidedly different direction. The past weekend with Roarke had been so incredibly wonderful that she questioned if it had really happened. But it had. All she had needed to do to confirm the reality of their uncontrollable passion for each other was to glance across the room at Roarke. Every time he'd looked at her during the past few days, she'd seen the desire in his eyes and had known he wanted her. And just that one look had set her pulse to racing. Dear Lord, would it always be that way? Would she never get enough of loving and being loved by Simon Roarke?

With Roarke in the same room with her, she hadn't been

able to think straight. She kept thinking about Saturday, when they'd gone riding and spent the day making love outside, in the creek, under the willows, in the woods. And Sunday, when she'd caught Daphne trying to seduce Roarke. How good it felt to know that she could trust her husband. After Roarke had carried her into their suite, they hadn't come out again until that morning, when they'd left for work.

Roarke had been such a distraction she'd finally asked him to leave, to send Kane or a member of his security force to guard her for a few hours. Roarke had put a man named Tom Brown outside her office, kissed her goodbye and told her he'd be back around noon with their lunch.

How could she be this deliriously happy when her life was in constant danger? Because she had fallen in love with her husband, that's how. She'd been attracted to him since the first moment she saw him in his Atlanta office, and with each passing day that attraction had grown. The more she got to know Simon Roarke, the better she liked him. He was everything a man should be. Intelligent. Strong. Courageous. Understanding. Loving. Gentle. And an incomparable lover. But her perfect husband had one slight flaw. He wasn't a man for long-term commitments. He hadn't signed on for the long haul.

She hadn't planned on falling in love with him. He'd been a means to an end. Their marriage a business arrangement. But somewhere between the judge pronouncing them man and wife and Roarke kissing her for the first time and this weekend, when their passion had known no bounds, she'd fallen head over heels in love with Simon.

How would she ever be able to let him go? Without him, her life would be meaningless. But when the time came she'd have no choice—if he chose to leave her. Maybe he was beginning to care for her. Maybe he wouldn't want to end their marriage. Whatever his reasons for stipulating that he wouldn't stick around to see her through the pregnancy might no longer be valid. Not if he loved her the way she loved him.

But Simon had never mentioned love, not even during their most intimate moments, when they were as close as two people could possibly be. She had no doubts that he would die for her, that he'd lay his life on the line to protect her, but what she didn't know was whether his actions would be prompted by duty or love.

Did she dare bring up the subject of their marriage? Question him about his true feelings? What if he didn't love her? What if he intended to follow through with the stipulations of their marriage contract and get a divorce?

A knock on the outer office door brought Cleo out of her thoughts. She glanced up just as Audrey opened the door.

"Mr. Winfield is here to see you, Mrs. Roarke."

Tom Brown stood in front of Hugh, obviously waiting for Cleo's answer before either stepping aside to allow Hugh entrance or escorting the man outside.

"Tell Hugh to come on in." Cleo checked her watch. Twelve-twenty. Roarke would return with their lunch shortly.

"Thanks for seeing me, Cleo." Hugh pranced into the office like some spirited young colt, blithely slamming the door in Tom Brown's scowling face. "We haven't had a chance for a private conversation since you married."

"Is that what this is—a private conversation?" Cleo asked. "I assumed you needed to speak to me about a business matter."

"I thought we were friends." He perched his skinny butt on the edge of her desk. "Can't friends have a private conversation?"

"Yes, of course." Cleo scooted her swivel chair up to her desk and looked at Hugh.

"We are still friends, aren't we?" he asked. "I mean you're not still upset about what happened between Daphne and me, are you?"

"No, Hugh, I'm not still upset. As a matter of fact, I was never that upset. I was disappointed more than anything else. Disappointed in your judgment. We've known each other since we were kids and I always thought you were a reasonably intelligent guy."

"You are still upset." He slid around the desk, grabbed her chair and turned her where she was directly facing him. "Cleo, sugar, Daphne is an exciting woman and very...well, shall we say, talented. But sleeping with her while I was dating you was a big mistake. And I'm sorry it happened."

"What's the purpose for rehashing old news? You've al-

ready apologized and begged my forgiveness." Cleo wondered just what Hugh wanted. He hadn't stopped by to renew
their old friendship. He was after something else.

Leaning forward, Hugh reached out and grasped Cleo's chin
in his hand. "It's not as if Daphne and I are in love or anything
like that. I mean, if you'd accepted my offer when I found out
you needed a husband, we could have worked something out.
You didn't have to pay a stranger to marry you."

Cleo sucked in her cheeks, then relaxed them and ran her
tongue over her teeth in an effort not to laugh in Hugh's face.
The dirty dog. The scheming, lying cheat. He actually thought
she would have preferred marrying him to marrying Simon
Roarke. Obviously Hugh's ego was inflated. Didn't he know
that he wasn't even close to being in Simon's league?

"What would you have done if I'd accepted your offer?"
She tried desperately not to smile.

"Why, I'd have married you, of course. Obviously your
uncle George wanted us to marry. What other reasons could
he have had to put such ridiculous stipulations in his will?"

"But if I'd married you to fulfill the stipulations in the will,
what would you have done about Daphne?"

"Well, I don't know. Daffie and I are pretty heavily involved sexually. But since my marriage to you wouldn't have
been a love match—"

"Are you saying that you could have married me, gotten
me pregnant to fulfill the stipulations of the will and continued
your relationship with my cousin at the same time?"

"Well, when you put it that way, it does sound rather crude,
doesn't it?"

"Hugh, let's cut to the chase. I'm not pining away for you.
I never loved you. I never wanted to marry you. And the only
reason I dated you was because it pleased Uncle George."

Her declaration wiped the smile off Hugh's face. "Well, I
see. I see. But still, wouldn't it have been better to have married me than to have paid some stranger to marry you and get
you pregnant? After all, what do you know about this Roarke
character? Do you have any idea who his people are?"

Cleo grinned. Laughter bubbled up inside her. "For your
information, Simon Roarke is the most wonderful man I've
ever known and my marriage is a real one, despite what you

and my dear family want to believe." Unable to contain it any longer, Cleo burst into laughter. "Why did you request this little private visit? What is it that you want, Hugh?"

"I certainly didn't request a visit so that you could laugh in my face."

"I'm sorry, it's just that you're so transparent." Cleo laid her hand on his shoulder. "You forget that I've known you a long time."

"Meaning?" Tilting his chin haughtily, he stuck his nose in the air and turned from her.

"You found Daphne irresistible, but you've finally figured out that she might have been using you to hurt me. After Uncle George died, you found out about his will, and hoped you could have me, my money and Daphne, too."

"How can you accuse me of being so mercenary?" He displayed a properly wounded expression.

"But recently, you've begun to wonder if maybe you made a mistake, that perhaps I'm going to win this battle and retain control of McNamara Industries." Cleo shot up out of her chair, placed her hands on her hips and looked Hugh square in the eye. "Is that why you've offered yourself to me again? Did you think I still wanted you?"

"You've made it perfectly clear that you don't want me, that you never did," Hugh said. "There's no need to rub it in."

She put her arm around Hugh's shoulder. "Thanks for the offer, old friend, but I already have exactly what I want. I'm married to Simon Roarke, and if I'm very lucky, I'll have his baby."

"God, Cleo, you're in love with him, aren't you?"

"What's wrong with that?" she asked coyly. "After all, he is my husband."

"Yeah, well, I hope he doesn't break your heart the way I thought I had." Hugh slipped his arm around her waist. "You know, you'd probably have been better off if you had married me. At least when our marriage broke up, neither one of us would have gotten hurt."

She knew that in his own misguided way Hugh might actually have meant what he said, and it was obvious that his statement had made perfect sense to him.

She kissed him on the cheek. "You can always marry Daphne. After all, she's a wealthy woman. Just not quite as wealthy as she would be if we had to sell McNamara Industries."

"You'd be better off if you did sell." He sighed, then hugged her to him. "But I know you won't ever do that willingly."

Just as Hugh kissed Cleo, a hasty, goodbye kiss, Roarke walked in. She glanced over Hugh's shoulder at her husband, who stood in the doorway glaring at her.

The sight of Cleo in Hugh Winfield's arms hit Roarke like a blow from a sledgehammer. He wanted to march across the office, rip Cleo from Winfield's arms and beat the hell out of the guy. How dared he touch Cleo! She belonged to him. She was his wife.

Some primeval instinct rose inside him, heating his jealousy to the boiling point. If Cleo knew what he was thinking, she'd skin him alive. He wanted to place a brand on her. One that read, Roarke's Wife.

Every muscle in his body tensed. He took several deep, calming breaths. Winfield was kissing Cleo, not the other way around. This was pretty much the same scene Cleo had walked in on in the study yesterday between Daphne and him.

Taking one more deep breath, Roarke lifted the two paper bags he held in his hands. "I brought lunch, honey. Are you finished with Hugh?"

Smiling at Roarke, Cleo stepped out of Hugh's embrace. "Yes, I'm finished with Hugh." Dismissing her former boyfriend without another word or glance, she motioned for her husband to come to her. "I'm starving. I hope you brought dessert, too."

"As a matter of fact—" Roarke ignored Hugh as he walked by him and over to Cleo and set both sacks on her desk "—I drove over to the River Bend Café."

"Lemon icebox pie?" She groaned. "Tell me you brought me a piece of lemon icebox pie, and I'll be yours forever."

"You're mine forever," Roarke said, then took Cleo in his arms and kissed her.

The kiss was long and wet and deep, and when he allowed

Cleo to come up for air, Hugh Winfield was nowhere to be seen and the office door was closed.

Roarke removed the two lunch sacks, placing them in her empty chair, then lifted Cleo off her feet and set her down on the edge of her desk. Kissing her deeply, he pushed her skirt up her thighs until it bunched around her hips, then slid his hands inside her panty hose and bikini briefs and tugged them down and off.

"What do you think you're doing?" Her heartbeat drummed in her ears. Her body throbbed with anticipation.

"I want dessert, too," he told her as his lips moved down her neck and his hands unbuckled his belt and unzipped his slacks. "And I want mine before we eat our corned beef sandwiches."

"Am I your dessert, Mr. Roarke?" She draped her arms around his neck when he spread her legs apart and situated himself between them.

"Yes, Mrs. Roarke, you most definitely are." He cupped her hips and brought her forward, then thrust into her, bouncing her hips off the desk.

They made love with wild abandon, oblivious to the outside world. Later they ate their corned beef sandwiches, and when Cleo started to eat her pie, Roarke took it from her and fed it to her. In the middle of the sensual feeding, Cleo gasped.

"Oh, my God, Simon, we didn't lock the door. Anyone could have walked in on us."

"It wouldn't have happened," he said.

"Why wouldn't it have happened?"

"Because when I came in, I told Tom Brown that no one was to enter this office until I told him otherwise."

"You're a wicked, wicked man, Simon Roarke." Cleo smiled, then opened her mouth, asking for another bite.

"And you're glad that I am, aren't you, my Cleo Belle?" Roarke cut off a piece of the pie with the plastic fork and put it in Cleo's mouth.

The following Friday night, Hugh Winfield dined with the family. During after-dinner drinks in the front parlor, Oralie Sutton announced that Daphne and Hugh were engaged. Hugh made a big production of placing a rather large diamond on Daphne's finger. Cleo congratulated them and wished them well, and considered herself lucky not to have married Hugh.

While Oralie discussed plans for a huge engagement party at the country club, Daphne gloated, smiling cattily at Cleo. But when Roarke nuzzled Cleo's neck and she giggled, the glint of triumph died in Daphne's green eyes.

That night Roarke gave Kane orders to have Ellen Denby ready the following Monday night to spring the trap that would hopefully catch the McNamara Industries saboteur. The odds were even. Fifty-fifty. Especially now that Winfield had officially cast his lot with the Suttons.

Which would the trap ensnare? Roarke wondered. A hot-headed, angry young cousin or a money-hungry, disloyal old friend?

Chapter 13

Cleo tossed back her head and laughed. Despite the overcast sky and the prediction of isolated showers, the day was perfect. Perfect because she was going to spend it with Simon, just the two of them alone together. Riding Sweet Justice and Valentino out to the Great Mississippi and into Sherwood Forest again this Saturday. Pearl had prepared them a picnic lunch that Cleo planned for them to spread out beneath the two willows. But what if it rains? she thought, then smiled secretly to herself. She'd never made love outside in the rain.

"What's that impish smile all about?" Roarke squeezed her hand as they walked down the path leading to the stables. "You worry me, woman, when you get that wicked look on your face."

"Wicked?" Pulling on his hand, she urged him to run with her. "Come on, and I'll show you wicked."

Releasing her hand, he grinned and checked his small backpack. "That's an invitation I can't refuse." Roarke raced with her, reaching the stables first. Not even winded from his run, he leaned against the fence and waited for her to catch up.

Breathing hard, but not out of breath, Cleo slowed her pace as she neared him. "No fair. Your legs are longer." She glanced at him, surveying him from the tip of his boots to his silver belt buckle, then moving her gaze down again to focus on where his jeans formed a triangle. "Much longer."

He grabbed her by the shoulders and pulled her up against him. "You are wicked, Cleo Belle. Wonderfully wicked."

Reaching up on tiptoe, she circled his neck with her arms and gave him a quick kiss. Thunder rumbled off in the distance. She tilted her head to listen. "It might rain."

"It might," he agreed.

"I've never made love outside in the rain," she said.

"You haven't?"

"If it turns out to be only a light summer shower, we could stay under the willows."

Lifting her off her feet, Roarke took her mouth hungrily. She clung to him, responding fervently.

Willie cleared his throat. "Excuse me, Cleo." He led Sweet Justice out of the stables. "Got Sweetie all saddled up and ready for you." He held out the reins to her.

Roarke set Cleo back on her feet. She eased out of his arms and took the reins from Willie. "Thank you." She smiled at Willie, who beamed with pleasure.

"I'll go get Valentino for you, Mr. Roarke."

Roarke threw up his hand in greeting. "Okay. Thanks."

When Willie returned to the stables, Cleo whirled around and faced Roarke. "How would you like to race over to the Great Mississippi? The winner gets to name his or her prize."

"I think this race just might be rigged," Roarke said. "Considering the fact that you'll be riding a young filly and I'll be riding a much older horse."

"What if I give you a head start?"

"How much of a head start?"

"Two minutes."

Willie led Valentino out of the stables. "Here he is, all ready for a good gallop this morning."

"Here are the rules," Roarke told her. "We mount at the same time, then you time yourself two minutes after I start off, and whoever gets to the Great Mississippi first gets to throw the other one in before he gets to name his prize."

Cleo clicked her tongue against the roof of her mouth, rolled her eyes heavenward, then pursed her lips. "Sounds fair enough, I suppose."

"Oh, yes," Roarke said. "There's just one more thing." He removed the backpack and held it out to her. "You have to carry our lunch with you."

Cleo groaned. "That won't be a disadvantage." She took the backpack and strapped it on, then lifted her foot into the stirrup and swung her leg over Sweet Justice's back.

Following Cleo's lead, Roarke mounted his horse. He glanced over at his wife, who smiled at him, then puckered her lips and blew him a kiss. He loved her smile—beautiful, joyous and genuine, like the woman herself.

Sunlight reflected off the decorative silver trim on Cleo's hand-tooled, leather saddle. The minute Cleo eased her bottom into the saddle, Sweet Justice whinnied loudly and reared her front legs into the air.

Roarke's heartbeat accelerated. What the hell had happened? Something had spooked Sweet Justice. But what? He hadn't heard or seen a thing. He sat in the saddle, watching helplessly while the skittish filly bucked Cleo off and onto the ground.

Dear God, it had all happened so quickly that Cleo must not have had a chance even to try to calm the panicked animal.

"Cleo!" Roarke heard the sound of his own voice as if coming from a great distance.

Willie rushed over to Cleo, who lay unmoving on her side. Roarke dismounted hurriedly.

"Don't touch her, Willie," he shouted. "Just get hold of Sweet Justice's reins and keep her away from Cleo." When the stable hand jerked around and looked at him with fear in his eyes, Roarke cursed under his breath. "I know you want to help her, but if she's injured, you would hurt her more if you try to move her."

Nodding his understanding, Willie grabbed the filly, who'd stopped prancing and casually kicked at the earth near Cleo's head. While Willie spoke softly to the horse, Roarke bent down and ran his hands over Cleo's prone body. She didn't move or speak.

He didn't think she'd broken any bones, but there was no

way to be certain without X rays. He stroked her cheek tenderly with the back of his hand.

"Cleo? Honey?" She didn't respond. "Cleo Belle, can you hear me?" She lay deadly still.

Roarke unzipped the backpack Cleo wore and removed his cellular phone. His hands trembled as he dialed 911. He told the operator what had happened. She warned him not to move Cleo and assured him that an ambulance was on its way.

"What—what can I do, Mr. Roarke?" Willie asked.

"Tie Sweet Justice to the fence over there," Roarke said. "Then go up to the house and tell Miss Beatrice what's happened. Tell her to call Sheriff Bacon. And Willie—" Roarke hesitated while his mind tried to absorb the implications "—don't let anyone get near Sweet Justice except the sheriff himself. Do you understand? Something caused Sweetie to throw Cleo off and I want the sheriff to examine the horse, her saddle and her food."

"I got all that." Willie kept nodding repeatedly. "I'll go tell Miss Bea to call the sheriff."

Roarke sat down on the ground beside Cleo, wanting more than anything to lift her into his arms and see her open her eyes and smile at him. God, please, don't let her be seriously injured. Maybe she'd just gotten the breath knocked out of her. No, if that was all it was, she'd be coming around by now and gasping for air.

He looked at her pale face, wishing that her long, dark-auburn lashes would flutter. They didn't. Suddenly, he noticed fresh blood ooze out from underneath Cleo's head.

Closing his eyes against the sight, Roarke clenched his teeth and screamed silently. His hot anger raged, boiling inside him, threatening to explode. How could he have let this happen? Why hadn't he seen it coming? He should have done something to prevent this. Dammit, if anything happened to Cleo…

"Cleo Belle." He caressed her cheek, then checked the pulse beating in her neck. "You're going to be all right. The medics are on their way."

When Beatrice and Pearl reached the stables, Roarke sat beside Cleo, stroking her hand and speaking softly to her.

"God in heaven, she's not moving," Pearl said. "She's not—"

"Hush up, you silly goose," Beatrice scolded the other woman. "Of course she's not."

"I'll take care of Sweetie until the sheriff gets here." Willie untied the filly and led her toward the stables, stopping just before entering. "You'll take care of Cleo, won't you, Mr. Roarke? You're her husband and you love her."

Roarke swallowed hard, downing the pain and anger and regret. "Yeah, Willie. I'll take care of Cleo."

Beatrice rushed over to Cleo, Pearl on her heels. "Willie said Cleo fell off Sweetie. How could that have happened? She's a good horsewoman. She's been riding since she was a girl."

"Something frightened the filly," Roarke said. "Sweetie was fine until— Oh, God!"

"What is it?" Beatrice asked.

"Sit down here beside her." Roarke shot to his feet. "I don't want her to be alone. If she wakes, I want her to see a familiar face."

He helped Beatrice sit down, then called out to Willie. "Hold up there."

"Where are you going?" Beatrice asked.

"Sweet Justice was fine until Cleo sat in the saddle. The minute her back end pressed down, Sweetie reared up as if she'd been shocked." Roarke clamped his big hand down on Willie's shoulder. "Keep her still while I check out something."

"Yes, sir."

Beatrice and Pearl watched while Roarke ran his hand over every inch of the hand-finished, floral-leaf-patterned saddle. He tugged on the silver swell plates and did the same with the full cantle plates and the corner plates. He inspected the skirts, the stirrups, the fenders and the horn. Then he lifted the saddle and turned it upside down, running his hand over the leather belly.

His fingers encountered four small, circular objects about the size of quarters. He flung the saddle on the ground, kicked it and cursed loudly. "Dammit to hell!" He stomped the ground.

"What in heaven's name is wrong with you?" Pearl asked.

"Must be something mighty bad for you to be cussing a blue streak."

"Did you find something on Cleo's saddle?" Beatrice looked up at him, her eyes misty with tears.

"Yeah, I found something, all right. Four small buzzers. The kind you can buy at any party store. A practical joker can put them in his palm and shock somebody when he shakes hands with them."

"Someone put them under Cleo's saddle deliberately," Pearl said. "Someone wanted Sweetie to buck Cleo off and kill her, yes?" The housekeeper's cheeks flared scarlet. Her wide, fleshy jaw clenched. "You've got to find out who's doing these things, Mr. Roarke, and put a stop to this person!"

"I've done a poor job so far." He blamed himself for this. Why hadn't he checked out Cleo's horse and saddle before she'd mounted? He should have realized that everyone in the family knew that he and Cleo were going riding this morning. Any one of them could have attached the buzzers. But he hadn't been thinking about the possibility that someone would tamper with the horses. All he'd been thinking about was spending the day making love to his wife.

He was too damn close, too personally involved, to do his job right. And if Cleo died—dammit, no! He wouldn't let himself think about losing her.

Roarke lifted Beatrice to her feet and resumed his place at Cleo's side. Beatrice and Pearl hovered over them, and Willie stood beside Sweet Justice, guarding Cleo's filly and her dust-covered saddle.

Roarke paced the floor in the waiting room. No amount of reasoning from Beatrice or finger-shaking from Pearl stopped his relentless prowl. What the hell was taking those damn doctors so long? Didn't they have any idea what he was going through, not knowing if Cleo was alive or dead?

When the medics had moved her, Roarke saw blood on the hand-size rock that was three-fourths embedded in the ground. The side of Cleo's head had hit the rock when she'd fallen.

Please, God, don't let there be any internal bleeding. Don't! Don't! Don't! Roarke hadn't prayed in fifteen years. Not since the night he'd been notified that his ex-wife and daughter had been in a serious automobile accident. In those few moments between being given the information and being told that Laurie had died on impact, Roarke had prayed more fervently than he'd ever prayed in his life. He'd said one final prayer at his little girl's funeral, begging God to forgive him for not taking better care of the precious life that had been entrusted to him. After that Roarke had never prayed again. Not until tonight.

He'd never cared enough about anything to seek divine intervention again. His life hadn't been worth a prayer, and praying for Hope was useless. But Cleo was worth a thousand prayers, a thousand promises to God.

Tilting his head, Roarke lifted his eyes heavenward as he stood at the far end of the waiting room, his back to Beatrice and Pearl. *What do you want?* he prayed silently. *Whatever it is, I'll give it. Just let Cleo be all right.*

"Oh, Dr. Iverson," Beatrice cried out.

Roarke spun around just as Pearl and Beatrice rushed toward the doctor, who walked out of the ER examining room.

"How is Cleo?" Beatrice asked. "May we see her?"

"It's certainly taken you long enough," Pearl said. "We've been out here for hours."

"Mr. Roarke," Dr. Iverson said.

The sound of his blood rushing through his body momentarily deafened Roarke. His heartbeat accelerated. Sweat coated his palms. He moved forward, every step an effort.

"Cleo?" Roarke asked.

"Her vital signs are good," Dr. Iverson said. "We've done a series of tests and X rays. There are no broken bones and no internal injuries, but…"

Roarke let out the breath he hadn't even realized he'd been holding. "But what?"

"She suffered a concussion and she's still unconscious. I think that's only temporary. I expect her to come around soon. She'll have a headache and probably be nauseated."

"What if she doesn't regain consciousness?" Beatrice asked.

Dr. Iverson patted Beatrice on the shoulder. "Now, Miss Bea, let's not borrow trouble." He looked at Roarke. "There's something else, though."

"What?" Roarke asked.

"Did you know that Cleo is pregnant?"

Roarke felt as if someone had punched him in the stomach. Shivers raced along his nerve endings. "Pregnant?"

"Oh, isn't this wonderful." Beatrice giggled. "A baby. My little Cleo is going to be a mother."

"Well, not for about eight more months," Dr. Iverson said. "I doubt Cleo realized she was pregnant."

"Did her fall jeopardize the pregnancy?" Cleo is pregnant, Roarke thought. *Already.*

"It doesn't seem to have caused any problems, but we'll keep her monitored," the doctor told Roarke. "You can go in and see her for just a few minutes before we transfer her upstairs to a room."

"Go on, dear," Beatrice said. "You're her husband. Pearl and I will wait here for you, and we can all go upstairs together."

Roarke followed Dr. Iverson into the ER cubicle where Cleo lay, her auburn hair gleaming red against the pristine whiteness of the sheet beneath her. She looked so small and helpless lying there with her eyes closed. Roarke neared the bedside, hesitating as he gazed down at her.

She was going to be all right. No internal injuries. Only a concussion.

He wanted to lift her into his arms and hold her. He wanted to kiss her awake and hear her sweet laughter. But he didn't even take her hand in his. He just stood there staring at her.

Did you know that Cleo is pregnant?

She was pregnant. Pregnant with his child. No! Not *his* child. *Her* child. Hers and hers alone.

"Talk to her," Dr. Iverson said. "It's possible that she'll be able to hear you. It might even help her come around sooner." The doctor put his hand on Roarke's back. "She should be all right. And there's no need to worry about the baby. Your son or daughter is safe."

No, my daughter isn't safe, Roarke wanted to shout. She's dead. She died fifteen years ago, and I wasn't even there to say goodbye.

Swallowing the emotions that threatened his sanity, Roarke took a deep breath. "Cleo. You're going to be just fine. You

took a bad spill off Sweet Justice, but that hard little head of
yours didn't get much more than a scratch.''

A nurse and an attendant entered the cubicle. "We're all
set to take Mrs. Roarke to the fourth floor. Her room's ready,"
the nurse said.

Roarke stepped back out of the way and waited until the
attendant rolled Cleo out of the cubicle and toward the inside
exit leading to the private elevators.

"Give them a few minutes to get her settled in," Dr. Iverson said, "then y'all can go on up."

Roarke heard Beatrice's voice before he entered the waiting
area. "She's going to be just fine. But no thanks to one of
you," Beatrice said sharply. "I wish I knew which one of you
is trying to hurt Cleo. I'd—I'd—" She choked on her tears.
"I'd strangle you with my bare hands."

"Yeah, and I'd help her," Pearl said.

When Roarke walked out into the waiting room, all eyes
turned to him. Dammit, the whole Sutton clan had arrived,
swooping down like a bunch of buzzards waiting for their next
meal.

"What the hell's going on out here?" Taking each Sutton
in turn, Roarke glared menacingly, giving each a deadly dose
of his killer stare.

"How is Cleo?" Perry Sutton asked.

"Do you really care?" Roarke had just about had his fill
of Cleo's bloodsucking relatives.

"How dare you question my husband's concern." Oralie
puffed up like a bullfrog. She titled her head and lifted her
nose with a regal air.

"Aunt Beatrice says that Cleo has a concussion," Daphne
said. "Is she conscious?"

"Not yet," Roarke said. "But Dr. Iverson thinks she'll
come out of this with nothing more than a bad headache."

"That's good to know," Marla said meekly.

"What happened to her?" Trey asked. "When we arrived
home, Ezra said that Cleo had had a riding accident."

"Yeah, she did." Roarke paused, waiting to see if he could
discern any type of suspicious reaction from Trey and the others. "I'll wait and let Sheriff Bacon fill you in on the specifics
of what caused the accident, but I will tell you that something

spooked Sweet Justice and she threw Cleo." Roarke looked meaningfully at Beatrice and then at Pearl, warning each silently not to reveal any specific information to the Suttons.

Oralie gasped and clutched her chest. "Oh, how dreadful. I've warned Cleo and Beatrice about riding those beasts. I despise the smelly creatures."

"There's no point in y'all being here," Roarke said. "I plan to stay with Cleo until she's released from the hospital. Aunt Beatrice, I know that you and Pearl want to see Cleo before you leave."

"We'd all like to see Cleo." Oralie strutted over and stood directly beside Beatrice, slipping her arm around her cousin's shoulder. "I, for one, will feel much better once I see for myself that she's all right."

Beatrice eased herself away from Oralie and glanced over at Perry, then lowered her head and looked down at the floor.

"Nobody's going to go in and see Cleo except Beatrice and Pearl. Then I'll send them home in a cab," Roarke told the Suttons. "The rest of you can leave now."

"We have every right to—" Trey said.

"If Mother wants to see Cleo—" Daphne spoke at the same time.

"Let me make this perfectly clear." Roarke's voice was deceptively calm and steady. A steaming volcano raged inside him, ready to erupt with the least provocation. "Someone has tried, unsuccessfully, four times to kill my wife. And each one of you is on my list of suspects. So there's no way in hell I'm going to allow any of you near Cleo until she's fully recovered. Do I make myself clear?" He spoke the last sentence slowly, enunciating each word.

"Well, I've never been so insulted in my life." Oralie huffed indignantly. "Take me home this instant, Perry. I will pray for Cleo's recovery and ask the Lord to remove Mr. Roarke from our lives. He's been nothing but a heartless bully since the day Cleo brought him home."

Confident that he'd made his point to the Suttons, Roarke dismissed them from his mind. He escorted Beatrice and Pearl out of the emergency room waiting area and into the hall. While they waited for an elevator, Pearl put her arms around Roarke and hugged him.

"I've been waiting a lifetime to hear somebody tell that bunch where they could get off." Pearl grinned from ear to ear. "Poor old Perry's too timid to control his own children, and Lord knows he's never been able to handle Oralie."

"Perry does the best he can," Beatrice said. "He's far too gentle and easygoing for a woman as high-strung as Oralie."

"Yeah, you're right about that." Pearl glanced sadly at Beatrice. "What he always needed was a sweet, kind, loving woman like you."

The elevator doors opened and the three of them stepped inside. No one said a word during the ascent to the fourth floor.

Cleo came in and out of consciousness several times during the afternoon. Once she called Roarke's name and smiled when he lifted her hand to his lips. He sat beside her bed waiting impatiently, his mind tormenting him with images of Cleo as her body gradually ripened with their child. As hard as he tried not to think of the child as his, he couldn't change the fact that he had ignited that tiny spark of life growing inside her.

Was the baby a girl? Would she have big blue eyes like Laurie's? Would she have the same loud, ear-splitting cry when she was a newborn and wanted attention?

Hell, what difference did it make if the baby *was* a girl? What difference did any of it make? He wouldn't be around to see her, to hold her, to rock and sing to her. He'd never see her smile or listen to her laugh or hear her call him "Daddy."

He had to destroy any paternal feelings that he had, and do it immediately. He could not allow himself to take any interest in Cleo's baby. They had made a bargain. And he intended to see that Cleo kept her word and set him free.

She awoke in the late afternoon, coming fully alert by degrees. Roarke held her hand and watched her. She smiled at him.

"Hi, there," he said. "How do you feel?"

"I've got a humdinger of a headache," she told him. "What happened to me?"

"Don't you remember?"

She thought for a minute. "We were going on a picnic, weren't we? We went to the stables and... Something scared Sweetie. She threw me! Roarke, what...who...? Did someone deliberately spook Sweetie?" She lifted her head, then groaned when intense pain exploded inside her brain.

"Don't get upset, Cleo. Lie back and rest." Taking her by the shoulders, he eased her down on the bed. "Dr. Iverson says you have a concussion, but no broken bones or internal injuries. You're going to be fine."

Reaching out, she sought his hand. He grasped her hand, squeezing reassuringly.

"I'll lie still and be good," she said. "If you'll tell me what really happened."

"All right. If you have to know right now, then I'll tell you." He sucked in a deep breath, held her hand tightly and looked directly at her. "Somebody stuck four whoopee buzzers under Sweet Justice's saddle, so that when you mounted her and put your weight on the saddle, the buzzers would give your filly a shock and make her go wild for a few minutes. Long enough, this person hoped, for Sweetie to throw you off. I'm sure the plan was for you to break your neck."

"When is it going to stop? When they've succeeded and I'm dead?" Jerking her hand out of his, she turned from him and buried her face in her pillow.

"I know I let you down." Getting up out of the chair, he stood beside her bed. "You could have been killed out there this morning. I had my mind on making love to you, instead of protecting you."

She turned around slowly, intensely aware of the pain in her head, and looked at Roarke's haggard face, his bleary eyes and slumped shoulders. He was blaming himself for what had happened to her. She couldn't let him do that.

"Simon, this wasn't any more your fault than the spiders in my bath towels or the poison in the tea Aunt Beatrice drank. There was no way you could have predicted any of those things happening and no way you could have prevented them."

"You shouldn't be staying in that house. Hell, you shouldn't even be living in this town!"

"What are you talking about?" she asked.

"The danger is here, in River Bend. The Suttons are dangerous. One of them. Two of them. Or all of them. When you're released from the hospital, I'm taking you away from here until I can guarantee your safety."

"I can't leave River Bend. I can't go away at a time like this, when McNamara Industries is in trouble. People are counting on me. I can't let them down."

"Dammit, woman, don't you understand that I can't promise you that another one of these unpredictable accidents won't happen? The person behind these accidents is covering his tracks well. The police haven't turned up any real evidence against anyone other than your uncle Perry in the poisoning incident. And that evidence was circumstantial." Sitting down beside her, he leaned over and gently grasped her shoulders. "You've got to stop worrying about everyone else and start worrying about yourself."

"You sound as if you want to put me in some sort of glass bubble and not let me have any human contact."

"If I could do that, I would."

She reached up and stroked his face. He pulled away from her caressing hand. "I promise that I'll cooperate with you in every way possible," she said. "No more horseback riding. No more risks of any kind. But I can't leave River Bend. McNamara Industries can't do without me. Not right now."

"Damn McNamara Industries!"

"Roarke, how can you say such a thing when you know how much my company means to me?"

"If you can't leave your damn business behind in order to protect your life, then at least we can move out of the mansion and get you away from your 'loving' family."

"How will we ever catch the person or persons who are trying to kill me if I'm not available to them?" Cleo placed her hands over Roarke's where they gripped her shoulders. "Moving away isn't the answer. This isn't going to end until either they kill me or we catch them."

Releasing his hold on her shoulders, he lifted her hands in his and held them against his chest.

Hell, he knew she was right. But he didn't want to admit

it. What if this unknown assassin tried again and succeeded? What if, despite his best efforts, he couldn't stop them?

"No more horseback riding," he told her. "At home, you'll eat and drink only what everyone else does. I'm going to do a thorough check of our suite every time we leave and return. At McNamara's, you'll run everything from your office and won't go out into the plant."

"I won't like it, but I'll do it," she said. "I don't want to be unreasonable about anything. It's just that I have obligations that I can't turn my back on, despite the risk I'm taking."

"Well, from now on you won't be just putting your life at risk." He released her hands.

She spread her palms out flat against his chest. His heart beat wildly. "What do you mean?"

"You're pregnant, Cleo," he said.

"I'm... Already?" Instinctively she laid her hand over her belly. "Oh, Simon. It's too soon. It shouldn't have happened. Not yet."

"I know. I was hoping our would-be killer would have tipped his hand by now. But whoever it is, is taking his own sweet time. He's not in any hurry because he knows he has a whole year."

Cleo realized that Roarke had misunderstood what she'd meant, although he was right about the fact that not only was she now in danger, but so was her unborn child. And whoever had attempted to kill her would want to see her child dead, too.

But Cleo had meant it was too soon to have to worry about Roarke leaving her. He'd made it clear that he wouldn't stay with her through the duration of her pregnancy. How soon would he leave and turn her case over to someone else? Surely he'd changed his mind. He wouldn't leave her now, not the way things were between them.

"Simon, you won't leave me, will you?"

"What?"

"Just because I'm pregnant, you won't leave me."

"No, Cleo, I won't leave you." Not now. Not yet. Not until I know that you and our...your child are out of danger.

She smiled contentedly. "I knew you'd change your mind.

Everything is going to be all right for you and me and our baby. We're going to be so happy.''

Now wasn't the time to tell her that nothing had changed. That as soon as she was safe and they had her would-be killer behind bars, he was going to leave. There could never be a happily ever after for Simon Roarke.

Chapter 14

Cleo dug her bare toes into the soft love seat cushions and lifted her knees. Hugging the cream knit afghan to her, she draped her arms around her legs. Alone in the solitude of her sitting room. Ah, home sweet home. But since Uncle George's death this house hadn't seemed like home. Not even here in her own suite did she feel perfectly comfortable. Knowing that a member of her own family had tried to harm her—four times—created a morbid air of suspicion and hostility. She didn't want to believe that someone hated her enough to want her dead. But since Aunt Beatrice's close call with death after drinking the poisoned tea and her own riding accident yesterday morning, she could no longer delude herself. Someone wasn't just trying to scare her—someone was trying to kill her!

Simon had wanted her to stay another day in the hospital, but since Dr. Iverson had said she would be as well off at home, she'd insisted on leaving. Simon hadn't liked bringing her home, but he hadn't argued with her about it. In fact, since their heated disagreement about their leaving River Bend and his announcement that she was pregnant, her husband hadn't said much of anything. Every time she'd tried to talk to him about their marriage and their child, he had changed the subject.

Yesterday, she had chalked up his moodiness to his fear for her life and his ridiculous guilt over not foreseeing the accidents that had occurred. She'd tried to tell him that he was a bodyguard, not a mind reader.

Simon had stayed by her side at the hospital all night, sleeping in the chair beside her bed. Whatever she wanted, he was one step ahead of her, waiting on her hand and foot, with gentle patience. He had kissed her good-night and held her hand until she'd drifted off to sleep. And when she had awakened this morning, he'd been sitting there staring at her.

Cleo knew that something was wrong, something that had nothing to do with the threats on her life or with McNamara Industries. Simon was worried. She hadn't known her husband long, but they had become so close, so intimately connected, that she could sense the change in his mood.

She wasn't sure what was wrong, but she suspected the worst. Her greatest fear was that he hadn't been completely honest with her when he'd told her that he wouldn't leave her. She had assumed that he was beginning to feel for her what she felt for him. Maybe he didn't love her—not yet. But she was certain that he cared deeply for her. Did he care enough to stay with her, to be a father to their child and a real husband to her for the rest of their lives?

When she'd tried to broach the subject this morning, he'd cut her off sharply, mumbled something about getting Kane to keep an eye on her while he went out for some fresh air. A couple of minutes later, Morgan Kane told her that he'd be right outside her door if she needed him.

Simon had been gone for hours. Something was definitely wrong. The massive oak grandfather clock in the hall struck twice. Cleo jumped. Her nerves were shot, and her husband's mysterious need to be alone had increased her anxiety.

She glanced at the lunch Pearl had brought up for her around noon. She'd taken a couple of sips of the iced tea, nibbled on the potatoes and taken a bite out of the yeast roll. The remainder of the meal lay untouched on the tray atop the round end table.

She glanced up when she heard the outer door open. Her

heart skipped a beat when she saw Simon enter. Kicking the afghan off onto the floor, she stood up and walked to the open French doors that connected the sitting room to the bedroom.

"Simon?"

He looked at her, his face hard, his eyes cold. She shivered, apprehension spreading through her like wildfire.

"You shouldn't be up," he said. "Go back and sit down and rest."

"Where have you been? You've been gone for so long I'd begun to worry."

"I'm sorry, Cleo, if I worried you. That's the last thing I wanted." He moved across the room, taking slow, cautious steps, as if he had to be careful not to come too close. "I just needed time alone, to think things through."

"What things?" Her heart raced madly. She clutched the sides of her satin robe.

"You're recovering from a pretty bad fall, and you've just found out that you're pregnant. This can wait, Cleo."

"Wait until when?"

"Until you're better." He turned around, removed his jacket and tossed it on the bed.

She stood there in the doorway, looking at his broad back and his wide shoulders. He removed his hip holster and laid his Beretta on the nightstand by his side of the bed.

"I want to know now," she told him. "This mood you're in is all about my being pregnant, isn't it? About the bargain we made and the contract we signed when we got married."

"I said this can wait!"

When she gasped, he turned sharply and saw the stricken look on her face. Dammit, why was she pressing him so hard? Why couldn't she just leave it alone for now? He was going to have to tell her the truth; she was going to force the issue and make him hurt her. He hadn't planned for this—for her wanting them to stay married. In the beginning, he'd been sure she'd be able to handle ending their marriage without any messy emotional displays. Now he wasn't so sure.

"You're going to leave, aren't you?" She looked at him, all the pain and disappointment showing plainly in her misty green eyes.

"Eventually," he admitted. "But not yet. Not until I know

you aren't in any danger. I'm going to stay as long as it takes for us to catch both our problem maker and our would-be killer.''

"I see." She sighed deeply. "You still think they're two different people, don't you? Well, if that's the case, you might have to hang around longer than you'd intended. You wanted to be gone before my pregnancy became advanced, didn't you?''

"You knew from the beginning that this marriage was temporary," he said. "You hired me for specific reasons, and once I've done my job I'll move on. I have plans for my future that don't include a wife or a child."

Cleo could not control her tears. They gathered heavily in her eyes and spilled over, running down her face in torrents. "I—I don't mean anything to you, do I? What we've...these three weeks together, making love, sharing our days and nights, learning to truly like and trust each other. Has it all been a lie? Was being my passionate lover just a little something extra you threw in for no extra charge? Dammit, Simon, have you been pretending to care about me?''

Why was she doing this? Why couldn't she just accept things the way they were? Why did she have to analyze their relationship to death? Because despite her cool, levelheaded, businesswoman demeanor, Cleo was a loving, giving woman. A woman who felt things deeply. A woman who, when she gave herself fully and completely to a man, gave him her heart.

But he didn't want her heart. And he had no choice but to give it back to her, broken into pieces.

"I wasn't pretending," he said truthfully. "I do care about you, Cleo, just not the way you want me to care. And not enough to stay with you and be a father to your child."

She doubled over with the pain of understanding. She loved Simon Roarke. He did not love her. What could be more simple?

When he saw her double over, he rushed across the room and reached out for her. She jerked up and spread her hands in front of her, warning him off.

"Don't touch me." She spoke the words in a low, calm, chillingly frosty voice.

"I want you to understand." He dropped his outstretched hands to his sides. "I owe you that much."

"You don't owe me anything, except to finish your job." She turned around and went back into the sitting room.

Roarke followed her. "Don't walk away from me, Cleo. Even if you hate me right this minute, give me a chance to explain."

She sat down on the love seat and crossed her arms over her chest. "What's there to explain? I thought that there was something between us, something strong enough to build a real marriage on, but obviously I was mistaken. You want to finish this assignment and then you want out."

Roarke entered the sitting room. "Yeah, you're right. I want out. I don't want to be married. And I do not want to be a father."

"Fine. Good. We understand each other perfectly. Enough said." Cleo clenched her teeth, trying not to cry. A lump the size of Texas formed in her throat, threatening to cut off her breathing.

Roarke sat down in the wingback chair across from Cleo. "You know that I was married once, a long time ago." *Why are you doing this?* he asked himself. *What good will it do to bare your soul to her? It won't change anything.*

"Married and divorced," Cleo said. "Yes, I know. That information was in your files."

"What the files didn't tell you is why my marriage ended and why, seventeen years after my divorce, I'm still taking care of my ex-wife."

Cleo uncrossed her arms and sat up straight, staring inquisitively at Roarke. "What do you mean you take care of your ex-wife?"

Leaning forward, he rested his arms on his thighs and dropped his clasped hands between his legs. "My mother died when I was too young to remember her, and my father got killed in a tractor accident when I was nine. He'd been a good guy, treated me okay, but wasn't much on affection. His sister and her husband raised me. They treated me like a hired hand on their farm. I couldn't wait to get away, so I joined the army at eighteen and never looked back."

"What does your childhood history have to do with your ex-wife?"

"No one had ever loved me. Really loved me." He bowed his head, hesitant to make eye contact with Cleo. "I met her when I was on leave, on vacation, in Florida. She was blond and beautiful and she smothered me with love."

"Your ex-wife?"

"Hope. Hope Allister. We had a wild fling. I thought we were both in love. Before my leave ended, we got married. That's when things changed."

Part of Cleo wanted to know more, to know every detail of Simon's life, then maybe she could make some sense of what was happening to them. Another part of her wanted to tell him to stop talking, that she didn't want to know any more about Hope, the beautiful woman he'd once loved.

"How did things change?" Cleo asked.

"She wanted me to leave the army. She didn't want me going away on assignments. She didn't understand that I was doing what I wanted to do. That being in the Special Forces was my life. It's what I'd trained for, what I'd gone through hell to achieve."

"So you got a divorce because she wanted you to leave the army and you wouldn't," Cleo said.

"I wasn't quite that simple. It might have been if…if Hope hadn't gotten pregnant."

Cleo felt as though someone had hit her square in the stomach and knocked all the breath out of her. "Pregnant?" Suddenly her lungs filled with air. She gasped. "You have a child?"

Not answering her question, Roarke continued, knowing if he deviated from the linear retelling of his past history, he might not be able to tell her everything. And Cleo had a right to know. Then maybe she'd be able to understand and someday forgive him.

"Even though the relationship was doomed, I stayed married to Hope until Laurie was nearly two years old. Looking back, I've wondered why the hell, if I'd stuck it out that long, I couldn't have just hung in there a few more years. Long enough to realize what was happening with Hope." Roarke rubbed the palms of his hands up and down his thighs, then gripped his knees. "I was gone a lot. Off on assignments around the world. I thought our being apart would make things easier for both of us. It did for me, except I missed Laurie. But it didn't help Hope. As a matter of fact, it made things more difficult for her."

"You have a daughter? She must be nearly grown now." Cleo laid her hand over her tummy, the gesture purely protective maternal instinct. Her child had a half sister, one that she'd never know.

"Dammit, Cleo, will you stop interrupting!" Roarke shot out of the chair, every muscle in his body tense, his back ramrod straight, his big hands clenched. "If I didn't think I owed you this much—this truth about myself—I wouldn't relive the past. I wouldn't reopen all my old wounds. I wouldn't do this for any other reason, for any amount of money."

Cleo slipped off the love seat and walked over to where Roarke stood gazing sightlessly out the windows, his back to her. She raised her hand, holding it over his back, but didn't touch him. Knotting her hand into a fist, she lowered it to her side.

Suddenly she knew, as if the truth had been staring her in the face all along, and someone had just now removed the veil from her eyes. Something terrible had happened to Roarke. Something so unbearable that it had changed his life forever and sealed off his heart, made it impossible for anyone's love to ever reach him again.

Something had happened to Laurie. Roarke's little girl hadn't grown up. She had died and Roarke had buried all his love along with her.

"Go on, please," Cleo said. "I won't interrupt again."

His wide shoulders lifted and fell as he breathed deeply. "I found out later, from a distant cousin, that Hope had suffered from depression for years. Ever since she was around twelve and her father committed suicide. Hope had found his body. Her mother had a nervous breakdown shortly after that and died in a mental hospital."

"Oh, how awful."

"Anyway, when Laurie was two, Hope and I got a divorce. She even agreed to it. Of course she got custody of Laurie, and I got visitation rights. But I didn't see much of Laurie that next year. I was away most of the time. My career was very important to me.''

Cleo longed to put her arms around Roarke and comfort him, but she knew he wouldn't welcome her embrace. Not right now.

''Hope started drinking, but I didn't realize how bad the problem was until it was too late.'' Roarke fingered the moiré drapes, then shoved aside the sheers and looked down into the yard. ''One evening she got in the car with Laurie. According to the police, Hope was so intoxicated—'' Roarke paused. His body jerked several times. ''It was a one-car wreck. Laurie was thrown through the windshield. When the ambulance arrived, she was dead. Her neck was broken.''

Cleo laid her hand on Roarke's back. She eased her hand upward and gripped his shoulder. Sobs lodged in her throat. Dear God, what it must have been like for him to have lost his child. And how tragic that it had all been so senseless. So preventable. If Hope hadn't been drinking. If. If. If.

''My drunken, mentally unbalanced ex-wife put my three-year-old baby girl in her car and I didn't do a thing to stop her. And you know why?'' Roarke's voice rose to a shout. He spun around, knocking Cleo's hand off his shoulder. He glared at her with dry, pain-filled eyes. ''Because I was halfway around the world playing soldier. I was in the middle of a jungle with a Special Forces group doing a dirty little job for Uncle Sam.''

''Oh, Simon.'' Tears distorted her vision so completely that she could barely make out her husband's face. ''You blame yourself. You think Laurie's death was your fault.''

''It was my fault.'' His tone lowered to a soft, calm lifelessness. ''I was more concerned about my military career than I was about my child. I left Laurie alone with a woman who couldn't even take care of herself, let alone a three-year-old.''

''You didn't know. You said you had no idea how much Hope was drinking, and you didn't realize that mental instability ran in her family.''

''I didn't take the time to find out. I had more important things to do. My daughter was not my first priority. She should have been.''

"How long ago did Laurie die?" Sniffling, Cleo swallowed her tears.

"Nearly fifteen years ago."

"Where is Hope now?" Running her fingertips under her eyes, Cleo wiped away the moisture.

"She's in a private sanitarium in Florida. She's been there over fourteen years, and the doctors say that after all this time, there's not much chance for a recovery."

"And you take care of her," Cleo said, understanding her husband more completely now than many women understood their husbands after years of marriage. "You pay all her bills, don't you?"

"I let Hope down. She needed help back then and I just didn't see it. Maybe if I had—"

"Don't do this to yourself." With quivering hands, Cleo reached out and cupped Roarke's face. "You've been living with this guilt all these years and it's nearly destroyed you."

"I don't want to hurt you, Cleo." He covered her hands with his, then pulled them away from his face and held them between their bodies. "I should have known I was playing with fire when I agreed to take this job, especially when one of the stipulations of our agreement was that I father your child."

"You must have had a very good reason for agreeing."

"Yeah, I thought they were good reasons. Now I'm not so sure."

"Security for Hope?" Cleo asked, certain of his answer.

"Partly." He held Cleo's hands, encompassing them with his. "I'm nearly forty. I want out of the cloak-and-dagger business. I told you that last year I got shot up on an assignment and nearly died. If something happened to me, there would be no one to pay Hope's expenses."

"So you agreed to marry me, be my bodyguard and father my child so you'd have the money to take care of Hope after you retired from the Dundee agency?"

"I'm going to buy a small farm somewhere." He released Cleo's hands. "The rest of the money is going into a perpetual trust for Hope."

"Thank you for telling me about Hope and about Laurie. I know it must have been painful for you. I'm sorry."

"You had a right to know."

"Yes...well...I—I appreciate your..."

He didn't touch Cleo. He didn't trust what he might do if he touched her now. She looked so small standing there, so forlorn and lost. He'd done this to her. He'd taken the light out of her eyes. She had thought something magical was happening between them, and selfishly, he hadn't been honest with her. He'd let her believe.

"I won't leave until you are no longer in danger. I promise you that." He looked directly into her moss green eyes and saw the rage inside her. Outwardly she was calm, totally unemotional. Roarke knew she'd already put up a defensive barrier between them. He had hurt her. She wasn't going to allow him close enough to ever hurt her again.

"Thank you." She walked away from him, then paused as she stepped into the bedroom. "I think I'm going to lie down and take a nap. I'm very tired, and I want to make sure I get plenty of rest. I intend to take very good care of *my* baby." She emphasized the word "my."

Her sedate composure worried him far more than if she'd thrown a temper tantrum. He wished she'd throw something at him. Beat her fists against his chest. Call him names. But that wasn't Cleo's style. She had a temper, but it had a low boiling point and her expression of anger was more subtle than hysterical outbursts.

He followed her out of the sitting room.

"Lock the door behind me. I'm going to Kane's room to discuss a scheme we've been working on to capture our problem maker at McNamara Industries."

"Fine. Go ahead. You can tell me all about it later."

Roarke walked outside. Cleo closed the door and locked it. He leaned back against the door, resting his head for a second. He'd give anything if he could take away Cleo's pain, the pain he'd caused. But he couldn't ease her suffering. Hell, he couldn't even ease his own.

Suddenly, he felt something moist on his face. He touched his cheek, removed his hand and looked down at his fingers. They were damp. Wet with his tears.

But that wasn't possible. He hadn't cried in fifteen years.

Chapter 15

Cleo insisted that she was well enough to go to work. Nothing Roarke, Beatrice or Pearl said changed her mind. She reminded Roarke that just as he had a job to do, so did she. He thought if he heard her say one more time that people were counting on her, he'd shake her until her teeth rattled.

They'd slept in the same bed last night. The bed they'd shared since the first night of their marriage. The bed in which they'd made love so many times. But he hadn't touched her. He knew that if he had, she would have refused him. He'd been right all along about Cleo. She was the kind of woman who'd get sex and love all mixed up.

"What if your and Kane's little scheme doesn't work?" Cleo placed her empty cup down on the tray. "You don't know for certain that Trey or Hugh is the person we're after, and even if one of them is, he might not step into your trap."

"Ellen Denby has been playing the blond airhead around Trey and Hugh, letting bits of so-called secret information accidentally slip out." Roarke tossed his napkin down on the tray beside his breakfast plate. "She's led them to believe that she's totally incompetent and can be easily manipulated. She's even hinted that for the right amount of money, she'd be willing to look the other way while someone tampered with the computer again or created another accident.''

''Do you honestly think Trey or Hugh is gullible enough to believe her?'' Cleo asked. ''Don't you think they're smart enough to figure out that she's lying? After all, they know Kane is a professional. He'd hardly hire a bimbo to be on his security force.''

''You don't know what a talented actress our Ellen is. She's pulled the wool over brighter minds than Trey's or Hugh's. Believe me, she knows what she's doing. She's implied that her intimate relationship with Kane is what got her the job.''

''Something my cousin and future cousin-in-law are just the types to believe.'' Cleo got up and walked into the bedroom. She picked up her black jacket off the bed, put it on and fastened the gold buttons. ''If you're right, then tonight we should know who was behind all our problems at the plant.''

''Maybe. If we're lucky,'' Roarke said as he followed her into the bedroom. ''Ellen's going to let it slip that she'll be alone on duty tonight inside the plant and there'll be no one else around except for the guard at the front gate.'' He lifted his holster from the nightstand, removed his Beretta, checked it and replaced it, then strapped on the holster. ''We're giving our saboteur a perfect opportunity to wreak havoc at the plant without getting caught. Or so we hope he thinks.''

''Hugh and Trey both have security clearance at the back entrance, so they could enter the plant without the guard seeing them.''

''Exactly.''

''So it's possible that by morning, all my problems will be over and neither I nor McNamara Industries will be in any more danger.''

''If we catch our man,'' Roarke said. ''And if he and the person who's been trying to kill you are one in the same.'' He lifted his jacket off the back of the chair.

''If he is, then your job will be finished and you can leave. You can get a divorce, collect your payoff and be long gone before I even have a bout of morning sickness.''

''Yeah. Sure. That's what we both want, isn't it?'' Roarke put on his jacket, walked across the room and opened the door. ''Are you ready to leave for the plant, Boss Lady?''

* * *

The day had seemed endless. Cleo discovered that ignoring Simon Roarke was easier said than done. She found it impossible to pretend he wasn't around when he was at her side constantly. After all, he *was* her bodyguard. And he could hardly guard her if she was one place and he another.

She supposed that if Simon hadn't told her the truth about his past—about Hope and Laurie—she might have gone on thinking that there was a chance he'd change his mind and stay with her. That he might actually want to spend the rest of his life with her. That someday, he would grow to love her.

But there was no hope now. No false dreams to hang on to. No illusions about a marriage of convenience that she now realized could never be anything more.

There was no love in Simon to give. The anger and guilt and remorse he felt over Laurie's death had slowly killed all the love inside him. And no matter how much she loved him, Cleo knew she couldn't bring his deepest emotions back to life. Only Simon could do that. And he never would. Loving someone meant taking a risk on being hurt. He'd been hurt too deeply, had endured an agony that would be a part of him forever. A man who walked around with third-degree burns scarring his emotions would never again take a chance on getting burned.

She glanced over at Roarke. He sat behind the Jacobean desk, while she curled up on the leather sofa. They had agreed to wait downstairs together in the study. Wait for Morgan Kane to call and tell them that they'd caught their man. That either Trey or Hugh had walked into their trap.

Roarke flipped through the pages of a book on farming techniques, which he'd found in Uncle George's library. Cleo held a biography of Amelia Earhart on her lap. The minutes dragged by, making the waiting unbearable.

They'd eaten dinner with the family and tried their best to keep up appearances, but Cleo suspected that they'd failed at presenting the happy newlyweds act they'd finally perfected. But it didn't matter. What difference did it make anymore whether the family believed theirs was a real marriage? They'd all know the truth soon enough, once Simon left. Once they got a divorce.

Both Daphne and Trey had excused themselves from a family night at home, Daphne saying she had a date with Hugh and Trey telling them that he was going to the country club to play cards with a group of his friends. Both explanations were reasonable. Daphne saw Hugh almost every night and Trey did play cards at the country club fairly often.

Cleo glanced down at her watch. "It's ten o'clock. You'd think if something was going to happen, it would have happened by now."

Roarke closed the book and laid it on the desk. "Not necessarily."

"If it has to be Trey or Hugh, I hope it's Hugh," she said.

"You're thinking of your family, aren't you? That it would be easier all the way around if Trey isn't guilty."

"Do you have any idea what it will do to Aunt Oralie if it is Trey? She dotes on her children. She thinks they can do no wrong."

The telephone rang. Cleo jumped. Roarke picked up the receiver.

"Roarke here. Yes. I see. No, go ahead and call Phil Bacon. Cleo and I will meet you at the sheriff's department." Roarke hung up the telephone.

"That was Kane, wasn't it?"

"Yes. Our simple little trap worked."

"Who?" Cleo asked.

"Trey," Roarke said. "They caught him red-handed. He's trying to talk his way out of it, but there's no question that he got into the computer again and deleted several files. Of course he had no way of knowing that he was destroying useless files, dummy orders that we'd entered today, or that he was being videotaped."

Cleo could tell by the look on Roarke's face that there was more to what had happened than he was telling her. "What else? You're not telling me everything."

"Trey had rigged some explosives that he planned to set off in the main production room of the plant."

"What! How would Trey know the first thing about explosives?"

"Every man and his brother can find that information on

the Internet or order it through the mail," Roarke told her. "It doesn't take a genius to assemble a simple little bomb."

"Trey." Cleo gritted her teeth. "I didn't want it to be Trey. I can't believe he'd try to kill me. Aunt Oralie raised him to be selfish and greedy, but I never thought he was capable of murder."

"He may not be." Roarke shoved back the chair and stood. "He may be guilty of only sabotage. Kane's calling Phil Bacon, so I imagine by the time we get down to the sheriff's department, they'll have brought in Trey for booking."

"He'll be arrested and put in jail, won't he?"

"Yeah, and if I have anything to do with it, he won't be getting out on bond anytime soon."

Roarke wished he could have spared Cleo from this ordeal. If the saboteur had been anyone other than a member of her family it would have been easier for her. But then, she'd known all along that it had to be someone with something to gain. Someone who would benefit if she agreed to sell McNamara Industries.

Trey Sutton had called Hugh Winfield, who had shown up at the county jail shortly after Roarke and Cleo had arrived. Cleo had reminded Hugh that as one of McNamara Industries' lawyers, he could hardly represent someone who'd tried to sabotage the plant. Hugh in turn had called Drennan Norcross, an old warhorse of an attorney, who, with his white hair and thick mustache looked the part of a forties-style Southern lawyer. Drennan actually wore white suits in the summertime and carried a gold-tipped black cane, which he said helped him get around better since his rheumatism had gotten so bad.

While Drennan spoke to his client, Cleo and Roarke waited, along with Morgan Kane and Ellen Denby. But Hugh Winfield suddenly disappeared.

"He's gone to the house to tell the family," Cleo said. "They'll all be down here in a little while."

"We'll handle that when it happens," Roarke told her. "I don't want you to worry. You're recovering from a concussion. You just got out of the hospital yesterday. Getting upset isn't good for you. Or for the baby."

She noticed that he hadn't said *your* baby or *our* baby, just *the* baby. Of course he was right. Getting upset and worrying about how she was going to handle Trey's capture and the family's reaction weren't good for her or her baby. And her child had to be her number-one priority. Regardless of the fact that she had conceived this baby to fulfill a stipulation in her uncle's will, she already loved her child and wanted it desperately.

In the future, she might have other children, but they would not be Simon's children. This tiny life growing inside her would soon be all she had of Simon. Their child and her few precious memories of the days and nights they'd shared during their brief marriage.

Drennan's cane tapped along on the hardwood floor as he shuffled down the corridor leading from the jail cells that were located in a separate west wing of the sheriff's department.

"Well, Phil, Trey's ready to sign a statement." Drennan clasped Sheriff Bacon's shoulder. "But he wants to talk to Cleo first."

"What sort of statement is Trey willing to sign?" Phil Bacon asked.

"The boy knows he's been caught red-handed, so to speak." Drennan chuckled, the sound a smirky good-old-boy laugh. "He's willing to own up to playing around with the computer and to rigging up some little old homemade bomb that probably wouldn't have done more than cause a loud sound and create some smoke."

Cleo rolled her eyes heavenward. Drennan Norcross was making Trey sound like a misguided Boy Scout who'd been caught putting a garden snake in the Scoutmaster's cot.

"Is he willing to confess to trying to murder his cousin?" Roarke asked.

"Hell, no. Trey Sutton is no murderer, sir. The boy doesn't have it in him to try to harm Miss Cleo." Drennan smiled at Cleo, his white teeth glistening.

"I want to talk to Trey," Cleo said. "I want him to look me in the eye and tell me that he didn't try to shoot me or poison me or—"

"Cleo will agree to speak to Trey, but not alone," Roarke said.

"Of course," Drennan agreed. "He said you'd want to come along with her."

"Are you sure you want to do this, Cleo?" Phil Bacon asked. "We don't need a signed confession, not with eyewitnesses—" Phil glanced at Kane and Ellen Denby, who waited discreetly just outside his open office door "—who caught Trey in the act." Phil lifted a videotape off his desk. "And even recorded what he did."

"I understand," Cleo said. "I'm glad that we've caught our saboteur, but unless Trey was behind the attempts on my life, then I'm still in danger. And so is my baby."

"Baby?" Phil looked from Cleo to Roarke. "Well, congratulations, folks. Hell, Cleo, this is hardly the place for a pregnant lady. Down here at the jail having to deal with a mess like this."

"I promise that as soon as I talk to Trey and hear what he has to say, I'll go home."

"Come on, then," Phil said. "I'll walk you and Mr. Roarke on back. If you'd like, I'll dismiss my deputy and stay in the room with y'all."

"Could we speak to him privately?" Cleo asked.

"I'm afraid not." Phil shook his head. "Sorry."

"All right. Let's go get this over with." Cleo turned to her husband. "He'd be a fool to confess that he's tried to kill me."

Roarke nodded, then slipped his arm around her. She didn't resist the comforting, protective gesture. They followed the sheriff down the hall and into the small, private inquisition room that also served as a private meeting area for lawyers and their clients.

Phil dismissed his deputy, who exited the room before Cleo and Roarke entered. Trey stood up the minute Cleo entered the room.

"I'm sorry, Cleo," Trey said. "I did what I had to do, what I thought was best for the whole family. We'd all be better off if we sold the company while it's still worth something. The way things are these days, there's no way for a small plant like ours to survive."

Roarke watched Cleo's face, the tensing of her jaw, the slight flaring of her nostrils, the narrowing of her pensive green eyes. She was trying to control her anger, trying to stay calm.

"Don't apologize to me," Cleo said. "There is no excuse for what you did, for the thousands of dollars you lost for McNamara's, the lives you put in danger."

"I never meant for anyone to get hurt." Trey came toward Cleo, his hands open in supplication. "You've got to believe me. When I took that shot at you right after Uncle George's funeral, I had no intention of harming you. I just meant to frighten you."

"You were the one! My God, it was you all along." Cleo curved her fingers into claws and lifted them toward Trey. "You put spiders in my bathroom and poison in my tea. You—"

"No, Cleo. No! I didn't. I swear I didn't. All I did was take a shot at you to try to scare you."

When Trey reached out for Cleo, Roarke stepped between them. Trey gazed into Roarke's stern face and backed away.

"Do you expect me to believe that you haven't been behind the other three attempts on my life?" Cleo wanted to put her hands around Trey's throat and choke the life out of him for what he'd put her through, for what he'd done to her and Aunt Beatrice and all the employees at McNamara's.

"I don't know who's been trying to kill you," Trey said. "But I would never hurt you. Scare you into selling McNamara Industries? Yes. But try to kill you? Never."

"Come on, Cleo, you don't need any more of this. Not tonight." Roarke put his arm around her shoulders. "Don't do this to yourself." Leaning over, he whispered in her ear, "Think of the baby."

She allowed Roarke to lead her out of the interrogation room and back down the hall toward the sheriff's office. When they reached the end of the corridor, Cleo heard her aunt Oralie's voice.

"Oh, God, they're here." Cleo leaned against Roarke.

"You don't have to see them tonight, honey. I can take you out of here the back way. We can check into a motel. You can face them tomorrow."

"No. I'm not running away. It's past time I took charge of

this situation.'' Cleo moved out of Roarke's arms and walked down the hall.

He followed her, but stayed several steps behind, ready to come to her aid only if she needed him.

Daphne caught a glimpse of Cleo and called out loudly, ''There she is mother! You tell her to get Trey out of this jail right now.''

Oralie rushed toward Cleo, hysterically waving her arms in the air. ''What have you done to Trey? How dare you have him locked up in this awful place. I demand that you have him released this very minute.''

''How could you allow the sheriff to arrest Trey?'' Daphne pursed her lips and glared at Cleo.

Cleo marched past Daphne, past Oralie, and stopped dead still in front of Perry Sutton. Aunt Beatrice stood several feet away, her arm around a weeping Marla. Aunt Beatrice shrugged her slender shoulders and smiled sadly.

''Trey was caught tampering with the computer system at McNamara's as well as placing a small bomb in the main production room at the plant. He's confessed to being behind all the sabotage that's taken place since Uncle George's death.''

''That's not possible,'' Oralie cried out. ''You're framing Trey. You want him out of McNamara's. You never wanted him working there in the first place.''

Cleo ignored her aunt's outburst, keeping her eyes focused on her uncle Perry's somber face. ''Trey also admitted to being the one who took a shot at me right after Uncle George's funeral.''

''You're lying!'' Daphne shouted.

''Trey has been arrested and is facing some serious charges, Uncle Perry,'' Cleo said. ''If he's convicted, and I have no doubt he will be, he's going to be in prison for years.''

''I understand.'' Bowing his head, Perry looked down at the floor.

''Well, I don't understand,'' Oralie said. ''This is a family matter. There was no need to turn Trey over to the sheriff.''

Cleo spun around and faced her wild-eyed, angry aunt. ''Trey tried to shoot me, Aunt Oralie, and he put McNamara Industries' employees in danger, as well as cost the company

thousands of dollars. He committed more than one crime.
What do you think I should do—slap him on the hand and
tell him to be a good boy from now on?''

''You—you can't let him go to prison. I won't allow it! Do
you hear me? I won't allow it.'' Oralie pointed her finger in
Cleo's face.

''Get your finger out of my face right now, Aunt Oralie, or
I'm going to bite it off!''

''How dare you threaten me!'' Oralie lowered her finger.

''If you think that was a threat, you haven't heard anything
yet.''

Phil Bacon walked up the hall and stopped by Roarke's
side. ''What's going on?''

''Shh, I think my wife is just about to set up some new
ground rules.''

''Trey is going to have to pay for his crimes. He'll go to
trial and if he's convicted he'll be sentenced to prison,'' Cleo
told her aunt. ''I will not lift a finger to help him.''

''You're cold and heartless and—''

''I will not discuss this with you ever again after tonight. I
want you and your family to move out of Aunt Beatrice's
home. Uncle George left the house to her, you know. After
all, it did belong to her mother's family. Aunt Beatrice has
been far too generous allowing y'all to make her home yours
all these years.'' Cleo took a deep breath. ''I'll give y'all one
month to find somewhere else to live.''

''You don't mean what you're saying.'' Oralie stared at
Cleo in disbelief.

''Yes, I mean every word I've said. I'm going to have a
baby and my child is my first priority. I don't want my son
or daughter living in a house with y'all.''

Oralie glanced across the room at her cousin, who still had
her arm around Marla's trembling shoulders. ''Beatrice, you
won't let her do this, will you?''

Beatrice looked at Perry, who had his back to her. ''Yes,
Oralie, I'm afraid I will let her. It's long past time that you
left.''

Oralie fussed and fumed and cried. Roarke walked around
the edge of the room and watched Cleo as she came toward
him.

"I'm tired," she said. "There's nothing else I can do here tonight. I'd like to go home now, Simon."

She looked so pale and delicate, as if the lightest breeze might blow her off her feet. He wanted to lift her in his arms and carry her away from everything and everyone who'd ever hurt her. But he didn't. He knew she needed to walk away on her on two feet, under her own steam. Cleo McNamara Roarke had finally taken complete charge of her life, and he, for one, felt like applauding her.

Chapter 16

Roarke lay in the darkness, listening to Cleo breathe. She had slept restlessly, tossing and turning most of the night. He'd slept very little and had been awake for quite some time. Dawn light came through the windows and French doors, permeating the room with a muted, rosy glow. He looked at Cleo, her face partially in shadow as she lay on her side, her back to him. She was so lovely, her features so utterly, completely feminine.

The oddest thought went through his mind. He wanted to memorize her face, so that over the years he would never forget exactly how she looked at this precise moment.

Cleo awoke with a start. Gasping for air, she shot straight up in bed. Roarke sat up beside her and pulled her into his arms. Maybe she didn't want his comfort, but he knew she damn well needed it. She was a strong woman, but sometimes the strongest people needed someone to lean on, someone to let them know they weren't all alone. He halfway expected her to resist him, but she didn't. Relaxing against him, she laid her head on his shoulder.

"You're safe, honey." Brushing away an errant red strand

of hair that had fallen across her forehead, Roarke kissed her temple.

He hadn't realized how much he'd missed her girlish giggles or her breath-stopping smiles or her warm, enthusiastic loving. He'd become used to Cleo. As the old song went, he'd become accustomed to her. That had been his mistake—his letting himself get emotionally involved. There hadn't been a woman in his life on a steady basis since his divorce from Hope. Women had come in and out of his life over the past fifteen years, but not one of them had put a dent in his defensive armor.

But Cleo had.

"Is it over, Simon? I mean really over?" Lifting her head off his shoulder, she looked at him, her eyes pleading for reassurance. "Now that Trey is in jail, am I safe?"

He wished he could tell her that it *was* over, that she *was* safe. But he couldn't. His gut instincts told him that Trey Sutton was telling the truth, that he had been responsible for shooting at Cleo right after George McNamara's death, but not for any of the other attempts on her life. If Trey had been honest with them, that meant the greater danger to Cleo still existed. Whoever wanted her dead was still free to try again.

Holding her securely in his embrace, Roarke stroked her arm tenderly. "I don't know. I honestly don't know. I'd like to think that we don't have anything else to worry about, but I tend to think Trey was telling us the truth last night."

"If he was, that means Daphne or Hugh or Uncle Perry or maybe even Aunt Oralie or Marla was the one behind the other three attempts on my life." Cleo shuddered, then draped her arms around Roarke's waist and buried her face against his chest. "Don't leave me." She whispered the plea, her lips brushing his collarbone. "I need you. The baby and I need you. Just for a little longer."

He grasped her chin with one hand. She gazed up at him. "I'm not going to leave you, honey. I'm not going anywhere until I know you're safe. You and the baby."

The baby. His baby. God help him, he'd tried so hard not to think of the child as his, but it was his. Nothing could ever change that fact.

He saw the need in her eyes, felt the hunger in her quivering body, and knew that Cleo could no more resist him than he could her. An overwhelming passion existed between them, a desire so strong that it overrode their common sense.

Lowering his mouth to hers, he consumed her with a kiss that combined tenderness with savagery, a gentle conquest, but a conquest all the same. Cleo pressed her body against his. Placing his hand in the center of her back, he shoved her harder against him, rubbing his chest over her aching nipples. Her satin-covered nipples hardened, jabbing into his chest.

He deepened the kiss, his tongue thrusting, mimicking the most intimate invasion of all. She clung to him, urging him, encouraging him, returning in full measure the fury of his loving attack. When they were both breathless, Roarke slowed the kiss and turned his attention to her neck.

She moaned softly, then whispered his name. He slipped his hand under the cover, up beneath her gown and between her thighs. He sought and found her hot, moist core.

"Let me love you." He murmured the words against her neck.

"Yes." She sighed. "I need you so much."

He tossed the covers aside, eased Cleo's gown over her head and threw it on the floor. Lifting his hips, he eased his briefs down his legs and flung them into the air. He mounted her slowly, forcing himself not to move too quickly, not to rush this sweet, sweet moment.

Roarke tormented her breasts with his lips and tongue, creating an unbearable urgency within her. Grasping his buttocks, Cleo urged him to take her. He cupped her hips, lifting her to meet his forceful plunge. Her body welcomed his entrance, claiming him completely.

They made love in quiet, hurried desperation. Each in such urgent need of the other. Each aware on some level that this might be their last time. Their fulfillment came too quickly. White-hot. Rocking them to the depths of their souls.

She would never know this ecstasy with anyone else. Only with Simon. Only with the man she loved with all her heart. Only with the father of her child.

Several hours later when Cleo and Roarke came downstairs for breakfast, they found the house unnaturally quiet. On their way to the dining room, they encountered Pearl pushing a serving cart toward the open French doors leading to the patio.

"Good morning, Pearl," Cleo said. "Are you serving breakfast outside today?"

Pearl continued pushing the cart, laden with a coffeepot and a pitcher of orange juice, toward the patio. "Perry called down an hour ago and said Oralie wanted me to set things up outside. He said the sunshine and fresh air might do her some good."

Cleo tensed at the mention of her aunt and uncle. Last night she had given them their walking papers, ordering them out of the house within the month. But this morning, it was business as usual, Oralie presiding over the household as if she were the queen bee.

"Has anyone come down yet?" Roarke asked.

Pearl stopped in the doorway. "I haven't seen anyone except Daphne. She was asking about you, Mr. Roarke. Wanted me to let her know the minute you and Cleo came down for breakfast. She's on the phone in the study."

"You might as well find out what she wants," Cleo said. "I'll walk on outside with Pearl and pour us both a cup of coffee."

"No," Roarke said. "I'll go on outside with you. Pearl can tell Daphne where we are."

Pearl pushed the cart over the threshold and out onto the patio. "I know the sheriff arrested Trey last night. Hugh Winfield came by and told the family that Mr. Kane had caught Trey up to no good at the plant." She paused momentarily, turned her head around and looked directly at Cleo, who stood in the doorway. "I didn't hear you and Mr. Roarke come in last night, but when the rest of them returned, Oralie was making enough noise to wake the dead. She was crying and screaming and carrying on like you wouldn't believe. I heard her say that you was kicking them all out of the house. Is that true, Cleo Belle—are you getting rid of that bad rubbish once and for all?"

"Yes, Pearl, she is." The feminine voice came from behind Roarke, who had stopped just inside the house, a couple of feet away from Cleo.

They all glanced back at Daphne. She ran the tip of her index finger up Roarke's arm, but she gazed past him at Cleo. "She's given us a month to get out. Generous of her to give us that much time, don't you think?" She looked at Roarke then, her full, red lips curving into a forced smile. "I'd like to ask a favor of you, Mr. Roarke." She emphasized the word *mister* when she spoke. "You're the only one I know who might possibly help me."

Pearl turned back around and went about setting up the coffee and juice for the family's breakfast. Cleo followed Pearl.

"Wait, Cleo," Roarke called after her.

"No. It's all right. Find out what you can do to *help* Daphne. I'll fix us some coffee."

"I'll join you in a minute," Roarke said.

Cleo nodded and waved at him, then headed straight for the silver coffee server that Pearl had just filled. The housekeeper handed Cleo a china cup, then waddled off toward the house.

"I'll be back directly, as soon as I take my apple cinnamon rolls out of the oven," Pearl said, disappearing inside the house.

As Pearl passed them in the dining room, Roarke noticed her disapproving glare aimed directly at Daphne. He grinned at Pearl. Her lips twitched, but she didn't return his smile. She just stared at him briefly, shook her head and headed toward the kitchen.

He glanced outside, watching Cleo as she poured one cup of coffee, set it down on the table, then repeated the process.

"What can I help you with, Daphne?" Roarke asked.

Daphne walked around Roarke and closed the French doors. He glanced outside, checking once again on Cleo, who he knew was deliberately ignoring him and her cousin.

Daphne danced the tips of her long red nails up the front of his shirt. "You can intercede with Cleo for us. You're the only one she seems to listen to these days. The only one who has any influence over her."

"Why would I intercede for your family? I hardly know any of you, and what I do know, I don't like."

Laying her hand flat on Roarke's chest, she rubbed her palm around and around. Roarke grabbed her wrist. They glared at each other.

"If you got to know me, you'd like me. I promise." She licked her moist red lips. "If you'll help us, I'll be very grateful."

"Exactly what do you think I can do?"

"You can persuade Cleo not to kick us out. After all, we are family. And you could ask her to help Trey. He didn't actually try to kill her. He told you himself that he only wanted to frighten her, scare her into selling the damn company."

When Daphne wiggled her fingers, trying to caress Roarke, he tightened his hold on her wrist. "The only person who can help Trey now is Drennan Norcross. A good lawyer might get him a reduced sentence since he has cooperated and confessed."

"Cleo cares more about McNamara Industries than she does her own family." Daphne twisted her arm, trying to pull free of Roarke's tenacious grip. "She'd rather save the jobs of a few hundred people than do what's best for us."

"Cleo has done more for your family than most people would have under similar circumstances. She's had to put up with your jealousy and greed all her life, and since her uncle's death, someone in this family, if not Trey, has attempted to kill her more than once."

Glowering at Roarke, Daphne tugged on her wrist. Releasing his hold on her, he shoved her hand toward her. "I can't help you, *Daffie*. Not you or Trey or your mother or father. For once, y'all are going to have to help yourselves."

Cleo knew that Roarke wasn't going to fall for any of Daphne's persuasive promises, but years of losing boyfriends and even a fiancé to Daphne made Cleo uneasy. What could Daphne possible want from Roarke? Why had she waylaid him in the dining room? Probably for no other reason than to aggravate her.

Nervous and restless, Cleo shoved back her chair, lifted her cup and saucer and stood. She looked up at the clear, blue sky, at the beautiful morning sun shimmering an orange gold on the eastern horizon. The day was Southern summertime beautiful.

She walked around the pool, careful not to get too close to

the edge. She didn't want to accidentally slip in and have to change clothes before she went into the office for a few hours this morning.

Sipping her coffee, occasionally glancing toward the dining room, where she could see Daphne and Roarke, and enjoying the fresh, morning air, Cleo continued her stroll around the pool.

She heard a noise from behind her. Thinking Pearl had returned with warm apple cinnamon rolls, Cleo started to turn around. Something hard and heavy hit her across the side of her head. A hand reached out and shoved her into the pool. Cleo opened her mouth to scream. A thick, heavy darkness surrounded her, silencing her cry for help.

Opening the French doors, Roarke looked outside. Cleo wasn't walking around the pool as she'd been doing only minutes ago. He glanced around the patio area. Cleo wasn't there. Where was she? His heartbeat accelerated, the thunderous roar deafening him to any other sound. He ran outside, his gaze searching. Suddenly he saw her—in the pool. God, no!

Fully clothed, Roarke jumped into the pool and lifted Cleo's head out of the water. She lay lifeless and unbreathing in his arms. He swam with her to the pool's edge, hauled her up onto the patio and laid her down on the stone floor. He straddled her hips.

Daphne hovered over him. "What happened? Is she all right?"

"Call 911! Get an ambulance here on the double!" Roarke shouted.

Daphne ran into Pearl when she rushed toward the house. "Call 911," Daphne said. "Something's happened to Cleo. I'll go get Mother and Father and Aunt Beatrice."

Roarke had performed resuscitation techniques before. He knew the drill. But this wasn't just anybody lying beneath him. This was Cleo. His wife. The mother of his child.

Forcing himself not to think, not to feel, only to perform, to do what he had to do, Roarke opened Cleo's mouth and positioned her tongue. Pinching her nose shut, he breathed into her mouth. He removed his mouth, allowing time for her lungs to empty. He repeated the process quickly, again and again.

While he gave Cleo artificial respiration, he concentrated fully on the task at hand. But while his mind focused on what he could do to save her, his heart prayed for divine assistance.

"I called 911." Pearl scurried out onto the patio, halting at Roarke's side. "The ambulance is on its way."

On some level he heard her, but didn't take time to acknowledge her presence.

Beatrice rushed outside, followed by Oralie and Perry. Daphne waited in the doorway.

"Come on, honey," Roarke said, then breathed into Cleo's mouth again.

She choked, then spit up mouthfuls of water. She gasped for air. Relief relaxed Roarke's tense body. He laughed as he ran his hands up and down her arms. She coughed repeatedly. When she tried to sit up, he put his arm around her shoulder and lifted her.

"You scared the hell out of me, honey." He grasped her shoulders, bunching the sleeves of her jacket. The light pressure of his fingers drew droplets of chlorinated water out of the linen material.

Cleo reached out and touched Roarke's cheek. "What— what happened?"

"I found you in the pool, unconscious."

"Someone hit me." She coughed again and again, then breathed deeply. Her lungs ached as the air entered them. "They hit me over the head and—" she coughed once more "—they pushed me into the pool. I tried to call out, but everything went black."

Roarke ran his hand over her head gently, threading his fingers through her wet hair. Lifting his hand, he looked at his palm and saw fresh, bright red blood. Maneuvering himself around without moving Cleo, he inspected her head, and discovered a small tear in the skin an inch or so above her right ear. A thin, water-mixed rivulet of blood seeped down the side of her neck.

"Did you see anything?" Roarke asked. "Do you have any idea who hit you?" Where the hell was that ambulance? Despite the fact that Cleo seemed all right, he couldn't help but wonder if this second blow to her head in such a short period of time might not have done some unseen damage. And what about the baby? Would those few minutes Cleo's body was without oxygen have harmed their child in any way?

"I heard something behind me." Cleo tried to get up. Roarke held her, forcing her to stay seated on the stone floor. "I want to get up. I'm wet and soggy. My head hurts. Take me upstairs and let me change clothes."

"No, no, you must stay still, dear," Beatrice said, moving closer to Cleo. "An ambulance is on the way. You need to go to the hospital and let Dr. Iverson make sure you're really all right."

"I am all right." Cleo crossed her arms over her chest. "Look, I don't want to waste time on an unnecessary trip to the hospital. Someone just tried to kill me." She turned her head, then cried out in pain. When Roarke reached for her, she brushed his hand aside. "One of you—" Cleo pointed to Perry Sutton, then to her aunt Oralie and finally to Daphne "—tried to kill me."

"Nonsense," Oralie said. "You must have slipped, hit your head and fallen into the pool. It had to have been an accident."

"It was no accident!" Cleo grabbed Roarke's hand. "And you were in the dining room with Daphne, so…that leaves only Aunt Oralie or Uncle Perry."

"Honey, I want you to stay calm and take it easy until Dr. Iverson checks you over," Roarke said. "Think about the baby, if not yourself."

"I am thinking about my baby," Cleo told him. "I'm thinking about what would have happened if you hadn't found me so soon."

"Good thing he was close by, like he always is," Pearl said. "You was keeping an eye on her through them doors." Pearl pointed to the open French doors, where Daphne stood. "Didn't you see anybody?"

"Daphne!" Roarke bellowed her name. Releasing Cleo, Roarke stood and glanced at Beatrice. "Aunt Beatrice? Please?"

He nodded toward Cleo, and her aunt immediately understood that he was turning his wife over into her care. Roarke glared at Daphne. "Come here," he said. She took several hesitant steps toward him, then when she looked into his angry eyes, she hurried to him.

"Don't harass my poor baby," Oralie said. "Isn't it enough that you've put one of my children in jail? Must you persecute Daphne?"

"You stopped me from going out on the patio with Cleo. You closed the doors and tried to divert my attention. You knew I wouldn't help you, knew talking to me would be useless," Roarke said.

Daphne turned to flee, but Roarke caught her wrist. "Let me go. I've done nothing wrong."

"Oh, but you have. You helped someone scheming to harm Cleo. You tried to separate me from Cleo just long enough for your partner to make another attempt on Cleo's life."

"I don't know what you're talking about." Daphne's eyes widened. Her chin quivered. She tugged on her wrist, trying to free herself from Roarke's grasp. "All I did was ask you to help Trey and help us. Mother insisted I talk to you as soon as possible this morning. She believed that I could convince you to use your influence with Cleo."

"Your mother?" Roarke jerked Daphne by the wrist, pulling her around to face Oralie. "Is that right Mrs. Sutton? Were you the one who sent Daphne to divert my attention?"

"I most certainly did not!"

"Mother?" Daphne stared questioningly at Oralie.

"Where were you five minutes ago, Mrs. Sutton?" Roarke glanced at Perry Sutton. "Was she with you?"

"No," Beatrice answered for him. "Perry was with me. We had—" she lowered her voice, as if what she was about to say was a secret "—we went for a walk together this morning, as we often do. We had just returned, when we ran into Daphne in the hall."

"When you went upstairs to get your parents and your aunt, did you find them?" Roarke asked Daphne.

"You don't have to answer him!" Oralie backed slowly toward the house, all the while glaring daggers through Roarke.

"Mother?" Daphne asked. "Please, Mother!"

Oralie turned quickly and ran from the patio, brushing past her daughter as she fled inside the house.

"Oralie!" Perry called to his wife as he rushed after her, following her inside the house.

"Your mother wasn't upstairs, was she, Daphne?" Roarke asked. "She was already downstairs somewhere, waiting and hoping for another chance to kill Cleo."

"No!" Daphne cried. "No. She just wanted me to talk to you. She didn't want Cleo to throw us out of the house. Please, try to understand. She didn't…she wouldn't…"

"Simon?" Cleo fought off Beatrice's attempts to keep her seated on the patio floor. Grabbing a chair for support, Cleo rose to her feet.

"Stay here. Wait for the ambulance," he told her. "Let me handle this."

"Do as he asks," Beatrice pleaded.

Cleo sat down in the chair. "You think Aunt Oralie—"

"Hush, sweetheart." Beatrice patted Cleo and hugged her head against her stomach the way a mother would in comforting a child. "Oralie has always been jealous of you, but I never dreamed that she…it isn't in her to murder. I thought she'd gotten over her…but she hasn't. Why didn't I realize that she's been pretending all these years?"

"What are you talking about?" Cleo lifted her head and stared up at Beatrice.

"Oh, my dear, dear girl, it's all my fault." Tears streamed down Beatrice's face. "When your father was killed and your mother deserted you, Daddy and I brought you home to live with us. You were such a tiny little thing. None of us had ever seen you. You were born after James went to Vietnam and Arabelle wasn't on good terms with us."

"Please, Aunt Beatrice, what does all this have to do with Aunt Oralie?"

"Oralie has always been terribly jealous of me, of my relationship with Perry." Beatrice hung her head, avoiding any eye contact. "After I brought you home and made such a fuss over you, and when Oralie saw how Daddy doted on you, she got the ridiculous idea in her head that you were my child, and not really James's little girl."

"What?" Cleo turned around too quickly. Pain shot through her head. She suddenly felt very dizzy.

"You've always resembled me a great deal, Cleo." Beatrice

smiled sadly. "We both take after Daddy's mother. She was a petite, green-eyed redhead."

"Oralie assumed that Perry was Cleo's father," Roarke said.

"Yes," Beatrice replied. "For quite some time nothing we said or did could convince her otherwise. She tormented us with her accusations. But finally, she said that she would accept Cleo into the family and forgive Perry, as long as he stayed away from Cleo and never paid any attention to her."

"That's why Uncle Perry—"

"He didn't dare be more than civil to you." Beatrice wept openly, gasping with sobbing breaths. Calming herself, she looked directly at Roarke. "Please, Simon, go on and do what must be done. There's no telling what Oralie will do now that we've found her out."

Roarke shrugged off his wet jacket and tossed it on the table. "Stay put," he told Cleo.

Roarke found Perry Sutton standing in the middle of his and Oralie's sitting room, his arms outstretched to his wife. Oralie had opened the double doors leading outside onto her balcony. She stood facing Perry, her back to the balcony. Daphne sat rigidly on the edge of the bed in her parents' bedroom. Her eyes were dazed, her face deathly pale. Roarke halted a few feet behind Perry. But Perry didn't turn around. With his arms open wide, he kept saying, "Come to me, Oralie," over and over again.

Oralie pointed a finger at Roarke and laughed hysterically. "If she hadn't married *him,* it would all be over now. She'd be dead and my children would be safe. It would all be ours, not hers. Not Bea's."

"Oralie, honey, everything will be all right if you just come on back in here with me." Perry took a tentative step toward her.

She backed all the way onto the balcony until her hips rested against the wooden banister. "Don't! I'm not going to let you trick me. Not any of you."

"No one's trying to trick you," Perry said. "I just want you to come back in here and let's talk this over. We can make everything all right. Cleo's fine. You didn't hurt her."

"I wish I'd killed her. I tried!"

"Hush, honey, you're only upsetting yourself." Perry stood perfectly still.

Roarke placed his hand on Perry's shoulder. "Has she threatened to jump?" Roarke whispered.

Perry nodded affirmatively.

"What's he saying to you?" Oralie screamed. "Don't you believe anything he says. He's Cleo's husband. He'll take her side. But you mustn't take her side. You have to be on my side. Mine and *my* children's."

"I am on your side."

"No, you're on Cleo's side, too. Because she's Beatrice's child. Yours and Beatrice's. You lied to me. All of you. Uncle George. Beatrice. You. But I knew better. I couldn't allow you to love Beatrice's child more than my children. That's why I tried to drown Cleo when she was a little girl. If only I had succeeded then, everything would have been all right."

Marla Sutton gasped loudly. She halted in the doorway of Perry and Oralie's suite. Cleo and Aunt Beatrice stood directly behind her.

"Yes, Oralie, I know," Perry said. "Remember? You promised me then that you'd never try to harm Cleo again."

"Yes, I promised."

"You broke your promise, didn't you?"

"It was easy, you know." Oralie put her hands behind her back and grasped the banister. She tossed back her head and laughed. "I almost got caught getting those spiders out of the science lab at Covenant. I did run into Professor Martindale, but he didn't remember who I was. Wasn't that fortunate? And the poison was so simple. I just got it out of a smelly old sack in your greenhouse. I remembered that one day when I went down to the greenhouse, you said you needed to get rid of some of those old insecticides and a sack of rat poison. But you never did. Wasn't that lucky for me?"

Cleo gripped Beatrice's hand. "Did you know that Aunt Oralie tried to kill me years ago? Did Uncle Perry tell you?"

"No, I had no idea," Beatrice said. "We all assumed that your nearly drowning when you were a child was nothing more than an accident. We were always having to scold you children for playing around the pool unsupervised."

"The little buzzers under the saddle were the most fun."

Oralie's voice boomed with a maniacal strength. "I found those in a sack in Trey's dresser. They'd been left over from some party that he'd given a few years ago, before he and Marla married. I had so hoped that when Sweet Justice bucked her off, Cleo would break her neck."

Marla gasped a second time. Cleo tightened her grasp on Beatrice's hand.

Oralie lifted one of her legs and swung it over the banister.

"Don't, Oralie," Perry pleaded. "We can fix things. We can make things right again."

"I tried to make things right and I failed," she said. "I can't let y'all call that silly Phil Bacon to come and get me. He'd put me in jail, just like he did Trey. I'm not going to jail. They'd take away all my jewelry." She fiddled with the rings on her fingers. "And I couldn't wear my nice clothes." She stroked her silk blouse. "And they wouldn't let Pearl bring me breakfast in bed when I'm having one of my bad days."

"You won't have to go to jail." Perry turned around and looked at Cleo and Beatrice. "Please, tell her that she won't have to go to jail. Please."

Cleo closed her eyes momentarily. A part of her didn't care if Oralie jumped to her death. Another part of her wanted desperately to save her aunt.

"Aunt Oralie, please come back inside." Releasing Beatrice's hand, Cleo walked over and stood beside Roarke. "No one is going to take you off to jail."

"You're lying!" Oralie laughed again, the hysteria accelerating, the laughter growing louder and louder.

"Mother." Daphne rose from the bed and walked into the sitting room. "Please, don't do this. Don't. I love you. I—"

"I'm sorry, my darling girl. So sorry." Oralie lifted her other leg over the railing and sat on the narrow banister, her feet dangling over the side.

Perry rushed forward, crying out his wife's name. She turned, looked at him and smiled. "I love you," she said, and jumped off the balcony.

Perry grabbed for Oralie, his fingers brushing her silk blouse as he reached for her. But she was too far away. He gripped the banister. Helpless to stop her descent, he watched his wife fall to the ground. Daphne dropped to her knees and wept. Marla screamed, then fainted dead away. Beatrice ran onto the balcony; she held out her hand to Perry, but didn't touch him. Roarke draped his arm around Cleo's trembling shoulders. Off in the distance an ambulance siren wailed.

Chapter 17

Dr. Iverson had assured Roarke and Cleo that their baby apparently hadn't suffered any damage from Cleo's accident. Cleo had cried tears of joy, and Roarke had held her in his arms, grateful that the baby was safe. He wished he could share Cleo's joy. He couldn't. And she seemed to understand. Although they continued making love, Cleo never again told him that she loved him, never again asked him to remain in River Bend permanently.

He did stay for Oralie Sutton's funeral. The family kept it a private affair, which everyone agreed was best, considering the circumstances. In the days following Oralie's suicidal jump from the balcony, Daphne clung to her father instead of Hugh. Perry turned to Beatrice for solace and support. And ever reliable and dependable, Cleo made all the arrangements, sparing no expense. Trey Sutton was released on bond in time for the somber event, and after his preliminary hearing, he and Marla stayed with her parents while awaiting his trial.

Roarke had remained at Cleo's side, still her bodyguard, still her husband, until all the loose ends were tied up. He had fulfilled his obligations to her, above and beyond those required in their legalized agreement.

She was two and a half months pregnant, but still as slender as a reed. She hadn't been bothered much with morning sickness and she glowed with good health and vitality. He didn't dare let himself imagine how she would shine with maternal beauty as her pregnancy progressed.

Roarke placed the last item in his suitcase, then snapped the lid shut. He glanced at Cleo, who sat at the writing desk at the foot of the bed. She ripped out the check from her checkbook, pushed back her chair and stood.

She held the check out to him. "This should buy you that farm you want, and take care of all Hope's needs as long as she lives."

"Thanks." He took the check without even glancing at it. He folded it in two, pulled out his wallet and slipped the check inside.

"I won't go down with you," Cleo said. "I'd rather we said our goodbyes here."

"That's fine with me." He reached out and took her hands.

She didn't move in closer; he didn't bring her toward him. They kept a foot of space between them.

"Take care of yourself," she said.

"Yeah, I will. You take care of yourself, too. And the baby."

"We'll be just fine."

"I'm sure you will. You're a strong woman, honey. A survivor." He released her hands, turned around, lifted his suitcase off the bed and walked toward the door.

"Simon?"

He paused, his hand on the doorknob, and looked back over his shoulder.

"Do you want me to let you know when our baby is born?"

He opened the door and stepped into the hall. "No. I don't want to know."

He closed the door behind him. Cleo slumped onto the bed, curled into a ball and cried. She had hoped and prayed something—anything—would change his mind and he would stay with her. It had taken every ounce of courage she possessed not to beg him to stay. But if he didn't love her, if he could never risk loving another woman and child, then nothing she said or did would have kept him at her side for a lifetime.

Cleo laid her hand over her tummy. "We'll be all right without him, my sweet baby. But I'm afraid your father's never going to be all right without us."

In the first week after he left Cleo, Roarke set up a fund that would take care of Hope's bills, now and in the future. He made a trip to Florida to see her, but she didn't recognize him. She seldom did. He took her a box of her favorite candy mints and she smiled that childlike smile that always reminded him of Laurie's.

The second week, he visited with his old buddies at Dundee Private Security in Atlanta and haunted a few nightspots with Gabriel Hawk and Morgan Kane. He got rip-roaring drunk and suffered a hell of a hangover.

The next night, he picked up a bosomy, petite redhead in a bar and took her back to his apartment. Before he got her halfway undressed, he called her "Cleo Belle." He apologized, gave the lady cab fare and sent her packing.

The third week he hired a real estate agent and started searching for a small farm, anywhere in the South. He told himself that time would take care of everything. That given enough time, he'd forget the way Cleo laughed. The way she walked and talked. The way she clung to him, calling out his name when he pleasured her. The way she made him feel when they were together. The fact that she was carrying his child.

Beatrice called him to tell him that Trey had been sentenced to ten years, a split sentence—five years in prison, five on probation. Cleo had testified in his defense.

"Cleo's well," Beatrice said. "She's gained three pounds. But I worry that she's working too hard. She practically lives at the plant since you left."

The fourth week, his agent showed him pictures of six different properties. One in particular caught his eye. It was a forty-acre spread in Franklin County, about twenty-five miles outside River Bend, in a rural community called Laurie Falls. His heart skipped a beat when he read the name. Laurie Falls.

The fifth week, he bought the farm at Laurie Falls, packed his meager belongings and drove straight through to Alabama.

The sixth week, he picked up the newly installed telephone in his den and called his wife.

"I don't see why you have to move out." Beatrice followed Cleo as she buzzed around the kitchen, preparing herself a sandwich for lunch. "What with Trey in prison and Daphne off in Europe, and Marla back home with her parents, if you leave, whatever will Perry and I do but rattle around all alone in this big house?"

"I'd think you two would enjoy having the house to yourselves and the chance to be alone." Cleo took an enormous bite out of her sandwich. In the past couple of weeks, her appetite had surged out of control. She went to bed hungry and woke up hungry. She wondered sometimes if she was eating for more than two, but Dr. Tanner assured her that she wasn't having twins.

"But buying a house and moving out on your own when you're four months pregnant seems a bit foolhardy to me."

"If Daphne can break her engagement to Hugh and move to Europe in search of a new life, then why can't I simply move across town and start over again? I want to give my baby and me a fresh start, away from all the memories this house holds. Good memories, and bad."

"I think you should go to Atlanta and tell Simon Roarke that he's damn well going to live up to his responsibilities as your husband and the father of your baby." Beatrice opened the refrigerator door, removed a bottled fruit drink and unscrewed the lid.

"I've been telling her to do just that for weeks now," Pearl said. "But she's too stubborn, too filled with McNamara pride, to go after her man. She reminds me of you sometimes, Bea."

"Are you implying something, Pearl?" Beatrice asked. "I wish you'd just say what you have to say and stop beating around the bush."

"All right." Pearl pointed a meaty finger at Cleo. "Go to Atlanta and get Mr. Roarke. Do whatever you have to do, but convince him that you're not letting him go. I don't think it would take much convincing. After all, he's been gone six weeks and he hasn't done a thing about getting a divorce, has he?''

"Pearl is absolutely right!" Beatrice took a sip of her drink.

"And you—" Pearl pointed at Beatrice "—you stop twiddling your thumbs while Perry Sutton plays the grieving widower. You've waited nearly thirty-five years for that man. Why wait any longer?"

Beatrice gasped. "My heavens, Pearl. Oralie hasn't been gone two months yet."

"What difference does it make how long she's been gone? Dead is dead. She ain't going to be no deader two years from now."

"Oh, hush up. You say the most outrageous things and still call yourself a good Christian woman."

The ringing telephone interrupted any reply Pearl might have made. She wiped her hands on her apron and lifted the receiver from the wall phone.

"McNamara and Sutton residence," Pearl said.

"Hello, Pearl, my love, how are you?" Roarke asked.

"I'm fine. And you?"

"Fine," he said. "Finer than I've ever been in my life."

"Well, I'm glad to hear it. It's about time you were coming to your senses. Did you want to speak to someone other than me?"

"Is Cleo there?"

"She might be."

Cleo and Beatrice stared at Pearl. Cleo mouthed the question "Who is it?"

"Before I let her talk to you, I want to know exactly what you're going to say," Pearl told Roarke.

"I'm going to tell her that I'm not giving her a divorce. Not now. Not ever."

"Hold on just a minute." Pearl held out the telephone toward Cleo. "It's for you. Some man who says he's your husband."

"Simon?" Cleo almost strangled on a piece of bread that had lodged in her throat. She grabbed Beatrice's drink out of her hand and took a hefty swallow.

Walking across the kitchen, she stared at the telephone in

Pearl's hand as if it were a live snake. She hesitated when Pearl tried to give her the phone.

"This is the call you've been waiting on, girl. Take it."

Cleo grasped the telephone. "Hello."

"Cleo, I want you to drive out to Laurie Falls today and meet me," Roarke said. "I'll give you the directions. Will you come?"

"Laurie Falls? Over in Franklin County? What are you doing there?"

"I'm living on my farm," he said. "It's not big. Just forty acres, and the house needs some work. But I like the place. I want you to see it."

"You're going to live in Laurie Falls? But—but that's only twenty miles or so from here."

"Yeah, I know. That'll make it convenient for you to visit Aunt Beatrice and Pearl whenever you want, and it won't be too long a drive back and forth to work."

Cleo wondered if she was dreaming, if any minute now her alarm clock would ring and she'd wake alone in her bed. She held the phone with white-knuckled fierceness.

"Are you all right, Cleo Belle?" Pearl asked.

"Is that Simon on the phone?" Beatrice glanced from an unresponsive Cleo to Pearl.

"Cleo, honey, did you hear me? Will you come out to the farm today? We need to talk," Roarke said.

"Yes, you're right. We need to talk." Cleo sucked in her breath. "Give me the directions to your farm."

An hour later, Cleo drove her Jaguar up in front of a two-story frame house badly in need of paint. Simon Roarke stood on the wide, wooden porch. He looked wonderful in his faded, worn jeans and cotton shirt. When he walked toward the driveway, the first thing she noticed was that he wasn't wearing a gun. By the time she opened the car door, Roarke was there to meet her.

"Thanks for coming," he said.

"I don't understand." She closed the door and walked away from the car and toward the house. "Why did you buy a farm so close to River Bend, so close to me and...and my baby?"

"Our baby."

She snapped her head around and stared at him. "What did you say?"

"I said *our* baby. That is, if you're willing to stay married to an idiot like me and allow me to help you raise our child." He looked at her with a mixture of hope and pleading in his eyes.

"You've changed your mind? Six weeks away from me and you suddenly change your mind? What happened? Did you get an attack of conscience and decide that you should be a part of your child's life after all?"

"I want to be a part of your life, Cleo." He held out his hand to her. "I want us to stay married and build a life together. Here. On this farm."

She didn't take his hand, didn't even look at it. "Why, Simon? Six weeks ago, you couldn't wait to get away from me and this—" she laid a protective hand over her stomach "—child. What changed your mind?"

"You're not going to make this easy for me, are you?"

"Why should I? You certainly didn't make things easy for me when you left me."

"Will it help if I get down on my knees and beg?" He bent down on both knees and folded his hands together in front of him. "Marry me, Cleo. Marry me for real this time."

Her lips twitched with an almost smile. "It seemed pretty real to me the first time," she said. "Besides, we're still married, as far as I know. Unless you got a divorce and forgot to tell me."

Roarke grabbed her hands. "All right, if the first time was good enough for you, it's good enough for me." Still holding her hands, he rose to his feet. "So when can you move in? Today, I hope."

"I can't just move in here with you." Cleo tugged on her hands, but Roarke held tight. "I have no idea what's happened to you. Why you—"

He silenced her with a kiss. She struggled to get away from him. The harder she fought his embrace, the harder he kissed her. When he finally let her come up for air, he looked into her moss green eyes and smiled.

"I love you, Cleo. That's what happened to me these past

six weeks. I found out that I love you and that without you, I don't have a life.''

"Oh, Simon.'' Tears gathered in her eyes. "You love me? You really love me?''

"With all my heart and soul.'' He lifted her into his arms and walked toward the house. "Can you ever forgive me for being such a jerk? I couldn't let go of the past, of all my old hurts. I was afraid to love you, afraid to reach out and grab the happiness you offered. But with every passing week we were apart, I realized that I was more afraid to go on living without you.''

"Are you sure?'' she asked.

"Yeah, honey, I'm sure,'' he said. "When the real estate agent gave me pictures of this house, in Laurie Falls, so close to River Bend, I knew we were meant to be together here. You. Me. And our baby.''

He carried her into the house, through the empty living room and down the hall. He kicked open the door to the only furnished room in the house. A huge, antique brass bed dominated the room. Roarke laid his wife on the bed and came down beside her.

She draped her arms around his neck. "I love you so much, Simon. And I've missed you.''

"Ah, Cleo Belle, I've missed you like crazy.''

He started to kiss her again, but Cleo turned her head to one side.

"Simon?''

"Yes?''

"How do you feel about the baby? I have to know.''

"I'm scared, honey. I messed up real bad at this father business the first time around and my little girl died. I don't want to ever fail this child.'' He laid his hand lovingly on Cleo's stomach. "You're going to have to help me. I won't ever be able to forget Laurie, and I'll never completely forgive myself for what happened to her. But maybe, if I'm a good father to our baby, I can somehow redeem myself.''

"I'm giving you a son,'' she said. "I had the ultrasound done yesterday. He's perfect in every way and—''

Roarke kissed her again, and within minutes they lay naked atop the new beige sheets. They made love with a fast, furious frenzy the first time. But the second time they didn't hurry, as they learned each other all over again, pleasuring each other with slow, tormenting deliberation.

When the sun went down, they raided the refrigerator, the only appliance in the enormous farmhouse kitchen. And after they dined on milk and cereal, they returned to their bedroom and made love again.

At dawn, Roarke woke Cleo, wrapped her in the top sheet and carried her out onto the front porch. He sat down in the wooden rocker and held her in his lap. She laid her head on his shoulder and kissed the side of his neck.

"I wanted us to share the sunrise together on our first morning here at our new home."

"I love you, Simon Roarke."

"And I love you, my darling Cleo Belle."

Epilogue

Sitting in a wooden rocking chair on his front porch, Simon Roarke watched his sons, six-year-old Johnny and three-year-old Jimmy, frolicking in the front yard with the family's Irish setters, Brady and Corey. The sun lay on the western horizon like a scoop of orange sherbet, the edges melting into a pool of luscious colors. The evening breeze cooled the summertime heat, but did little to lessen the humidity.

Cleo walked out onto the porch, carrying two glasses of lemonade. She handed one to her husband, then sat down beside him in a matching chair. Rocking slowly, she sipped the cool, tart liquid.

Roarke leaned over and kissed her. She sighed, deep in her throat. "What was that for?" she asked.

"That's for being the most wonderful woman in the world and making me the happiest man alive," he said.

Cleo smiled broadly, and for one split second Roarke's heart stopped beating. Every time he looked at his wife, she took his breath away. Every time he touched her, he wanted to make love to her. And every time he thought about how much she'd given him, he ached inside with a pleasure almost too great to bear.

In the seven years since their hasty marriage of convenience, Roarke had gone from being a lonely, cynical man who lived his life on the edge, to a contented family man, a gentleman farmer living the good life that had once been only a dream for him.

"Who've you been talking to on the phone for so long?" he asked.

"Aunt Beatrice for a while, and then Pearl."

"What great news did those two have?"

"It seems Daphne got married again. To a European count this time."

"What does this make—husband number four or five?"

"Four, I think," Cleo said. "And Marla is pregnant. Isn't that wonderful? I think she and Trey are making a good life for themselves now that Trey's working at McNamara's again and they're living back at the house with Aunt Beatrice and Uncle Perry."

"I agree, honey. I never thought Trey would change. But I have to admit that he's a different man from the one who tried to sabotage McNamara's."

"I'm glad he accepted Uncle Perry's marriage to Aunt Beatrice. I was afraid he and Daphne would both create problems."

"Daphne can't cause too many problems thousands of miles away, and I don't think you have to worry about Trey any more."

"Oh, Simon!" Cleo gasped.

"What's wrong?" he asked anxiously, then relaxed when she smiled at him.

Laughing, she took the glass out of his hand and set her glass and his on the small, wooden table at her side. She reached out, grasped his hand and laid it over her protruding belly.

He grinned when he felt his child move inside Cleo. "She's got some kick, hasn't she? She's going to be a feisty little gal, just like her mama."

"Only two more months to wait for Miss Sara Ann Roarke to make her debut." Sighing contentedly as Simon rubbed her tummy, Cleo looked at her strong, healthy sons, both of them tall and big for their age. She knew they would grow to be large, handsome men like their father.

Johnny, their eldest, named after his paternal grandfather, was the spitting image of Simon, except for his auburn hair. Brown-haired Jimmy, their younger son, named after Cleo's dad, took after the McNamaras, with his fine, delicate features and his striking green eyes. They were perfect children at moments like this, and normal little heathens as a general rule.

Cleo was glad that their first two children had been boys. Simon would have had a more difficult time becoming a father again if they'd had a daughter the first time. Losing Laurie would always be a sorrow in Simon's soul, but realizing what a good father he was to the boys had helped him forgive himself and ease some of the guilt he'd always feel over his daughter's death. Now, after so many painful years of remorse and regret, he was ready to open his heart and love a new daughter. Sara Ann could never replace Laurie, but she would bring her father the joy only a little girl could give him.

Simon and Cleo were happier than either had once thought possible. From their deep and passionate love, they had created three children and shared a marriage that would last a lifetime.

* * * * *

An ex-Navy SEAL is sent to protect an old lover,
and discovers a new family in
A MAN LIKE MORGAN KANE (IM #819)
coming in November from Beverly Barton and
INTIMATE MOMENTS.

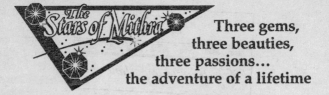

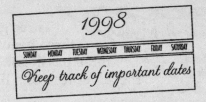

1998

SUNDAY MONDAY TUESDAY WEDNESDAY THURSDAY FRIDAY SATURDAY

Keep track of important dates

Three beautiful and colorful calendars that celebrate some of the most popular trends in America today.

Look for:

Just Babies—a 16 month calendar that features a full year of absolutely adorable babies!

1998 CALENDAR
Just Babies
16 months of adorable bundles of joy!

Hometown Quilts
1998 Calendar
A 16 month quilting extravaganza!

Hometown Quilts—a 16 month calendar featuring quilted art squares, plus a short history on twelve different quilt patterns.

Inspirations—a 16 month calendar with inspiring pictures and quotations.

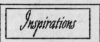

Inspirations

A 16 month calendar that will lift your spirits and gladden your heart

Steeple Hill™   ◆ HARLEQUIN®

Value priced at $9.99 U.S./$11.99 CAN., these calendars make a perfect gift!

Available in retail outlets in August 1997.   CAL98

SILHOUETTE WOMEN KNOW ROMANCE WHEN THEY SEE IT.

And they'll see it on **ROMANCE CLASSICS**, the new 24-hour TV channel devoted to romantic movies and original programs like the special **Romantically Speaking-Harlequin® Goes Prime Time**.

Romantically Speaking-Harlequin® Goes Prime Time introduces you to many of your favorite romance authors in a program developed exclusively for Harlequin® and Silhouette® readers.

Watch for **Romantically Speaking-Harlequin® Goes Prime Time** beginning in the summer of 1997.

If you're not receiving ROMANCE CLASSICS,
call your local cable operator or satellite provider
and ask for it today!

ROMANCE
CLASSICS

Escape to the network of your dreams.

TRINITY STREET WEST

**where danger lies around every corner—
and the biggest danger of all
is falling in love.**

Meet the men and women of Trinity Street West
in the compelling miniseries by

Justine Davis

continuing in September 1997 with

A MAN TO TRUST
(Intimate Moments #805)

Kelsey Hall was hiding secrets and needed
someone to trust, and Cruz Gregerson, the one man
she desperately wanted to trust with her secrets *and*
her heart, was the one kind of man she knew she
couldn't—a by-the-book cop. But this time, he wasn't
thinking with his badge....

INTIMATE MOMENTS®
Silhouette®

DIANA WHITNEY

Continues the twelve-book series 36 HOURS in September 1997 with Book Three

OOH BABY, BABY

In the back of a cab, in the midst of a disastrous storm, Travis Stockwell delivered Peggy Saxon's two precious babies and, for a moment, they felt like a family. But Travis was a wandering cowboy, and a fine woman like Peggy was better off without him. Still, she and her adorable twins had tugged on his heartstrings, until now he wasn't so sure that *he* was better off without *her*.

For Travis and Peggy and *all* the residents of Grand Springs, Colorado, the storm-induced blackout was just the beginning of 36 Hours that changed *everything!* You won't want to miss a single book.

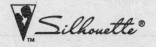

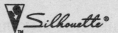

COMING THIS OCTOBER 1997 FROM

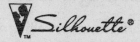

THREE NEW LOVE STORIES IN ONE VOLUME BY
ONE OF AMERICA'S MOST BELOVED WRITERS

DEBBIE MACOMBER

Three Brides, No Groom

Gretchen, Maddie and Carol—they were three college
friends with plans to become blushing brides. But
even though the caterers were booked, the bouquets
bought and the bridal gowns were ready to wear…the
grooms suddenly got cold feet. And that's when these
three women decided they weren't going to get mad…
they were going to get even!

DON'T MISS THE WARMTH, THE HUMOR…THE
ROMANCE AS ONLY DEBBIE MACOMBER CAN DO!

AVAILABLE WHEREVER SILHOUETTE BOOKS
ARE SOLD.